EACH VAGABOND BY NAME

a novel

Margo Orlando Littell

UNO Press
Manufactured in the United States of America
All rights reserved
ISBN: 978-1-60801-122-3

Cover illustration: Clare Welsh
Book and cover design: Alex Dimeff

Library of Congress Cataloging-in-Publication Data

Names: Littell, Margo Orlando, 1976- , author.
Title: Each vagabond by name : a novel / by Margo Orlando
Littell.
Description: New Orleans : University of New Orleans Press,
2016.
Identifiers: LCCN 2015050325 | ISBN 9781608011223 (pbk.)
Subjects: LCSH: Bars (Drinking establishments)--Fiction. |
Miners--Fiction. |
   Romanies--Fiction. | Choice (Psychology)--Fiction. |
   Pennsylvania--Fiction. | Life change events--Fiction. |
   Psychological fiction.
Classification: LCC PS3612.I874 E43 2016 | DDC 813/.6--dc23
LC record available at http://lccn.loc.gov/2015050325

UNO PRESS
unopress.org

EACH VAGABOND BY NAME

a novel

Margo Orlando Littell

To Andrew, Lucia, and Greta

There is something in the autumn that is native to my
        blood—
Touch of manner, hint of mood;
And my heart is like a rhyme,
With the yellow and the purple and the crimson
        keeping time.

The scarlet of the maples can shake me like a cry
Of bugles going by.
And my lonely spirit thrills
To see the frosty asters like a smoke upon the hills.

There is something in October sets the gypsy blood
        astir;
We must rise and follow her,
When from every hill of flame
She calls and calls each vagabond by name.

— "A Vagabond Song," Bliss Carman (1861–1929)

CHAPTER 1

1118 Trillium Street

They rang the doorbell once. They'd been watching the house—two stories, red brick—and knew someone was home. They'd seen her drive up and carry in two sacks of groceries half an hour before.

She opened the door, neat tan slacks and a pilled red cardigan over a white turtleneck. "Can I help you?"

They bowed their heads. "A glass of water, ma'am, if it's not too much trouble," one said. No explanation, no apology, no reason why they should be refused.

The woman glanced over their shoulders then said, "Wait here."

She left the door open when she went to the kitchen, the storm door unlocked. Quickly one of them slipped inside. He found the staircase and ran up as a cupboard banged shut. The bedroom he came to had not so much as a shoe on the floor. This one was easy. Top dresser drawer, behind the cupped white bras and rolled brown stockings, just as he'd thought. In a house like this, furniture matching, carpet old but carefully kept, things were always where they belonged. He took out the jewelry box and emptied its contents into a small cloth sack.

As he crept downstairs, he heard the woman open the porch door. "What happened to your friend?" she asked, her voice now suspicious. He ran to the kitchen and out the back door before he heard the other's answer.

Back in the mountains, they spread what they'd taken on the floor of their tent. A tangle of necklaces, a gold watch that had stopped, a few tarnished rings, a crystal brooch in the shape of a leaf. Two pairs of gold hoop earrings in small velvet pouches—fourteen carat at least, eighteen at the most. As soon as they'd seen the house and the woman, they knew what they'd find. They'd seen a lot of towns in their wanderings, and they'd learned early on that people and the things they loved were all the same.

It was an ordinary fall until the gypsies came. Leaves changed, fell, and clogged the curbside gutters. Crackling footsteps approached and receded, and the blue sky took Ramsy's breath when he glimpsed it through his bar's small window. For the first time in years, it made him feel hopeful, even though he knew better. There wasn't any more reason to feel hopeful in the fall than at any other time, and anyone who believed otherwise was setting himself up for a life of disappointment. The blue of the sky and the smoky burning leaves in the air didn't hold any magic, and they would disappear just like the hot yellow days of summer. Still, Ramsy felt something different this year, some stirring in his blood. Each morning, when he gazed at the maples like red smoke on the hills, he found himself unable to look away, as though something he'd been waiting for would fly out, any moment, from the branches.

Zaccariah Ramsy was a tall man, with long white hair and skin the color of whiskey. He had only one eye, bright blue and peering from a web of veins. The other socket was empty, sewn over with bits of skin, as red and raw as though the eye had been removed that day. It hadn't—he'd lost it in Vietnam—but it looked that way. The patch he used to wear made people too curious. Eventually he left it off. Few people wanted to look at Ramsy now, which gave him plenty of time to study them.

Ramsy's bar was at the end of a tree-shrouded road that curved into the mountains like S's end-to-end. The bar was a cabin really, built with logs and boards, and nothing about it suggested what lay inside. There were no beer signs in the window, no welcome mat by the door, no airbrushed sign calling out to drivers by the turn. The bar didn't make much of a profit, but it was somewhere to go, something to do in a small town like Shelk, and Ramsy was proud of it. The room was narrow, like a trailer. There were eight stools around the bar, and the walls inside were paneled with thin, dark wood. The only real light came from a wobbly lamp near the cash register and the portable, rabbit-eared TV. Only the people who knew about Ramsy's bothered driving out that way. Outsiders took the toll road, which wound around Shelk and other mountain towns and led, eventually, to the Turnpike.

Shelk had a small downtown of blackened storefronts and weedy vacant lots, a grocery store, a Dollar General, and some local businesses that had been around for years: a printer, a trophy and baseball card shop, and a music store where high school students rented band instruments. Shelk wasn't poorer than any other town. There was a decent public school, and the residential streets were clean. People didn't walk in the old Southside Park at night, and no one would want to go into the mountains after sunset, but most felt safe. They locked their doors when they left the house, but they didn't drive out of their way back home if they forgot.

In the three years past, Ramsy had seen nearby towns get wiped off the map. The bituminous coal that had fed the area for decades was harder to find now, but willing men could get in with one of the new companies shearing off the mountaintops to get to the coal inside. The blasts from the hilltops heaved silica dust and small pieces of rock over the towns like snow that wouldn't melt, forcing people who'd never gone more than twenty miles from home to pack up and move on. Whole families—three, even four generations—took the payout money and resettled, even though the idea of bulldozed homes wasn't easy to swallow. But Shelk was safe, nestled in coal-poor mountains that held nothing but white pines, eastern hemlocks, and American beeches.

Shelk was the kind of town where people were rarely disappointed. Pittsburgh and Morgantown were just over an hour's drive, but most folks were put off by the heavy traffic and stayed at home. Sometimes people camped for a weekend in the mountains, or drove through the counties in southwestern Pennsylvania just to say they'd been there. It was enough. Teenagers called it *boring*, but they, too, stayed on. No one forced them. The road was right there, crooked and potholed, but open.

*   *   *

Ramsy first heard of the gypsies in early October. He'd spent the day as he always did. He got up when he woke up. He counted the money from the night before and recorded the number in a small blue notebook. Then he headed into town, to the drive-through window of Pittsburgh Federal, and put the cash into a plastic capsule that whooshed through a tube to the teller inside.

Running a small bar wasn't a job that required too much thinking, but there were things he had to do.

Since it was a Monday afternoon, he drove to the beer distributor and backed into a parking spot in front of the open warehouse door. Inside, coolers of six-packs and cold cases lined the walls. He filled the truck bed with five cases of Budweiser, five of Coors Light, three of Yuengling, and two each of Iron City and Pabst Blue Ribbon. It had been a long time since he'd bothered keeping anything else on hand, save a bottle of whiskey or two. Light, bitter, cheap—these were what the men he served wanted.

Later, with his truck full of beer, he went to the bar. It was getting dark already—even in October you could smell winter in the air, clear as smoke from cigarettes— and he unloaded the cases in the last of the twilight. He filled the cooler with ice from the icemaker out back and broke down the cardboard cases as he emptied them. He put a few bills into the register for change. Then he turned the ballgame on, the volume low.

That night, Ash Haggerty and Charlie Snyder came in for drinks after working the mines, and they spoke of their wives while shadows slipped through the window.

"Junie was in one of her moods again," Charlie said. One or the other of them always started off this way— with a mood, with an irritated glance, with a remark said sharply for no reason at all. "Told her my chicken was a little dry, and she dumped the whole plate in the sink. Five bucks of chicken, wasted."

"Least she cooked," Ash said. "Meg flat-out refused last night. Said she's too tired. I had to go down to McDonald's and get us a sack of burgers. Then she complained she was gonna get fat. Jesus."

"It's the job," Charlie said. "Wears her out."

"Yeah. The job."

Ramsy had met Charlie and Ash's wives. Junie was a bus driver for the school kids, her voice harsh and quick to yell, her nails stained with the bus's black grease. Meg worked the breakfast shift at the Rowdy Buck, Shelk's diner, and knew most people in town. All of them had married young and settled close to where they'd been born, just a few streets away from the houses and rooms that had held them as infants.

Charlie and Ash were gentler about their wives, more likely to show their hurt and confusion, without Jack Kurtz there. No one could complain about their home life the way Jack Kurtz could. As far as Jack was concerned, his wife, Kitty, wasn't good for much more than spending his money without showing the proper appreciation. He complained that her need for attention could suck the air out of a room, and that her manufactured rage when people talked behind her back was equal only to her determination to keep them talking. Charlie and Ash were quick to complain but just as quick to defend, a habit Jack Kurtz ridiculed.

After their second round, Charlie asked Ramsy, "You hear the news?"

Ramsy didn't listen to the news. "News of what?"

Charlie leaned forward. "There's strangers in town," he said. "Gypsies."

"Gypsies?"

"We're not the first town they hit. Came over to us from Owl Creek."

"Gypsies? In P-A?"

"That's what they say," Charlie said. "They're break-ing into houses. Sneaking in. They're saying you gotta lock your doors now all the time, or they'll get inside. Heard they stole fifty grand in Owl Creek," he said. "People's life savings, for Chrissake."

Five houses had been robbed so far, every one of them during the day, and in three cases the owners had let in the gypsies themselves. "Gal named Mary Kolecik opened her own door for two of them," Charlie said. "Took her cash and jewelry when she went to the kitchen to get them some water."

Food went missing, too. Fruit bowls were emptied of oranges and apples. Milk, juice, and beer disappeared from refrigerator doors. Cheese, bread, peanut butter, crackers—the empty spaces on shelves sometimes went unnoticed until hours or even days after the crime, opening the wounds all over again. These weren't things that made the paper, but the missing food was what people talked about most among themselves. A few leftovers, a few canned goods—they weren't worth anything in the end, but, once they were gone, they were what people remembered. There, near the coffee, was where the Campbell's soups had been. Two pounds of ground chuck had been sitting on top of the eggs. Boxes of cereal, tins of homemade cookies, Tupperware containers of two-day-old chicken and rice—everyone who'd been robbed had a detail to add. *They even took the cake left over from Jenny's birthday,* they said, and it was this as much as anything that made people shake their heads and double-check their locks at night.

There seemed to be an understanding that the gypsies would soon move on, that the danger was mild and temporary, something to be put up with for a short, inconvenient while. A rolling feeling in Ramsy's gut told him otherwise—but he kept quiet and let the men in his bar believe what they liked. Outsiders always caused a stir in Shelk, and Ramsy wasn't in the habit of worrying about himself or others—he found it tiresome and with few rewards.

He made an exception for Stella Vale. Stella lived alone and wasn't the sort to open her door for strangers, but Ramsy still worried she'd let them in, offer tea or juice, linger in the kitchen while other gypsies took their time in her drawers and closets. Stella didn't have much that a gypsy might want, but it didn't matter. Ramsy didn't like the thought of anyone in her house at all.

So he was relieved when she came into the bar the next night and sat down in her usual spot, farthest from the door. Ramsy rose from the wooden stool he kept behind the bar, lifted a bottle of red wine from a glass-doored cupboard, and poured a good bit into a tumbler. Nobody else drank wine in his bar, but he kept it on hand for Stella. They didn't talk until everyone had left. Ramsy poured himself a drink, then leaned up against the bar near Stella.

"Two people came into the library," Stella told him. "It was a busy day."

"They take out any books?"

"They used the copy machine and left."

Ramsy hadn't been to the library for a decade, but he imagined Stella sitting behind the horseshoe-shaped desk with a newspaper or a water-stained book, waiting out the hours while the grandfather clock in the entryway *tick-tocked* its bulbous pendulum. It was how she spent her time in the bar, too, waiting out the hours with drink after drink.

Stella's hair was silver-streaked and long, her frame thin but womanly, her kitten-gray eyes unlined. In another town, where nobody knew her, she might have been mistaken for a younger woman. But in Shelk there was no erasing the years she'd endured.

Ramsy drank and felt the whiskey slowly seeping into his blood, his gums, the tissues of his throat. It felt warm and familiar. The wine relaxed Stella, too— he could see the tension leaving the sides of her jaw, her temples, and her neck. He poured her a few more glasses—three? four? He'd lost track. She was probably drunk by now, but Ramsy could never tell. The only sign was a slight downward slope of her eyelids when she smiled.

"I'd better get going," Stella said once the night tilted toward morning.

"It's cold," Ramsy said. "I'll drive you home." He wiped down the counter, drained the melted ice, straightened the stools around the bar, and emptied the cash register into a zippered rubber pouch. He turned off the lights, and Stella followed him outside to his truck. The mountain night was perfectly still.

Stella always walked to the bar, and Ramsy often drove her home when it was cold outside. He turned the heater on high and kept a steady speed around the sharpest curves, expertly balancing gas and brake, lightly steering with his fingertips. He knew Stella liked to watch him drive, and sometimes, if she was tired or had had too much to drink, she sat in the middle seat and rode with her head on his shoulder.

"Have you heard about the gypsies?"

"I've heard." She was looking out the window, and her breath fogged the glass.

"I want you to be careful," Ramsy said. "Lock your door when you take a bath. Lock it when you leave. You don't want them to get inside and take anything."

"Take anything?" Stella said. "Everything I have's been taken already."

Ramsy felt cold spread from his stomach through his veins. She meant, of course, her baby. Her Lucy.

"Thanks for the ride," she said when they reached her house, and she didn't look back as she walked down the path. Once she disappeared inside, Ramsy drove away, cursing himself.

*   *   *

It was dark on the road. Early snow clouds covered the stars and moon, and Ramsy's headlights barely broke the cold, bitter blackness. When he left Walnut

Drive and started down Linden Street, he saw red and blue flashing lights on the shoulder a few blocks down, by the turnoff to the road that led to the mountains. He slowed his truck. A state police cruiser crookedly nosed the curb, its back end sticking out into the road. Shelk didn't have a police department, and the state police handled domestic calls and quality of life complaints. The cruiser's siren was off, but Ramsy saw flashlight beams sweeping the ground. He knew many of the state troopers who rode through Shelk—a group of them used to come to the bar when Hawk, the old owner, was around—so when he pulled up alongside the commotion, he stopped and rolled his window down. There'd been a lot of talk about gypsies, and Stella's house wasn't far from here.

Against the cruiser stood three young boys, their hands flat on the hood, their legs spread. They wore baggy jeans stuffed into heavy, unlaced boots, and long coats that didn't look warm enough for October. Young faces, dark unkempt hair, in one kid's ear a thick silver hoop that glinted in the flashing lights, on another's head a close-fitting black hat. They looked at Ramsy. One of the troopers nodded. "Ramsy."

"Everything alright?" Ramsy said. There were three brown paper bags sitting in front of the car. They were wrinkled, clearly not new from the store, though they bore the Shop N' Save logo.

"Seems these kids thought they could take what they wanted from the Shop N' Save," the trooper said. He sneered at the word *kids*. It was clear he meant *gypsies*.

"We told you," said the boy wearing the hat. His dark hair reached his chin. He had a red scarf tied around his throat, but his coat hung open. "We bought that food. We're just getting it home now."

"At night? Shop N' Save closed hours ago." The trooper rolled his eyes at Ramsy.

"Seems suspicious, you're right, but they're telling the truth," Ramsy said evenly. The truck was still in drive, his foot on the brake. He hadn't planned to speak. He angled his face slightly toward the windshield so his missing eye was all the troopers could see. His heart pounded with the lie, but his face remained unreadable. "I was at the store this afternoon. They were in line ahead of me. Unloaded their cart and paid like anyone else." He hadn't been anywhere near the Shop N' Save that day. It was only a few bags of food. Wherever they got it, they must need it.

The kids didn't say anything, but the boy with the red scarf looked up and studied Ramsy, not looking away when Ramsy met his gaze.

The trooper frowned. "You sure about that, Ramsy?"

"Easy to remember seeing unfamiliar faces."

For a few moments, the troopers stayed where they were. Then one of the troopers kicked the cruiser's tire and said, "Get on out of here, then. You were lucky this time. Hear me? You won't always have no guardian angel."

The boys picked up their bags and walked quickly into the shadows. When the troopers looked at Ramsy now, their faces were hard.

"Appreciate you telling us what you remember," one said. "But maybe you just let us do our jobs from now on."

In the rearview mirror Ramsy saw them standing shoulder to shoulder, watching his truck for a long time after he drove away.

*   *   *

The next day, two more houses were robbed. Charlie told Ramsy the news when he came into the bar after work.

"More old ladies," he said. "Just trying to be nice. They lock their doors just like they should, then they open them up."

"How'd Owl Creek get rid of them?"

"They left on their own. Seems they stole so much they couldn't stick around. They've been all over— Jack heard they were as far as Philadelphia, then came all the way across the state. Maybe they like the mountains."

"Getting cold to be out there at night."

"My guess is they're up in the caves," Charlie said. "You get a fire going and those caves'll keep you warm."

There was more talk of the gypsies when Ash and then Jack came into the bar.

"Got my gun by my bed," Jack said. "That's all I know." Jack Kurtz had the lean, long-legged build of a former second baseman, but years of hard work and too much drinking had made him ropy and grim.

The other men murmured their agreement, though every one of them knew that Jack Kurtz was the kind of man who would shoot before making sure the rustling was a deer and not a person.

It was talk like this that made Ramsy uneasy. He knew about these men's wives. He knew about their affairs, if they had them, because indiscretions were meant to be aired in a bar like his. But he wouldn't say he knew them. He wouldn't call them friends. He didn't know what Jack or the other men would do with guns in their hands.

Near midnight, Ramsy's daughter, Liza, called the bar. "Ramsy," she said when he answered. "How are you?"

"I'm fine," he said. "You?"

She exhaled. Every week she seemed relieved when he said he was fine, as he had the week before, and the week before that.

"I'm good," she said. "So what's new?"

Liza had her mother's voice and her mother's face and hair, but Ramsy hadn't seen Marcie for thirty years other than a picture or two, so he couldn't say for sure. When he thought of Marcie, that's what he pictured: straight dark hair and clear pale skin that sunk purple and moist under the eyes. The kind of face that was ordinary enough to be remembered only by those whose remembering would mean something.

"When're you gonna move out here?" she said, as she did each time she called. Every week, she sounded disappointed when he said he had no plans to move. Every week, she said, "One of these days we'll get you to change your mind."

Ramsy had last visited Liza three years ago, a few months after her second baby was born. He wasn't the visiting type, and Liza knew that, but she insisted he come anyway. And Ramsy, since he was her father, after all, did. He drove the sixty miles into Pittsburgh to a neighborhood full of houses with the same white siding, red brick paths, and shiny lampposts at the ends of their driveways. The inside of Liza's house was shabby but bright, and she served him lunch in the kitchen while the two children cried.

"Welcome to my life," Liza had said, laughing, but Ramsy hadn't felt welcome at all. He was happy to return to the padded, tree-soaked quiet of Shelk and sit in his bar without the lights on.

*   *   *

Back in the days when he'd met Marcie, not long after coming home from Vietnam, there wasn't much to want, and he was grateful for what he had: an apartment with a bed, couch, and table with one curtained window and a door that locked, and a job at a bar whose owner, Hawk, was a vet of a different war and knew enough not to ask questions. Hawk had built the log-cabin bar with his own hands. Now he was getting old, and he needed someone he knew would be around for a while. Ramsy supposed it was easy enough to tell that he had nowhere else in the world to go.

He found peace at the bar. He preferred to be there than at home, where even the dark towel he'd draped over the window seemed to let in too much sun. He found peace, too, at a diner in town, where he sometimes went late at night after closing down the bar when he was too wired to sleep. He always sat on a counter stool and drank coffee while the night-shift waitresses wiped down the tables and closed out the register.

One night a waitress with *Marcie* on her nametag slid a wedge of apple pie in front of him. "Thought you could use it," she said. "Haven't seen you for a while."

"Been working more hours," he said.

"Well, glad you're here."

He was moved. He ate the pie and left a larger tip than usual when he saw it wasn't on the bill. He wanted to say thanks, but she was somewhere in the back when he got up to leave. It was for the best anyway. It was only a slice of day-old pie, intended for the dumpster, but he had so little in those days, and no one he could really call a friend. It warmed him to imagine there was someone who might care if he was gone.

He always ordered pie after this, whatever Marcie showed him in the scratched glass case, coconut, blueberry, lemon meringue. She told him about Shelk, where she'd lived her whole life, about the mines and the wealth they'd once brought. Her father died in a collapse when she was nine. But it didn't stop her brother from going in as soon as he turned sixteen. Not much else you could do in a town like this.

Marcie looked at him with a curious, expectant face when she said it, inviting him to explain what had brought him to Shelk, but Ramsy didn't know what to say. He'd never told anyone why he'd left Vietnam, and his chest still burned with humiliation when he thought of his buddies fighting in the jungle while he sat there, eating pie. So all he said was, "Not easy coming back from a war," and Marcie nodded like he'd said enough.

Ramsy had some money saved, and he bought a house on the west side of town, in a quiet neighborhood where the houses were small but had neatly kept yards. The street was a dead-end, so only his neighbors' cars drove by. Marcie moved in a few months later, bringing enough furniture and dishes and knickknacks to make it finally seem like a home.

"There," she said when she moved in, as though something were settled. She gave him that expectant look again, but Ramsy had nothing to add.

He hadn't married Marcie, but he'd given her a baby, which was all she'd ever really wanted. He was young then. He didn't know the first thing about what it meant to belong to a family. Marcie was the one who wanted the baby, and when she got her, after a year of being together, he left her to it.

Marcie was usually asleep when he came home from the bar, though the nights were dreamy spells of waking and crying and feeding and rocking and trying to sleep again. Some evenings, if the bar stayed empty, he mowed lawns and trimmed the bushes at the cemetery, then sat in front of the TV in the living room while Marcie took care of the baby at the back of the house. Through the hallway he could hear her talking to Liza and Liza squealing back. He never joined them. He felt it wasn't his place. There'd be time for the baby later, when she was old enough to go fishing or toss a ball in the yard. Ramsy tried his best to tune it all out. Marcie knew what she was doing, and Ramsy didn't want to get in the way.

She left in the summer of the cicadas. Every seventeen years they came to the mountains, a grotesque kind of plague. Shells wrapped the trees in their yard like bronze plating, and if the windows were open in the hot afternoons, the buzz was loud enough to drown out the TV.

It was early morning when she left, and the world outside the house was bright. She came down the hallway with a suitcase, the baby, and a light summer sweater over her arm. She looked at him, then walked out without a word. He followed her outside.

"You don't want to do this," he said.

"I'm gone already," she said. "Magic. Poof. You won't even miss us."

He stood in the yard and watched her drive off, then went back inside before neighbors could watch him from behind their screens.

She was back in twenty minutes. She'd forgotten her purse. She grabbed it from the bedroom, said, "Goddammit, Ramsy," and left again, and that's what Ramsy had never gotten over: that she'd come back for the purse and not for him. He could never forget how that final slam of the car door made him feel.

What no one knew was that he'd tried to find them. Not right away, but a few days later, when it became clear Marcie might just be gone for good. He'd chosen not to attend graduations and weddings and so had never met her family, but he knew their names and found them easily in the phonebook.

Marcie's brother, Don, frowned when he heard Marcie was gone, but he asked Ramsy in for a drink. "Now I don't mean nothin by this," he said, "but I think she probably had her reasons." He held up a hand. "Not sayin you're not a decent man. Have to trust Marcie on that. Just sayin maybe you should leave her be." Don's voice was friendly, but there was threat behind the words, and Ramsy made no more attempts to find out where Marcie had gone. It wasn't that he was afraid; he just knew Don was right. Marcie did have her reasons. And there was no promise he could make, no words he could say, to change her mind.

She lived in Texas now, with a man who rode horses for a living. Ramsy never had to wonder what life would have been like if Marcie had stayed. He already knew full well. Marcie would have gone back to waitressing, working herself to the bone like the wives of the men in his bar. Liza would have been one of the poor kids in school, without the right clothes, her hair a lopsided tangle of home-cuts and cheap shampoo. And the bills—the bills would have barely been paid, each month a highwire act performed on pennies and dimes. There would have been no joy in a life like that. There couldn't be.

*   *   *

Later, when Charlie and Ash were finishing up their drinks, Charlie said, "You tell your daughter the gypsies are here?"

"No," Ramsy said. It hadn't crossed his mind.

"She'd just worry anyway," Charlie said. "Women are like that."

"Good ones, anyway," Ash said.

"Good ones," Charlie agreed. "Don't want her lying awake at night worrying over her old man."

Liza had admitted she did that sometimes anyway, but Ramsy didn't give her worries too much thought. He was fine on his own and always had been, but if Liza wanted to worry, there was nothing he could do to stop her.

Nights like tonight, when Stella didn't come into the bar, Ramsy had worries of his own. He wanted to drive past her house. If she didn't show up for two nights, then he'd definitely go. But she was a grown woman, entitled to nights alone. There was a time when she would have told him where she was and what she did, but all that was a very long time ago.

CHAPTER 2

1209 Red Clover Drive

The man mowed his lawn in neat horizontal lines, starting at the sidewalk and working up to the house. He turned the mower off when he pushed it to the backyard, and when he started it up again, the boy slipped in the side door. It was a one-story house, an older person's home, and the smells inside—stale cigars, old beer, microwaved food—told him it belonged to a widower. The wife's jewelry would be gone by now, passed on to daughters and granddaughters and nieces, so the bedroom closet was where he turned first. On the shelf just above the clothes was a heavy wooden box. A quick peek inside confirmed that it was full of old coins on thick paper cards.

Downstairs, the mower was still grinding at the late-fall lawn. The boy opened the top dresser drawer, pressing the thin, silky socks with his palms until he found what he wanted: a wad of cash, twenties and fifties, secured with a rubber band and hidden in a sock's toe. And finally, almost an afterthought, the cash from the wallet on the dresser. A twenty and a five—not much, but not nothing. He had no use for credit cards, car keys,

IDs. Those things could be tracked and found. They could not easily be sold. But coins, cash—these things meant life would be easier for a few days.

The mower was still going, so the boy, for only a moment, sat down on the bed. It creaked and sagged. The flowered bedspread was frayed at the edges. There was a wooden crucifix above the headboard, a black-and-white wedding photo underneath in a frame, and reading lamps on both nightstands, and he felt a sudden pulse of sadness. Then the mower sputtered off, and he gathered his things and slipped out the side door while the man pushed the mower into the garage. The boy left him to face the rest of his day.

"The gypsies got the neighbor's house," Stella announced to Ramsy and the men when she came into the bar the next night. "Got in the side door and took Frank's coin collection. They got all the cash, too."

It took a moment for the men to get over the shock of her voice.

"Anyone home there?" Jack Kurtz asked.

"Frank was out front mowing the lawn."

"He got lucky," Jack said. "Gypsies'd kill you as soon as rob you. How'd you find out?"

"Saw troopers outside later. Asked them."

Ramsy held his breath. He knew everyone was remembering another time the authorities were out-side Stella's house. The men who drank in his bar were mostly good men, but Ramsy didn't trust them not to say something they shouldn't.

There was a pause, but then Jack Kurtz said, "Knew from the start they'd be trouble. Knew from the start they wouldn't move on." No one else said a word.

Ramsy could always tell how Stella was really feeling by the way she drank her first glass of wine. Sometimes she drank as though she'd mistaken the action for breathing, her hand moving from bar to lips with the same even in, out, in, out of the lungs. Tonight, though Ramsy expected her to be upset and careless, she sipped slowly, then let the glass go untouched for a while.

When the men finally left, Stella turned to Ramsy. "They say gypsies steal babies."

"Do they?"

"It's what I've heard," she said. "They take the babies and raise them to be thieves. They teach them their customs, tricks for stealing—like how to leave a jewelry store with diamonds in their mouths. If the parents ever find them, they don't even recognize them. Their children aren't their children anymore."

"This isn't a folktale, Stella."

"No."

"We've got some bad kids, that's all."

"I know. Still. I think if I had children I'd be scared to death."

"You shouldn't think about things like that."

"I know."

She was quiet for a while. Then she said, "Kitty Kurtz came into the library today."

Kitty Kurtz, Jack's wife, had been the Coal Queen in high school, but she'd aged just like all the other women in town—quickly, harshly, the ravages somehow equal whether you were thin or fat or in between. Kitty was thin, but it didn't suit her. Flesh sagged at her neck, and her clavicle stuck out like a clothesline. Her face was pinched and painted, her eyelashes very black, and her hair had been bleached into a frizzy mane she swept back with gold barrettes. She wore low-cut shirts that showed her leathery breastbone and favored metallic shoes. Everything about Kitty was too much, too young, and people instinctively stayed out of her way. In another kind of town, among people she didn't know, her old loveliness might have managed to overpower her bitterness and indiscretion, making her seem exciting instead of sorry and strange. But in Shelk there was something weightless about her, some untethered thing that set others on edge.

"She have a card?"

"Didn't come in for a book," Stella said. "She came to talk about Lucy."

Stella told him the story. Kitty had blown in as she usually did, all windswept hair and excited cheeks. On her feet were puffy boots, pink, and she wore a bright red ski cap with a tassel. She let the front door slam and went right up to Stella at the desk.

"I've been thinking about you," she announced. "Been thinking what you must be going through, with the gypsies and all."

"The gypsies haven't bothered me," Stella said.

Kitty lowered her chin and looked up at Stella in disbelief. "You can be honest with me," she said. "I'm pretty sure you and I are thinking the same thing."

"And what's that?"

Kitty put her elbows on the counter and leaned forward. "I think the gypsies have Lucy," she said. "How else could she have disappeared? I think they were here all those years ago when it happened, and I think they're here now to return her to you."

"That's ridiculous," Stella managed to say.

"Is it? Look, Stella, something is telling me the gypsies know about Lucy. Now, this is none of my business, and I'm not the type to pry. But I wouldn't be able to sleep if I didn't come down here and tell you what I believe."

She paused, as though waiting for thanks, but Stella was unable to do more than nod. Kitty left the way she'd come in—with a swoosh of coat and scarf into cold wind that slammed the door behind her.

There was no more to the story. Stella waited for Ramsy to respond.

"Lotta nerve she has, saying that to you," he said finally. "Always stirring up trouble. You alright?"

Stella waved him off. "Of course."

"You tell me if she bothers you again."

Stella never talked about the night Lucy disappeared, not directly, and sometimes Ramsy wanted to shake it out of her, make her speak the whole sordid story. Instead, he poured her wine and leaned across the bar to brush hair from her wine-sticky lips. She'd never asked if she could stay late or if Ramsy had something to do in the morning. He'd stay open all night if that was what she wanted, and he liked that she knew it.

When Stella's eyes began drooping, Ramsy said, "Come on. I'll take you home."

Her house was dark when they arrived. "No light?" Ramsy said.

"Forgot."

"You shouldn't forget a thing like that."

"I didn't mean to."

Drunk, she didn't protest when he parked the truck and followed her to the door. He wouldn't sleep if he didn't check the locks on her doors and windows, and be the first one to step into the dark and empty house. On the porch, while she fumbled in her coat pocket for the key, Ramsy imagined what might wait for them inside: drawers spilled open, an intruder sneaking down the stairs, knife in hand. But as soon as he slid Stella's key into the lock and stepped over the threshold, he knew no one was there. Living alone had taught him how to recognize that stillness.

Stella's house was overrun with things she'd bought and found. There were boxes and bags in the rooms upstairs, as well as pieces of furniture, large frames, some paintings on rain-warped canvas. Most were shoved in corners and closets, half forgotten, and Ramsy sometimes felt like the house was empty, as though the rooms were filled with ripped-open envelopes or books with the pages torn out.

She'd lived there for almost fifteen years, moving in not long after Lucy disappeared. She had a lawyer sell the house she'd shared with her former husband, Seth— it was in his name, and she wanted nothing more to do with it. She couldn't afford much, and though the house was big, parts were so decrepit they were almost uninhabitable. Years ago, Ramsy had tried to do some of the work. He replaced some wiring, repainted a few rooms, repaired the wooden floor where rot had eaten through. He bought some insulation to finish off the sunroom out back but never managed to put it in. The house needed new windows, and plaster from a caved-in ceiling still coated the closed-off dining room. He wouldn't make a dent if he worked every day for a year, and if Stella noticed when he stopped bringing over his tools, she never said a word.

He checked the back door, the cellar, and the latches on all the windows. "Everything looks fine," he said. "Safe and sound."

"I need something, while you're here," Stella said. "The storm window in the spare room upstairs is stuck. I can feel the draft across the hall at night. Can you get it down?"

"Of course," Ramsy said.

For the first time in years, he climbed the steps and turned left into Stella's spare bedroom. It was a small room, and though there was a window in the middle, heavy plum curtains blocked the light. Ramsy parted the curtains and raised the blind, then opened the window and reached up to jiggle the storm pane free. He lowered it and returned the blind and curtains to how they'd been. Then he sat down in the room's only chair.

Thick patterned wall hangings swaddled the upstairs into a hushed cocoon. He leaned forward and raised the blind again, peering down onto Stella's backyard. In the moonlight he saw a bird feeder hanging from an oak tree, bare now. Dry stalks of old hydrangeas huddled in a tangled clump by the garage. Ramsy didn't want to move, believed, in fact, he couldn't move, that the quiet and peace of this room were holding him to his chair, erasing the rest of the world and leaving him alone. He wondered how much time Stella spent sitting in this chair, looking out this window, while her mind found the quiet it needed to rest.

Ramsy roused himself. "Fixed," he said when he went downstairs. He squinted his eye in the light. "Drafts should stay out now. We can put plastic up if you still feel cold."

Stella was half asleep, but she smiled. "Thanks, Ramsy."

"I'm going to head home," he said.

"Okay." But then she paused. "Something feels wrong, Ramsy. I feel it in my gut. Something bad will happen. There's death in the air. These gypsies are here, and it's the same time of year Lucy disappeared."

"No meaning there," Ramsy said. "Thefts will happen, that's all. Don't need gypsies for that. Get some sleep, now."

"I will."

He waited while she bolted the door behind him, then walked briskly through the damp air to his truck. Just a few degrees colder and the roads would freeze over, form puddles of black ice where the road dipped and curved. His house would be dark and cold. It wasn't a place he looked forward to as he drove on the empty roads with the tires rattling underneath him. Stella's house had been warm. There was a time when he would have stayed there on a night like this, and on nights unlike this. It was so many years ago that the memory of it should have been dim, mottled, veiled with time, but it wasn't. It was crisp like a shadow against snow.

*   *   *

Ramsy didn't think of Stella's story every time he looked at her, but he did on nights like tonight, when her past rose around her like smoke. He hadn't been part of it—hadn't known Stella until later—but he'd heard the story many times, and could almost believe he'd been there.

Fifteen years ago, Stella Vale was thirty-one years old, newly married to Seth Kimmell and settling slowly into a small two-story house on Oak Road. With a ribbon in her braided hair and an ivory complexion, she was the prettiest waitress at the Unionville Country Club, a red-brick building set back on a golf green twenty miles outside Shelk. Stella kept to herself on her shifts unless Seth came in. They'd met at the country club—he'd flirted with her when he saw her in the pro-shop café, sent her blushing for extra rolls and refills, won her over with undisguised adoration and easy charm. The other waitresses, with dyed hair and out-of-season tans, deeply resented her. Though they dropped the names of country-club members who'd given them a compliment or a generous holiday tip, as though they'd somehow managed to forge a relationship, Stella had actually done what they'd pretended.

Stella continued to work at the club until she was eight months pregnant. She didn't have to. Seth encouraged her to quit. But Stella, prone to solitude and shyness, had grown used to the bustle of the restaurant kitchen, the rough joking of the cooks. She didn't talk much, but she liked the talk around her. Finally, when her back started aching too much to stay on her feet, she quit and stayed home to wait.

That last month, everything went wrong. A woman phoned one day, looking for Seth. "I'm his wife," the woman said. Even though Stella said, "So am I," and explained who she was and where she lived, the woman persisted. But how much could she persist, when Stella was the one with his baby inside her, and his scent on the sheets upstairs?

But when she confronted Seth, he said, "Shit. How'd she find this number?" When he saw the look on Stella's face, he said, "Please. This is my crisis, not yours." And he started staying away from home at night.

People whispered about Stella in Ramsy's bar, and everyone said that things would come to a bad end. They may have even hoped so. The news spread quickly, and with concealed excitement, when Seth came home drunk out of his skull one night not long after the baby was born, left the car running in front of the house, grabbed little Lucy out of her crib, and ran out the door. Stella's last glimpse was a flash of white sleeper, the kind of one-piece outfit Stella preferred: it made Lucy seem like a tidy, comfortable, happy little gift.

The cops found Seth passed out at the wheel three towns over. He said he didn't remember—that he *couldn't* remember—what happened to Lucy, and no one could really argue that it wasn't true. They found the other wife and questioned her. Frustrated with the angry inquiries and background checks, she gave a snort of derision and said, "Seth isn't someone who thinks too far ahead. If I was you I'd check the highway. Probably tossed her out of the car once he sobered up and saw what he did."

They scoured the highway, farther in each direction than Seth could have ever gone. They looked inside every bag, under every pile of leaves. Stella was with them every morning, and searched long after them at night. At first, people helped her. Ramsy had heard a lot about these searches. Each morning, before the sun rose, Stella led the group through the neighborhood until they hit Route 119. It was a narrow two-lane highway that connected some of the mountain towns, and tall, industrial streetlamps lit the way. Stella trudged ahead along the road, against traffic, her long hair lifting in the cold wind. When she came across a plastic bag on the shoulder, she untied the top and dumped its contents on the ground, sifted through them, and kept walking. Others did the same. They walked five miles south, crossed the road, and walked the five miles back on the opposite side.

Ramsy had heard about the things they'd found on their searches. In most bags were fast-food wrappers, empty cups, dirty napkins, pop cans, beer bottles, torn pantyhose, newspapers, rot. But they also found things that had once been living. There were mice and rats with their necks snapped in wire traps. There were birds and rabbits shot with BBs. Once there was a litter of kittens, their fur matted from drowning. And there was a dog, a dark brown beagle. Stella had opened the bag, then dropped it and ran.

They'd found bags full of bright, torn wrapping paper and ribbons, wax-dripped candles, and festive colored envelopes. The pastel papers from baby showers. Stella found a whole bag full of half-deflated balloons, which a breeze lifted out of the bag and scattered, bouncing, all over the highway, their colored strings trailing like second thoughts behind them. Some said Stella was bothered more by things like that than she was by drowned kittens or mice with broken necks.

As the days went on, Stella's helpers dropped out one by one. Stella's behavior had become a little strange. She'd stopped searching only the bags that looked suspicious and started searching every bag, even ones too small to possibly hold a baby. Even ones obviously filled with leaves or trash. Even boxes where people's attic junk peeked through. And she began taking things home with her, without explanation, slipping a piece of costume jewelry in her coat pocket or a photograph in her sleeve. At first, people asked her why. Stella said she could sense stories in tattered Harlequins, old beaded bracelets, yellowed snapshots. But when she found a box full of baby clothes—mostly blue, some white and yellow, some with the tags still on—people stopped asking questions. It was suddenly clear to everyone that going home with something was better than going home with nothing. They sensed that something had changed, and they slipped quietly, politely, back to their lives.

*   *   *

Seth disappeared for good after the investigation, to serve his prison time somewhere in eastern PA. Two months later, on a morning after a gusting blizzard that left snow piled high on shrubbery and parked cars, Stella held a yard sale outside the house they'd shared. She didn't post signs on telephone poles or put a classified ad in the paper. Instead, without advance notice, she emerged from her house that morning, bundled in coat, hat, and gloves, and snapped bed-sheets over the snow. Then she carried out armfuls of Seth's things: clothes, ties, shoes, socks, underwear. She hauled out plastic bags filled with shaving cream and shampoo. She piled the sheets with books and records and binders of old baseball cards, table lamps and straight-backed kitchen chairs, sturdy black lug-gage, jars of pens, a box of half-empty liquor bottles. Then she sat on the porch and kept the front door open, a sign taped to the doorframe announcing *Furniture for Sale Inside.*

It didn't take long for word to spread. As soon as the plows finished that morning, cars began filing down Oak Road, parking in a long line that stretched to the end of the block. The spectacle was what they'd come for—grim, bundled Stella. Seth's earthly possessions dumped in the snow. A peek inside the house where tragedy had struck. But there was no one in Shelk who didn't like a good yard sale, and after the spectacle wore off, they got out their money and started carrying things away.

The sale was the talk of the town for days afterward. Mostly people asked in hushed voices, *Where were the baby's things?* There had been no trace of Lucy in the items on the ground. When Stella finally moved out, leaving the cleaning and sale of the house to a lawyer, people said she must have left it all behind, crib and rocking chair and drawers of tiny clothes.

*   *   *

The first time Stella came into the bar, she'd been out walking, and her hands were red from the cold.

"Drink?" Ramsy asked her, and she said, "I suppose." He knew who she was. Everybody did. But he didn't ask any questions, and let her drink alone. After that, she kept coming back.

She sat there night after night with her red wine. Ramsy had never seen anyone drink so peacefully. Too often, men who drank in his bar did it desperately, with hard swallows that left drips on their wrists and shirtfronts and sadness and anger in their eyes. Stella drank for the same reasons they did—to erase, soothe, numb, dampen, weaken, blur, forget—but the Stella that emerged from the wine seemed better than before.

"You look at me like you want to say something," she said one night, "or like I'm supposed to understand something just by looking at you." She was drunk enough to look at his eye without flinching. "It's not pity—I know that look. What is it?"

"I lost a baby too," he said. He hadn't meant to tell her. Talking about his past wasn't his way, and the words felt stale in his mouth.

Stella didn't say anything, but he went on. "A baby girl, same as yours. Her mother took her seventeen years ago. Said I wasn't worth shit. Walked out with the baby and I never saw her again."

"You didn't chase her?"

"Not enough. But she was right to go."

"Then it's different," Stella said. "I tried to chase Seth. I just couldn't catch him." She left, and Ramsy was sorry he'd told her, sorry he'd made it seem like he would understand. Of course it was different. Of course it was. But then Stella started coming back, and he saw that maybe it had helped after all.

He was always glad to drive her home, and soon, he began spending the night when she said she was lonely or scared. Together, they didn't have to pretend normalcy, didn't have to lock away words like *daughter*, *lost*, or *grief*. The specter of the missing babies loomed over and around them, but they embraced it, swallowed it whole, used each other to remember and to forget. Some nights Ramsy lay awake, frightened that they could feel pleasure even after they'd lost so much.

It went on more than three years. They came together at Stella's nearly every night, and for the first time since Marcie left, Ramsy felt what he thought other men must feel, what he had once felt, a kind of warmth, a kind of happiness, that came from someone else's breath mingling in rooms with his own.

Then Liza called him. The kind of missing-daughter call that would never come for Stella. *I'm your daughter*, she'd said. His daughter. The long separation didn't make it any less true.

The night after Liza's first call, Ramsy drove to Stella's house to tell her the news. She greeted him sleepily in a robe and slippers. "It's late—come in. Let's go to bed." But she took his hand when she saw he was shaking.

"My God, Ramsy, what happened?"

"Liza called."

She looked like she'd been struck. "You said she was gone."

"She was. She found me."

"It's been over twenty years."

"If I was a praying man I'd say I got my answer." Gently he moved into the house and shut the door behind him.

"What will you do? What does she want?"

"Meet her, I guess. Says she wants to know me." Ramsy couldn't stop a tiny catch from hooking his words.

At this, Stella put her hand on his arm, made a visible effort to smile. "It's wonderful. It's really wonderful. I'm so happy for you. A miracle, really. They exist after all."

But her eyes went dark, and though he followed her upstairs, Ramsy wished he could leave.

It didn't take much more than a night for Stella's jealousy and pain to spring up around her. She asked him questions and expressed joy and amazement, but Ramsy could see that every mention of Liza—grown, newlywed Liza, living in Pittsburgh in an apartment she wanted Ramsy to visit—cracked pieces of her heart off like bark from a dry, rotting tree. It got so that Ramsy couldn't bear to say Liza's name, which was difficult as their calls increased, and they made plans to meet. Soon he stopped staying the night. Soon Stella stopped coming to the bar. Whenever he saw her he felt he was looking at her across a great distance, and soon they never saw each other at all.

Stella eventually started coming back to the bar, but what had been between them was now gone. Stella wasn't angry or hateful, and she lived a quiet life. But losing Lucy had cloaked her in a soft, muffling wall that Ramsy couldn't get through. Not that he tried— he respected her distance. Lord knew how she ever managed to live after searching in bags for her baby. All he knew was that on nights like this, with gypsies or what have you on the loose, a woman like Stella shouldn't have to be alone.

CHAPTER 3

24 Goldenrod Street

There was mail in the box outside, and the leaves were swept from the front steps, so the boy knew someone lived there. There was no back door—the house was one simple square—and the front door was locked. But the side window was easy to break, and he climbed inside.

He found the cash, in a drawer of the bedside table, a small stack of bills wrapped in a rubber band. But there was more here, he could feel it. The house had bare walls, bare surfaces, barely anything but food in the kitchen to suggest a living soul slept and woke here. He couldn't imagine this—this nothing—being the extent of someone's life. In a place like this, you had to hold onto something. There had to be more, and he set out to find it.

Living room first—nothing but one wobbly floor lamp and a pile of outdated Time *magazines on a tray table. Closet next. Clothes—flannel shirts and folded jeans—patted down and pulled from hangers. Boxes opened and rifled through. Nothing more than newspaper clippings and photographs, clearly long forgotten. There was a heavy black case of knives, twenty or thirty lying in rows like teeth. He yanked three small sharp ones free and tucked them into his satchel. Then, on a stepstool shoved deep into the back, a shoebox with a cloth-wrapped pistol inside. Standard military weapon, and loaded. He could see that much. He emptied the magazine and slid the gun into his waistband and the bullets into his pocket.*

In the kitchen, there was a small stand under the telephone with one shallow drawer. He yanked it out, spilling pens and rubber bands and a small box on the floor. He crouched and opened the box. A war medal, a bronze star hanging from a bit of red and blue ribbon. It was tarnished and smudged, as though at one time someone had held it for long hours in his hand. He shoved the medal back into the drawer. He'd seen enough. Whoever lived here had seen enough, too.

Whenever Ramsy was out in town, he found himself looking for gypsies. He'd been an outsider once too— hell, after thirty years, lots of people might say he still was—and he felt a strange kinship with the gypsies, whoever they were. They'd all come from somewhere else. The difference was that no one imagined Ramsy would ever move on.

Shop N' Save wasn't crowded when Ramsy stopped in the next afternoon. The floors were dirty, the shelves poorly stocked, and at the front of the store young cashiers with pale faces counted out change in their register drawers.

He saw Stella come in while standing in the checkout line. She was wearing jeans and boots and her bulky winter coat. Her hair was pulled into a ponytail. A large leather purse—something she never brought to the bar—hung from her shoulder. She walked straight in and headed for the produce aisle. Ramsy stepped out of line and followed her, a stranger in the middle of the day. It was different when they'd been together, when he could watch her face change as morning rose—from her face in the darkness to her face in the light. The change didn't seem so violent then.

Now, she looked tired in the fluorescent lights, and older than she seemed when she came to the bar. She was wearing lipstick but no other makeup, and her red-purple lips looked like they belonged on another woman's face. She filled a basket with vegetables, fruit, bread, rice, and cans of crushed tomatoes. Ramsy had a sudden urge to grab her arm and make her his again. But he hung back, behind the canned green beans, until she turned out of the aisle.

She saw him a minute later, when she doubled back for something forgotten. "Ramsy," she said. "Hello."

"Hello," Ramsy said. They smiled at each other. "How are you?"

"Fine," she said. "You?"

"Fine."

Why was it so much easier in the bar, or in his truck, late, driving home? Now, her face was filled with errands and the necessities of the day. They went through the checkout, and then the automatic door whooshed open and released them into the cold afternoon. Ramsy was about to say goodbye when Stella said, "Look. Is that a gypsy?" At the end of the shopping plaza, near an empty storefront that had once held a drugstore, a young girl sat on a milk crate, her arms crossed low in her lap. Two more milk crates stood beside her, and a cardboard sign rested against the middle one: *Palm Readings $5*. Her bored slouch said she'd been waiting for a customer for some time.

They watched her for a moment, and then Ramsy took a step toward his truck.

"Wait. I'm going to have a reading," Stella said. "Come with me?"

She didn't wait for Ramsy's answer. A worry flashed through his mind, too fast for him to stop it: that Stella had finally cracked, crossed a line anyone else would have crossed long ago. Ramsy angrily pushed it away. She was curious, that was all, and kind, happy to give a few bills to a young girl on a cold day. He shifted his grocery bag to his other arm and followed her.

He saw it too late: around the girl's chest, a many-layered strip of cloth was wrapped around a baby. Only the very top of its head was visible, tufts of wispy dark hair shivering in the wind. It was too late to block her from Stella's view, and Ramsy heard her surprised gasp.

"You have a baby in there," she said. "A baby without a hat."

"She's warm," the girl said. "She's got my body heat."

"But it's freezing today. Surely she doesn't have to be out here with you."

The girl's bored stare didn't change. "You want a reading or not?" she said, and after an agitated moment, Stella sat down on a crate across from the girl. She took Stella's hand in hers. For a long moment, she studied her palm, and then she studied Stella. Ramsy wondered how much she knew about Stella just from that long measured gaze. Stella's cheeks were flushed in the cold, disguising her usual pallor, and a warm hat covered her hair. She looked like any other woman out shopping, planning dinner for herself or a family back home. But then the girl looked at Ramsy, and he knew he was fooling himself. He and Stella stood out in this town as much as the gypsies did.

"Your heart line begins with the Mount of Jupiter, which means you're a romantic and believe strongly in love," the girl began. Ramsy hadn't expected the authority in her voice, the conviction.

"To you," she said, "even love that comes with difficulties is attractive, and you've often made decisions that may not make sense to people who don't know you well. You don't always choose the easiest partners, but this is out of your control. See—here—the heart line breaks. You gave yourself to something, and lost it. You came back from it—but here, where the line starts up again and then forms a chain—you weren't the same."

Ramsy saw Stella lean in toward the girl, staring hard at the palm she held. From where he stood Ramsy could see that Stella's hand was dry, with flaky white skin roughening the bases of her fingers. The line the girl was tracing was deep, and redder than the rest of Stella's skin.

"Below the heart line is the head line," the girl said. "Yours don't touch each other, which shows a strong self-reliance and a tendency to act without caring about others' advice. Your line also slopes dramatically, which means you're imaginative but also may be prone to insanity."

At this Stella laughed, a short, hard bark, and the girl looked up and frowned. In a hesitant voice she went on, "The line is deep, though, which shows a strong mind."

Stella said, "Well, that's a relief."

"You have good intuition," she said. "Here, at the edge of your hand—this line. You can't always account for how you know things, or why you feel the way you do." She studied Stella's palm once more.

"Finally there's the life line," the girl said. "Yours is long, and uncrossed by other lines, which means you'll have a long, healthy life. But here—it breaks, just briefly—and here, around the break, is a square." The girl traced four faint lines into Stella's palm. "A break on a long line like this can mean an accident, or a loss. But the square shows you'll recover." She released Stella's hand and sat back on her crate.

"Something is coming," the girl concluded. "A change, a discovery. Something you've been waiting for. You've lost something," she repeated, "and you're about to find it." Her voice was not ominous. She sounded bored, ready to take her cash and get back to waiting out the day. "Five dollars," she said.

Stella gave her the money. "How old are you?"

"Fifteen."

"And the baby?"

"Six weeks. A girl." She didn't offer a name.

Stella nodded and turned toward her car, her chin lowered against the cold, and Ramsy followed. He hurried after her, hoping to stop this now before it could get out of hand.

Ramsy waited by Stella's car while she put her bags into the trunk. "Don't say it," she told Ramsy. "I know what you're thinking, and I don't want to hear it."

"So you believe her."

"How did she know, Ramsy? How did she know?"

Ramsy couldn't tell Stella that loss was written on her face as grotesquely as a missing eye. Instead he said, "Not a person in this town hasn't lost something. Not a person in this town couldn't identify with that." Stella set her mouth. "She's just a kid," Ramsy said. "Learned palm reading from a book somewhere. People can promise you anything when they don't care whether it's the truth."

But Stella wasn't listening. Ramsy watched as she slid into the driver's seat, dug a pen from her purse, and jotted the girl's remarks on the back of her Shop N' Save receipt, as though they were a recipe she'd heard from a neighbor and wanted to remember when she got home.

He had to say one more thing. "Stella." She peered up at him from the car. "You know it's not her. This town is filled with fifteen-year-old girls, gypsy and otherwise."

Stella looked away. "You're always so certain of everything, Ramsy. The world doesn't hold any mystery for you, any promise. I'm not sure I'd want to live that way."

"Stella. You know it's not her."

Stella stared straight ahead and then started the car. "Of course I know it," she said finally. "After all these years, Ramsy, now you think I'm crazy?"

She looked at him, waiting, but all he said was, "See you tonight?"

Stella nodded, but he could tell her mind was far away. In his head, too, a new version of the night Lucy disappeared was taking shape: gypsies whisking a bundled child from the roadside. It hovered just outside the edges of his imagination, and then, as it should be, it was gone.

*   *   *

People in town had never been so sealed up. Doors that had once stood open were now bolted, barricaded, strengthened, chained. Even men out raking leaves locked their doors, fearful that they wouldn't see a gypsy slip inside. Ramsy heard from the men in his bar the things they did to their houses. Besides installing steel hardware that fastened door to wall, they pushed chairs under doorknobs, tied windows to sills with rope, stacked tin cans on windowframes. Few in Shelk could afford a home alarm system, so the methods were crude, makeshift, infused with fear and anger. Ramsy locked his door as he always did—a doorknob lock that twisted and a chain that wouldn't take much force to break. He had nothing any gypsies would want, anyway.

"Kitty's driving me crazy," said Jack Kurtz one night. "Five locks so far she's made me install. Big suckers, too. Takes a good chunk of time. Only way to get in our house now is to chop into it with an ax." He scoffed.

"Windows are next. Says she can't sleep at night with the gypsies out there. Seems to me getting rid of the gypsies is a better plan than locking us up inside."

The men added stories about their own wives' fears, but their complaints—even Jack's—were half-hearted. None would have put in those locks on their own, but Ramsy could tell they were happy to have them. That was the problem with living as they did. None had much money, but each had something prized or irreplaceable that they wanted passionately to protect. Mostly it was jewelry, nothing dazzling, but special in a town like this: a mother's gold-set engagement ring, sapphire studs passed down from a grandmother, a grandfather's watch, and necklaces and rings that were prized for sentimental reasons more than anything else. Caring about objects was a risky business. There was always the chance that someone else was going to step in and steal them away.

There was nothing in Ramsy's bar but beer and stools to sit on, nothing behind the counter but glasses, a mirror, and a lamp. Years ago, to make his bar more *personal*, he arranged his knife collection in a shadow box and stood it behind the bar. But the knives drew questions and requests for stories ("Where'd you get that one, Ramsy?" "Use that one to make anyone cry?"), and by the end of one week, Ramsy felt like he'd given too much away. When he took the knives home, the bar was empty again, and only then did it feel truly his.

Ramsy poured more beers for the men, and while he listened to them discuss locks and bolts and the expense of home alarms, he thought about Stella. So many times he'd wished he could've been there the night Seth showed up and took Lucy away. He would've held the door, pinned Seth down, tripped him on his way to the crib, anything to stop him from getting his hands on the baby.

When she came into the bar, later, she looked tired. She drank only three glasses of wine, slowly, and listened to the men talk of locks and work. The talk had nothing to do with her. Few things did.

"You want me to put some locks in at your place?" Ramsy asked her. He grew warm after he asked it. The men had been talking about their wives and Ramsy felt he was implying something he shouldn't.

"I'm fine," Stella said. "I've got nothing for them to take, Ramsy. You know that."

On the phone that night, Liza said, "We haven't talked about it, but I know there are strangers in Shelk. Gypsies. I don't like you being there, Ramsy."

"Just some kids," Ramsy said, because, in truth, they were. "Not much more than petty theft around here."

"Well, we heard it was worse in Owl Creek," Liza said. "Serious amounts of money. They seem reckless, Ramsy. Dangerous."

"I'll stay out of their way. They won't bother me."

"I don't like it. You're alone there—what if something happens?"

Something happening—a fear of Liza's that most women shared. It's why they kept extra bills in their purses, sewed nametags into children's clothes. It seemed an awful way to live, and he had a difficult time imagining what Liza had in mind. Was she afraid he'd fall and hit his head in the shower, lie in blood until, days later, he was missed? Those were foolish fears.

"I'll be fine," he said.

Liza's sigh scratched over the line. "You're alone," she said again.

"No."

"And you're lonely."

"No."

"You just don't think you are. What's normal to you is loneliness to the rest of the world. Move out here, Ramsy. Think about it. Please?"

Women like Liza didn't understand that *alone* did not mean *lonely*. It had taken Ramsy a long time to understand it himself.

It was easy to be alone in a town like Shelk. There was no hustle and bustle to be left out of, no festive places to dread going to alone. There were no couples to envy, no one walking arm-in-arm like there was all the time on TV. People were married, sure. Men loved their wives and women loved their husbands, or at least everyone tried to, the best they knew how. But when Ramsy saw couples in cars stopped at traffic lights, the man was usually driving, his arm hanging out the window with a cigarette, and the woman was staring out her own window, off into space. They could be any two people paired in that car, if it weren't for the ring that flashed on the man's hand when he lifted his cigarette for a drag. What Ramsy saw between most people didn't seem to be love at all. That wasn't what he wanted. Being with someone like that would be lonelier than being alone, which, if that was what you were accustomed to, wasn't so bad at all.

When he hung up, he looked at Stella and said, "That was Liza," as though having his daughter call him didn't matter. Stella nodded as she always did. Sometimes the way Stella looked at him made him think she wished Liza had just stayed gone.

"Liza knows about the gypsies," Ramsy said.

When Stella looked up at him, her eyes were distant and sad. "It's nice of her to call." She frowned then, and an uncertain look crossed her face. "I need to tell you something," she said. She'd been nursing the same glass of wine for an hour. "You'll think it's crazy."

"You know I won't."

"I can't stop thinking about what Kitty Kurtz said. That the gypsies know about Lucy. And that palm reading—that I'll find something I've lost. It's strange, Ramsy, don't you think? The gypsies being here, that poor cold baby, all of it together?"

Ramsy kept polishing a glass with his worn plaid rag. "Not sure it makes any sense," he said. "These are young kids. Anyone who knows about Lucy would be thirty, forty."

"Lucy would be young," Stella said. "She'd be fifteen— like the girl who read my palm."

"You think she's one of them?" He fought to keep his voice even. "You really think that girl was her?"

"How would I know either way? I need to ask them, Ramsy. And I can't stop thinking about that baby." Only now did Ramsy notice the grocery bag at her feet. Through the thin white plastic he saw diapers and a blanket printed with yellow ducks. "Thought I might help, somehow."

"You can't go up there by yourself," Ramsy said. "How will you find them?"

"I don't know. But I have to do something."

Her agitation pulsed across the bar. Ramsy wiped down the counter and emptied the register. "Let's go, then," he said. He knew already they'd see no one, that Stella's provisions for the baby would go undelivered. Then she would understand how it was, and that would be the end of the story. Better this way. Thoughts like these shouldn't have a chance to grow.

*   *   *

It was cold, bitter. Even through the closed truck windows Ramsy could feel it. There was little chance the gypsies would be out in the open, even around a fire. But he drove on because Stella's face was peaceful, as it must have been all those years ago when she searched bags each night along the highway. He was sure he'd never felt that peace and sure his face had never shown it. He'd buried his grief, quickly, and rarely looked back. Yes, Liza had returned. But if she hadn't, he wouldn't have gone looking for her each time a sliver of hope pricked his heart. He would never have expected her to be just around the corner if only he could find the right corner at the right time.

"How far?" Stella asked. They'd been driving uphill for ten minutes.

"Far as you want," Ramsy said. "They could be any-where. We're passing the caves now." There was noth-ing out the window but blackness.

Stella sighed. "Don't know what I was thinking. If we found them, what would I say? I'm sorry, Ramsy. Kitty got to me, that's all, and all the talk of gypsies. My imagination—" She waved a hand. "Just got it in my head to do something, that's all. Foolish. Let's go."

He pulled to the side of the road and was about to turn the truck around when he saw headlights approaching. He heard the car gunning its engine as it rounded a curve about half a mile ahead. Ramsy frowned. It was very late, and though he and Stella had their reasons for heading up the mountain, he doubted anyone else had cause to be here at this hour. When the car came into view, Ramsy closed his eye against the glare until the car was nearly beside him. Then he looked over. Kitty Kurtz was driving, leaning forward anxiously, her face taut. If she cared about passing a parked truck on the narrow road at a high speed, she didn't show it. Ramsy watched the taillights in his rearview mirror and heard Kitty's tires squeal around another turn.

"Was that Kitty Kurtz?" Stella said, turning to peer out the back window.

"Looked that way."

"Well, what on earth." Neither of them bothered to speculate. Truths about women like Kitty Kurtz had a way of coming to light on their own.

*   *   *

When Ramsy got home that night, he knew something was wrong. He could sense it as soon as he left his truck. Around him, neighbors' houses were dark, locked up tight. There were no sounds but night-sounds. His front door was shut. But when he walked alongside his house, he found it: a window broken from the outside, the latch undone, the pane raised. Scuff marks on the siding where someone had climbed inside.

Ramsy walked back around, unlocked his front door, and entered. He closed and locked the door behind him, then turned on the ceiling light. He heard a sound from the bathroom—a window shoved open.

"Who's there?" Ramsy shouted. He ran back outside and sprinted around the house, rounding the corner just as someone dropped from the window to the ground. The boy landed on all fours then pushed off at a dead run. "Stop!" Ramsy yelled, but the boy was already gone. Ramsy caught a glimpse of a black sweater and a flapping, unzipped jacket, but that was all.

Back inside, panting from the sprint and the shock, he surveyed the damage. His house was trashed. Someone had obviously tried hard to find things that were not there. Drawers hung out of their sockets, emptied. The floor was littered with clothes and all the things that made up Ramsy's home. Even the kitchen cabinets had been ransacked. Silverware, dishes, pots, pans—everything was in the open, in the light, as startled as Ramsy was.

Then he remembered the gun: a Colt .45 automatic, identical to the one he'd had in the war. He'd gotten it after he came home, when he was afraid his missing eye would make him a victim. The .45 was what he was familiar with, its size and weight, and when he bought it he felt a flickering of who he'd been before it all fell apart. But soon after moving to Shelk, he'd put it in a shoebox and never touched it again. He looked for it now, in the closet. Gone. It was an old gun, unpredictable. And with no children around, he'd kept it loaded.

He cleared a space on the couch and sat down. He should call the state police—had an obligation to, really, with the gun missing—but he wouldn't. The gypsies had ransacked his home as they'd ransacked so many others, and the anger in town was already growing. There was no telling what the cops—and the men—would do if they knew a gun was in the gypsies' hands. And other than losing the gun, Ramsy was just left with a mess. Calling the police would be an angry reflex, and Ramsy didn't feel angry. He just felt very, very tired.

He wanted to call someone. He wanted someone to exclaim over the mess and help him put things back in order. But who could he call? It was three in the morning. The men from the bar were at home, asleep with their wives. He couldn't call Stella. It wouldn't be right. He stood and began picking things up from the floor, putting them back where they came from. He put his few books on the shelf. He stacked dishes and pans. He swept up the glasses that had been broken. His boots thudded on the floor and his flannel shirt swished as he bent and straightened, again and again, each piece of his life a different size and weight in his hands. *Lonely*. The word slid into his mind like a thief through the window—quiet and smooth, and there to do harm. *Lonely*.

Finally, something had happened—just like Liza feared—and he was alone and didn't want to be.

Lonely. If there was another bar like his to go to, he'd go. He'd leave the mess and drive there now, sit with a beer and either talk or not talk to the man behind the bar. It wouldn't matter what he said. He knew from experience that it wasn't about the words. It was the being listened to, the being seen by someone, the being sure you were physically present when it seemed like you'd disappeared. All the things you didn't have—couldn't have—when you were by your-self at night.

When the sun lightened the rooms, he stopped clean-ing. He opened the front door to let in the fresh, cold air, and made coffee. He sat at his table and sipped it while it was still near-boiling. The heat burned his tongue. His eye watered, and he sipped again. The pale pre-morning light lapping at the sky made him feel old and even more alone. There were no night-sounds now, just the slam of someone's car door. It was that slam that did it, that slam that sounded like every other slamming door he'd ever heard in his life. Maybe Liza was right—maybe it was time he left. He could do exactly this—sitting and sipping—anywhere in the world.

Thirty years. That was how long he'd been in this town, and tonight the theft had shown him more clearly than ever that he didn't belong. Maybe he never had. But after all this time, didn't there have to be a reason why he couldn't just pick up and leave? Something had to be keeping him here. He was tired, was all. That was why he couldn't remember. He poured more coffee and drank it fast, willing it to his memory. He knew this place, every corner and street, every store and bridge. He knew people, their troubles and their families, the fights and affairs and bad debts. But in the end, what it came down to was this: he was on one side of the bar, and the townspeo-ple—and Stella—were on the other. He was no more capable of changing this than he was of growing a new eye in his empty socket. He had no more connection to this town than the gypsies.

He thought of all the people he knew who'd left Shelk. Marcie was one. He admired her for that, even though her leaving meant she'd left him here alone. There was Seth Kimmell, who'd left in violence and disgrace, and a teenage boy or two sent away each year to the Army. That was all. There were always a handful of high schoolers who made it out of town for college—into Pittsburgh or Erie, even West Virginia or Ohio. But unless they were girls who found someone out of town to marry, they usually came back home. There was no one who left for the sake of adventure, no one who left to find something new. It was like leaving town was something shameful: left to the desperate, the delinquent, and the insane. But the gypsies—couldn't forget about them. Gypsies would leave this town in a heartbeat and never think about it again.

His house was clean now. Tomorrow he'd wipe down the siding, clean the muddy footprints from the windowsills. He wondered where the boy who'd robbed his house was now, if he'd looked at the gun he'd stolen. If he'd fired it. Thin fingers of fear stirred Ramsy's exhaustion, but he pushed the fear away and faced the morning with determined resolve.

*   *   *

When Ramsy went to the bar that night, he brought a square of cardboard, a black marker, and a hammer and nail. *Closing,* he wrote, and posted the sign on a tree at the end of the drive. It didn't make him feel good to write the word, and when the men came in long-faced, he didn't have much to tell them.

"Just time to be moving on," he told Ash. "My daughter wants me to move near her. Now's as good a time as any."

"You don't belong up there," Ash said. "You belong in Shelk, Ramsy. You know that."

"Maybe so," Ramsy said. "But I'm getting older. What if something happened? It's not good to be alone."

"For Chrissake, Ramsy. You're not alone. What are we, nothing?"

Ramsy filled his glass and kept quiet. Ash wasn't someone he could call for help in the middle of the night. Ash might think he was, but he wasn't. Ramsy knew. And if Ash took some time to think it over, he'd know it, too.

"When?" Charlie asked.

"A couple of weeks."

"What're you gonna do up there?" Jack Kurtz asked. "Open another bar?"

"Haven't thought about it," Ramsy admitted. "Something will come along."

"You gonna live with Liza? Or get a place of your own?"

"Haven't thought about that yet, either," Ramsy said. The men looked at him with their eyebrows knitted close. Ramsy could tell they thought something strange was going on. They'd been giving him that look for as long as he'd known them. It was the eye that did it. Gave him a secret life he didn't really have. Mostly, he didn't mind it. Whatever it was they were thinking now, he let them go on thinking it.

"We're not going to know beforehand when you decide it's time to leave," Charlie said a while later. It wasn't a question.

Ramsy shrugged.

"Better this way," Ash said. "I'm not much for goodbyes."

"Sure will miss this place," Charlie said. "It's been good, coming here."

"There'll be other places," Ramsy said.

"Not like this."

It was as much of a goodbye as Ramsy wanted or expected. Soon they were talking as they always did, of ball games and hunting and wives, and drinking what he poured like it was an ordinary night. Deer season would start next month, and they shared past successes and failures. Charlie had bought a new gun—a Remington Model 700 bolt-action rifle—and described it to Jack and Ash.

"Been two years since I shot anything," he said. "This year'll be different."

Ramsy knew what each of the men had shot for many years back. A thought flitted in like a moth—he wouldn't know, anymore—then disappeared. He was unsentimental—always had been—but he thought he'd feel *something*. Maybe he would, in the next few days, when he locked the door for the last time. For now he turned the TV on mute for the ball game, and the blue light flickered across the men's faces.

Stella came in later and didn't say anything about the sign. The men tried to watch her without seeming that they were, but Stella gave nothing away. She drank slowly, joining the conversation when the talk turned to predictions of a hard, early winter.

"Snow and more snow, is what I heard," she said. "Snow and more snow."

But later, when they were alone, she put her drink down quietly and said, "So what's this all about?"

Ramsy filled the small sink behind the bar and began cleaning glasses with a wet rag, gripping them carefully in his soapy hands. "Just time for me to go," he said. "Liza wants me to move out there. I'm getting older. It's not good to be alone."

He knew his mistake as soon as he said it. "I'm alone," Stella said. "Tell me what's wrong with that."

"Nothing's wrong with it."

"Then why go?"

"I've been here a long time. I'll die in this town if I don't get out."

"Then you'll die in another town. I don't understand."

He wanted to tell her there was nothing keeping him here, that he had no reason to stay. But that would be cruel to say to Stella, and not exactly true. She could have kept him here, years ago.

"My house got robbed last night," he told her instead. "Kid got in through a window. Tore the place apart."

"Oh, Ramsy. Did he take anything?"

"I've got nothing to take." He turned off the water, rubbed his hands dry with another rag. "Some money, I guess. Just a little I had in the drawer by the bed." Better not to mention the gun. It felt like a secret, somehow, a secret between him and the gypsies.

"Call the police?"

"Not worth the trouble."

Stella nodded. Not many people would understand that, but Stella did. "Is that why you're leaving?"

"No," he said. "But it's as good a reason as any not to stay."

They didn't talk any more after that, and Ramsy was grateful. He was sure they'd talk more in the days ahead. But tonight they drank together quietly as frost crystallized on the grass outside and stars sparkled in the cold dark sky.

*   *   *

Word about Ramsy's leaving spread fast in town, and for a few days the bar was busier than usual. People who hadn't come in years suddenly reappeared, as though the bar's closing meant something to them. No one talked much, and those who weren't regulars didn't talk to Ramsy at all. Everyone took their time with their drinks and looked around before leaving. A few told Ramsy they were sorry to see the place go. But no one asked why he was leaving, and Ramsy got the feeling that they were afraid to hear his answer.

The regulars stayed late, talking and drinking like they always did.

"A whiskey," Jack said one night, running a hand through his hair. "And a bottle of Bud." Jack was unshaven and agitated, and he slid his wedding ring on and off, on and off, and then set it on the bar. He glanced over at Stella then glanced away. He asked for another whiskey and looked dully around the bar. "It's Kitty," he said loudly. "I think she's having an affair."

Charlie and Ash drew into themselves and stared into their laps. "Easy, Jack," Ramsy said, setting down a glass of cold water. He stood there as Jack sipped the water and took deep breaths.

When he spoke again his voice was lower. "She's not where she says she'll be," he said. "She says she's going for groceries, but when I go to the store she's not there. She says she's at her sister's, but when I call she's always just left on an errand. She says she's working late, but her car's not in the lot. She's sneaking around on me, Ramsy. Sneaking the fuck around."

"You're spying on her?" Ash said.

"She's my wife," Jack said. "I have a right." He slammed his glass down on the counter. "Goddamn gypsies," he said. "They get here and everything goes wrong."

A fight between Jack and Kitty was nothing new in Shelk. No one could fight like the Kurtzes. They lived on a street of close-set houses, and sound traveled easily through single-pane windows. They accused each other of ruining their lives—but it wasn't exactly clear what kind of life one would have without the other, or what exactly they'd sacrificed to be together. Neither one, most people in Shelk would agree, was any prize. Mornings after their fights, you might find a smashed mirror or broken chairback by the curb. They were violent with their words, and their things.

Ramsy dried a few glasses with a towel. He remembered Kitty Kurtz's late-night rush down the mountain—her grim white face, her grip on the wheel—and knew, if he wanted to, he could add fuel to Jack's fire. But if she was sneaking around like Jack suspected, Ramsy couldn't blame her. A young girl paid too big a toll for living with a man like him.

"Give her some slack," Ash said. "She's only a woman. She's not out to ruin you."

"You don't know her," Jack said. "You don't know what she's like."

"Seems to me you can leave the gypsies out of it," Charlie added.

"Jesus Christ, you're on their side now? You don't know anything about it," Jack spat. But he said nothing more.

*　　*　　*

Stella stayed quiet the nights people came. To a lot of people in Shelk she was simply the woman who lost the baby, and they snuck stares at her when they thought she wasn't looking. But Ramsy ignored their glances and poured what they asked, and each night, once the bar was quiet again, he and Stella looked at each other in the quiet for a long time. It wasn't pity, wasn't sympathy. It was closer to forgiveness than anything else.

"I don't like all those people here," Stella admitted a few days after Ramsy hung the *Closing* sign.

"Me, either," Ramsy said.

"You should be glad for the business."

"That's not why I have the bar."

Ramsy drove Stella home, happy for the empty roads and black sky. "Snow should be starting soon," he said.

"I'll miss the bar, Ramsy."

"You'll find another."

"No," she said. "In any other place I'll get those looks. You know those looks, Ramsy."

"I know."

"I hate them."

"I know."

"I'm safe in your bar. No one stares. They know you won't allow it."

She didn't say she'd miss him. He waited, but he knew better than to hope for it.

"Lock your doors," he instructed when they reached her house. She lifted the door handle and stepped down from the truck.

"You want me to come in?" he asked.

She looked at him. In another life her eyes would have said something different. "I'll be okay," she said. "See you tomorrow." He watched her walk to her porch. Once she was inside she flickered the porch lights, and he drove slowly away.

CHAPTER 4

139 Wild Sage Road

The white-sided split-level was a house where teenagers lived. He could tell by the clothes on the floor in the small rooms at the top of the stairs. In one, blue jeans, pink and purple sweaters, lipsticks and hair brushes strewn over the dresser. In a desk drawer, he found a sequined purse with some folded bills. He took the money and put the purse away. Tucked into the dresser mirror were pictures, girls together and girls alone, one girl with straight mouse-brown hair appearing over and over. It was her room, then, her sequined purse. What kind of girl was she, to choose a purse like that?

The next room smelled of sweat and socks. The intruder stepped over sneakers and sweatpants, kicked T-shirts out of his path. The hum of a computer filled the room with a strange and quiet peace. He took a wad of money from a football-shaped mug on the dresser. When he put it into his bag, a soft beep came from the computer. On the screen was a box, and in that box was a message: Hey, you there? *Next to the message was a tiny photograph, a quarter the size of a postage stamp, of a girl with long blond hair. She'd taken the picture herself—he could see the insides of her arms just at the edges of the photo. Her plum-purple lips were parted in a slight near-smile. Another beep from the computer, and another message from the girl appeared on the screen: Hello...Hello...Anyone there?*

He looked around the room, but there was no picture of the boy. And so he imagined himself in the oversized Steelers T-shirt, the worn black sweats, sitting at the desk with headphones on, listening to music while he wrote message after message to the girl with plum-purple lips. He slung his money-filled bag over his shoulder. He looked at the flashing cursor, the empty white space where the boy's message would go. And then he typed, I'm here. But he didn't wait around to see what the girl wrote back.

Over the last thirty years, the rhythm of Ramsy's solitary days had varied just a handful of times. It'd varied when he'd met Marcie, and during the year he'd shared his home with both a woman and a child. An empty spell of years followed, until he met Stella. Life had been different then, too. And when his relationship with Stella fell apart, he briefly left Shelk. That was the only time that he'd closed the bar and driven beyond the city limits with his mind focused on escape.

He'd left because being in Shelk had become a quiet torture. Stella was everywhere and nowhere, and he couldn't stand it. If he couldn't see her—her body, her hands, her face—then he didn't want to be around the things she'd touched. He needed relief, just enough time for his torn-apart world to sew itself up again. He locked the bar one night, put a handwritten sign on the door that said *Closed*, and walked away. He needed to give this daughter of his—this suddenly reappearing daughter—what he couldn't give last time. Ramsy knew now what was expected of him, what he'd shamefully failed to provide, and he packed his bags with a feverish desire to correct the past as quickly as possible. He reserved a room at an efficiency motel not far from Liza's. He didn't intend to stay long, but still he watched his house in his rearview mirror just as Marcie would have all those years ago, and said goodbye.

In the twenty years Liza was gone, he'd never imagined a reunion, and when he saw a young woman waving from the stoop of an apartment that matched the address on the paper he held scrunched against the wheel, he felt panic, not joy, and a dread he was embarrassed to acknowledge. He waved, and she smiled—Marcie's smile—and hurried to the truck.

Her hair was dark and long, tied back in a ponytail. She wore jeans and sneakers and a blouse with the sleeves rolled up to the elbows. She was a beautiful girl, and she beamed at him as he climbed out of the truck. He saw the moment when she registered the eye—a flick across her face like a light clicking off and on—and he was glad he'd worn his patch. No need to scare her with that.

"Well," he said.

"Hello," she said. She gave him a fast hug and stepped back.

"You're all grown up," he said. And then he couldn't say anything more.

She led him inside, where he shook hands with a young man who said, "Mark Cole. Nice to meet you. Welcome."

They sat in the living room, and from there Ramsy could see all the rooms of the apartment, no more than four hundred square feet—the narrow kitchen, tucked into the corner, had a refrigerator as high as his neck. "It's just a starter apartment," Liza said, serving coffee from a tray. "Just until we save some money."

"It's a nice home."

There was too much to say. Ramsy sat with his back straight, gripping his hot mug. Liza never lost her smile, but he could see a wobbly uncertainty in her eyes where excitement had been.

They spoke of their jobs, their towns. Liza explained how she and Mark had met. Then she reached for an envelope on the side table and handed it over to Ramsy. It held pictures of Liza—baby, toddler, child, teenager. Hair darkening from dirty blond to chestnut, body slimming and lengthening, smile changing from a baby's pure joy to something deeper. He could barely look at them. He could barely breathe. And he couldn't look at Liza, who was watching him expectantly.

As he shuffled through the pictures, he found one he was certain Liza hadn't meant to include. It was stuck facedown to the back of an engagement portrait of her and Mark that was tacky with old tape, as though it had hung on a mirror or refrigerator door. He peeled it away and felt the wind rush out of him like he'd fallen, chest-first, onto pavement.

She was on Liza's left, her arm around her waist, her other hand clutching a yellow satin pocketbook without any straps. *Marcie.* Her hair was above her shoulders, frosted blond and cut in layers, with bangs over her brow. She was smiling, her lips shiny pink, her face flushed. She'd gained weight—she was a woman now, heavy through the breasts and hips, matronly in a low-waisted dress. The old Marcie—his Marcie—was in her eyes and every inch of her skin, but in a crowd he'd miss her. She'd gone right on living, right on changing, unlike the pictures in his head.

She looked happy. There were wrinkles at her eyes, the good kind that came from laughing. At twenty-five she'd had wrinkles on her brow that appeared when she was tired—tired from always needing more money and raising a baby almost entirely alone. If she hadn't left him, what would she look like now? For a moment Ramsy hated himself for how he might have destroyed her.

There was a man on Liza's right—Marcie's husband. He was tall and dark, with gray-streaked hair and broad shoulders. He stood with his hands clasped in front of him, his smile indulgent and proud. He looked like the kind of man who could earn a decent living, raise another man's daughter, and make life easy so the woman beside him could sleep at night. Ramsy put the picture down. He'd known all along she was better off without him, but part of him had always believed she could have been happy with him, too. But now that he'd seen her, with that man and that smile, he knew he was wrong.

On the back of the picture, Liza had written *Me with Mom and Dad*. So the man had saved them both. Ramsy had never felt so weak.

"What's his name?" Ramsy said.

It took a moment for Liza to realize what Ramsy meant. "Oh my God," she said. "I didn't know that was in there. I'm so sorry, Ramsy."

"What's his name?" Ramsy asked again.

Liza took a breath and said, "Joe Pounds."

Ramsy nodded. "Okay," he said, "okay."

"He's a good man, Ramsy."

"I know it." He wanted to say more—that he was glad Pounds had been there, that he was glad she'd been happy. But he was afraid of what else he might say: that he hated this Pounds more than any other man in the world.

"It was a long time ago, what happened," Liza said. "Life goes on." She waved her hand at the room. This was life. This was what years could do.

"I know it," he said again.

Liza asked him to stay for dinner, but all Ramsy wanted was to get back to the motel, get a hoagie from the gas station across the street, and sleep.

Late that night, someone knocked on his door. He was awake, still dressed, and he said, "Come in." Liza pushed the door open, paused, and then came in and sat on the desk chair. He was too tired to be surprised.

"Mark said not to ask you, but I want to," she said.

"Go ahead. Can't think of anything I shouldn't answer."

"Do you want to know about my mom? What she's doing?"

He hadn't expected the question, and he didn't want to know. But he imagined Liza's home, her hope and good intentions shining on every surface like lemon wax. It didn't seem fair to pretend Marcie didn't exist. "I'd like to know she's doing well," he said.

Liza relaxed. "She is. She and my dad are retired. They like to RV out West. They stop their mail, get a kid to mow the lawn, and just go whenever the mood strikes. Their house is filling up with souvenirs of their trips. When they came back from New Mexico they brought enough dried chilies to string around their entire kitchen ceiling."

"Marcie never talked about wanting to travel."

"She came to it late. And it agrees with her. Dad gave her a push when he bought the RV."

"Sounds like he's a good man." It was the only thing he could think of to say.

Liza smiled. "We have work all week, but see you Saturday for lunch? Can you stay in town that long?"

"Lunch," he said. "Alright." Without Stella, Shelk held little to get back to.

*   *   *

Ramsy slept fitfully after seeing Liza and went out early to a Dunkin Donuts a few blocks from the motel. He ordered coffee and a glazed donut and sat in a booth where someone had left a paper behind. He spread it open but did not read. Now and then someone glanced his way, taking in his long white hair, the faded patch over his eye. He was a stranger here.

He'd been in Shelk over twenty years, and this was the longest he'd ever been away. He felt the distance more than he'd expected. He tried to follow a routine to give the days some shape. But despite his planning he felt unmoored, unsafe, as though he hadn't remembered to bring some vital part of himself from home. The rest of the week went on like this. Breakfast each day at Dunkin Donuts, working his way through chocolate frosted, old-fashioned, cruller, glazed twist. Walks and drives through town, down streets of two-story houses with fenced-in yards. Dogs barked at him from living room windows, and joggers gave him wide berth on the sidewalks. He drove into downtown Pittsburgh, where no one seemed to see him. But here he kept looking over his shoulder, worried he'd wander somewhere he wasn't supposed to be. He bought sliced bread and sliced cheese and had a sandwich each night in his room, watching movies on the classics channel, things he should have seen but never had: *On the Waterfront, Casablanca, The Sound of Music, All About Eve.*

When Ramsy pulled up to Liza's apartment Saturday at lunchtime, he idled in the truck, watching the windows for signs of life, hoping there would be none. Then he got out of the truck and knocked on the door, once again receiving a hug from Liza, a handshake from Mark, and the weight of too much history on his chest.

Lunch stuttered on, Liza and Mark valiantly chattering, Ramsy rarely able to speak in more than monosyllables. His presence here—with Liza, at this table—felt fragile, as though one wrong word would make the return of this daughter nothing more than a dream.

But at the end of lunch Ramsy could not hold back. "I should tell you I'm sorry," he said. His throat closed up, and he coughed before going on. "I should have tried to find you. I did try. I should have tried harder. Lots of things I'd do differently if life happened that way again."

For the first time Liza kept her eyes straight ahead. "I was angry about that for a long time," she said slowly. "But when I was older, I started to wonder what you would have done for me if you'd found me. And I realized I should be grateful for what I had. I don't mean to be harsh," she rushed to add. "I'm just saying I eventually understood what wasn't possible."

Ramsy's face grew hot. If he'd found her, what would he have done? What could he have done, except make a little girl's life sadder and harder? He'd known all this from the moment Marcie walked out the door. She was the one who left, but he was the one everyone knew—hoped—would stay gone.

"Besides, we had Joe," she said. "We weren't alone. For the first half of my life I never even knew I was missing a father."

"Glad you had a hero," Ramsy said.

"Look, Ramsy, this is hard," Liza said. "I had a whole life before I found you. And I still have it. I can't pretend it's not there. I can't replace it with an imaginary past with you I never had. It would have been nice if that existed. But it didn't. Remember, I tracked you down. You never found me." She got up from the table and went into the bedroom. Mark nodded at Ramsy as if to say *Don't worry*, then followed his wife.

Of course she was right. Even if Marcie hadn't left, he feared he still would have been absent, distant, visible only in the sad faces of these women who deserved— and, ultimately, got—much more.

He packed his bags that night, throwing away his leftover food and removing his few clothes from the bureau. He drove to Liza's early Sunday morning and found her and Mark dressed for church.

"Just wanted to tell you I'm leaving," he said. "Heading back to Shelk. Gotta get back to the bar before people start forgetting about it."

Liza nodded. "I understand. I'm sorry, Ramsy. Mark told me it was too much too soon, and maybe he was right. I'm just—happy to have found you."

"Not going anywhere now," he said. "Not going to disappear."

"I hope not. I love you, Ramsy. I barely know you but I do. You don't have to say it back."

Surely he loved her—his daughter—but what he felt now was more like weary affection. He tried to remember her as a baby, her plump pink arms and flower-bud mouth, when she'd inspired an instant kind of love that seared deep before she was even a person he could know, but he could barely call the image to mind.

"I'm sorry," he said, hating himself. And then he walked out the door.

*   *   *

In Ramsy's mind, Marcie had always been twenty-five. It was how old she'd been when she left, and that final image of her—brown eyes red-rimmed, long hair tossed over one shoulder and the baby over the other, her back arched for balance as she unlocked and opened the car door—was the one that stuck. She'd been slim, and her jeans hung a little loose at her waist. With her hands full, she couldn't pull them up, and when she bent to put the baby in the car Ramsy could see the thin blue elastic of her panties. That was when he said, *You don't want to do this.* But he was wrong—he could

see plain as day she wanted to. He was the one who
didn't want her to go. Now young, wounded Marcie
was gone all over again, replaced in his mind by the
woman Liza had revealed.

The day after he got back to Shelk, he backed his
pickup right up to the shed next to the garage, then cut
off the padlock with a hacksaw. Twenty years ago, he'd
been angry when he'd filled the shed with everything
Marcie left behind. The antique bureau she'd brought
from home, the head- and footboards she'd picked out at
Sears, the pieces of Liza's white crib, stacks of unmarked
boxes. He could still feel the ache and sweat of packing
and hauling, pushing and balancing, the late-summer
sun a burden, the dive-bombing cicadas a curse.

Now he knew it was no use keeping his shed like a
graveyard when even the ghosts had moved on. Maybe
he'd never forgive her. Maybe he had already. As for
himself—he'd never go that far. But maybe he was
ready now to let it all go.

He hauled and threw and stacked until his truck
was full of furniture, and he drove it all to the dump.
He hesitated over the boxes, then gave in and opened
the flaps of each before loading them up. Baby clothes,
blankets, towels, sheets, Marcie's clothes and shoes—
into the truck. In a box full of papers he found a small
album of photographs: Liza as an infant, red-faced,
desperately asleep. He set the album aside. Finally
a box of toys. On top was a small white bear, with a
stained ribbon around its neck that said *It's a Girl!*
Ramsy had bought it in the hospital gift shop the day Liza
was born. She'd taken to it, slept with it. It sliced him,
right through his heart, just as it had when he'd seen
it in Liza's crib that long-ago summer day and understood Marcie had left it behind. Not because the baby
wouldn't want it, but because it was something he'd
given her to love.

From then on, the bear and the album rode with him in the glovebox of his truck. He thought of them when he went to the bar and took down the *Closed* sign. He'd been gone a week, not even enough time for most people to notice. Eventually, Stella came back to the bar. The awkwardness between them weakened and died, and Ramsy didn't think about leaving anymore. A decade would pass, years of routine and sameness, before the gypsies arrived, and Ramsy prepared to leave Shelk again, for good this time.

He fl
Th
a

CHAPTER 5

52 Lupine Road

They were called magic flowers, tangled nests of dry brown twigs light and dead enough to blow away in the wind. They looked like nothing, revealed no hint of what they'd been or what they might be. It took a true believer to trust the magic and take it on faith that the flower would transform in water from death to life. The girls kept a box of the flowers in one of the vans, for when they needed money in a pinch. They couldn't get much for them, but it was something, and at least it gave them a way to get inside. In every town, it was easy to find people who wanted to believe, who'd open the door to examine the flower as they explained that its miraculous ability would bring about whatever dramatic change the purchaser desired.

A rail-thin man who opened his door cast furtive glances to the street before he took the proffered flower in his hands. He turned the brittle lump over and over, fingering the stumpy roots. He even brought it to his nose. "What kind of change is it good for?" he asked finally, and they knew they had a sale.

"All kinds of change," one of them answered. They'd been at this long enough to know, for this man, what they should say next. "Regarding love, especially."

...shed and said, "Come in. Money's inside."

...e house was airless and neat, couch cushions ...ranged just so, magazines fanned across the coffee table. The girls followed the man to the kitchen, where he filled a clear glass bowl with water and set it on the counter. They did not mention money as they gently placed the flower in the water and then joined their hands and chanted over the bowl. "What are you saying?" the man asked. They told him it was an old gypsy love spell. When green replaced brown, when life filled the flower, they told him, change would come.

The man stared at the flower. "If this doesn't work," he said, and they knew he wasn't speaking to them. But then he trained his sad pale eyes on theirs. "What if this doesn't work?"

They'd gotten twenty dollars for the flower but no chance to sneak into the man's upstairs rooms. They left the house disappointed, but forced themselves to laugh when they thought of the false hope they'd left inside. Later, when they were alone, they regretted their laughter, and they wondered what happened to the man when the flower bloomed without bringing any change at all.

Now that Ramsy knew he was leaving, he stayed at the bar later on the nights Stella wasn't there, watching the Weather Channel on mute, pink and blue and yellow spinning across the states. Warm fronts, cold fronts. Storms he'd never feel and never see. It was the same inside his bar whether or not it snowed in Wyoming, whether there were record winds in California, whether rain or sun appeared, or didn't, in places far away from Shelk.

On one of these late nights, in the middle of October—a night with record cold in Chicago, traveling their way—Ramsy saw movement through the thin-curtained window. Wouldn't be the first time a deer passed so close, but this shadow was thinner—a person. A man.

Ramsy heard footsteps crossing the gravel drive, and then the metal squeak of his trash bin's lid. He carried his trash down himself in his truck—no garbage service came this far up the mountain—but he kept a bin behind the bar to collect it.

He opened the cabin door. "Nothing to help a hungry man out there," he called. "Best you'll find is a little rice with canned soup, and that was from two days ago." Silence. "Close the lid before you leave," he said. "Do my best to keep the raccoons away, damn pests." He heard the lid close. "If you need it there'll be something more in there tomorrow," he called, surprising himself. There was no answer, just the fast crunch of feet over fallen leaves.

There weren't many homeless in Shelk—and none would survive this far up the mountain—so Ramsy suspected a gypsy. He had the reflexive urge to check the register and his wallet, and he shook his head. The men's talk got to him sometimes, and he pushed it away.

The next night he brought a sandwich—nothing fancy, just peanut butter and banana in a brown paper bag—and late, after the men left, he went outside to the bin. He hesitated. It felt wrong to be doing it this way, like he was leaving scraps for a feral cat, but he set the thought aside and dropped in the bag. He knew someone was watching him. As soon as he was back inside he heard the squeak of the lid being lifted once more.

The night after that: a sandwich again, butter and sliced American cheese. And after that, tuna salad with celery. This time, Stella was just arriving at the bar as Ramsy made his way back inside. "What're you doing?" she asked as he held open the door.

He cursed himself for being so careless. He didn't want to make a big thing of what he was doing, but he decided that hiding it from Stella would be impossible. "Been leaving food out back," he said. "Came across someone who needs it."

"Who?" Stella said.

"A gypsy," Ramsy said. "Haven't seen him, but I have a feeling."

"You sure you should get mixed up with them?"

"Wouldn't say I'm mixed up in anything. He's a young kid, looks like."

"This isn't like you, Ramsy."

He imagined what the men would do if they caught a gypsy scavenging in their backyards. "Running people off is what's not like me," he said. "I'm leaving what amounts to table scraps, that's all."

The next night, Stella brought something foil-wrapped in a small insulated bag. "Bring it out before it gets cold," she said.

"What is it?"

"Just some meatloaf on a roll," she said. "Even gypsies can't eat peanut butter every day."

The meatloaf was wrapped carefully, the ends of the foil folded and tucked neatly in. Ramsy put it in the bin along with a can of Coke.

The next time she came in, she brought a Thermos of hot chili and some sliced bread in a Ziploc bag. The empty Thermos was in front of the bar's door when Ramsy arrived the next day. Stella brought a square of lasagna, and then a chicken pot pie in a small foil dish. Each night for a week, he placed the food in the bin, uneasily. He was leaving soon—could be any day now—and he hoped the gypsy wasn't counting on this, that he wouldn't be in trouble when it stopped, like skittish, skinny birds at a suddenly empty feeder in the dead of winter.

He wouldn't always have done this—any of this: leaving food, or worrying about not leaving it. He would never have run the gypsy off, but he wouldn't have given him reason to hang around. Keeping his distance was just how he lived, and how he ran his bar. Years ago, after a night when Hawk's regulars had said too much about their wives and other women, Hawk had said to Ramsy, "You have a choice, you know. And you'll have to make it early on, once this bar is yours. Usually there's no changing your mind."

"A choice of what?"

"Whether to get involved. They'll want you to. First they'll want you to listen, then give advice, then step into their lives for all manner of reasons. It's what happens when you spend your life standing where we do—separate from them. Makes us seem safe, special somehow. Even wise. Best be careful or you'll start believing it."

"And your choice?"

"You can't tell by now?"

"You stay out of it."

"I do. Hasn't always been easy—you're proof of that. You get to know these men, you want to help out, you want to reach over the bar and wrap your hands around their throats and shake them. But it's too hard, living that way. Got troubles enough for myself. Don't need to be taking on anyone else's. Worry'll undo you. Always does."

*   *   *

On Thursday, a truck pulled up in front of the bar as Ramsy made his way outside, carrying an egg salad sandwich in a plastic container. It was late. The men had left nearly an hour ago. Charlie climbed out of the truck. The men looked at each other for a moment, their breath wispy clouds in the cold air.

"Left my scarf," Charlie said. He didn't move toward the door. Ramsy saw him glance at the sandwich. "What'cha doing, Ramsy? Awful cold to be having dinner outside, ain't it?"

"Been carrying this thing around in my truck for days," Ramsy said. "Thought it was time to throw it away." Charlie watched him walk to the bin and put the sandwich inside. "Let's get you your scarf," Ramsy said. "Time for me to be getting home."

Both men looked up at the sound of footsteps. A boy in black appeared at the edge of the woods then sprinted away when he spotted Charlie's truck.

Charlie stared, surprise giving way to anger. "That gypsy coming to see you, Ramsy?" he asked. "'Cause that's what it looked like. That's what it goddamn looked like."

Charlie was stocky and strong, the kind of man who needed extra-large shirt collars and whose jeans pulled tight over thick calves. He took a step toward Ramsy.

"He's hungry," Ramsy said. "Now maybe it's time you get on home."

Charlie didn't move. "Hungry," he said. "Even though they've been stealing food from our kitchens and taking our goddamn money. We're killing ourselves trying to keep them out of our houses, and here you are, hand-delivering dinner like a goddamn waiter. Well fuck you, Ramsy."

"Nothing wrong with helping out a man when he needs it."

"A man? It's a gypsy!" Charlie was shaking his head, punching one gloved fist against his other open palm, but he didn't come any closer to Ramsy. "The other men find out about this, you're done," he said. "Look, Ramsy, I like you. I don't want to see nothing happen to you, your bar, so I ain't saying a word. But I'm telling you right now, you're crazy. Acting like gypsies will just take your charity and that's the end of it—you'll pay for this, somehow." He backed away and opened his truck door. "You'd better figure out where your loyalties lie."

Ramsy didn't move until Charlie's truck disappeared down the mountain road.

There was no forgotten scarf inside the bar, though Ramsy looked under every stool. Charlie had come back tonight because he suspected something—that was clear. Ramsy had said too much, or too little. He had denounced the robberies too much, or not enough. Whatever the case, Charlie had found reason to believe that Ramsy wasn't being entirely honest, and he was right. Whose side was he on, when it came down to it?

He locked up the bar and checked the bin. The sandwich was still there. He hoped the kid would come back for it, but he'd be surprised if he did. Seeing that truck pull up tonight was a reminder that leaving food for a gypsy wasn't just about feeding and being fed. Maybe it should have been, but it wasn't. Not in a town like this.

*   *   *

A little over a week after he'd first seen the shadow pass by his window, Ramsy was closing the bin—a tuna fish sandwich and an apple tonight—when he heard a twig crack. He turned around. The boy, wearing an unzipped canvas coat, stood at the edge of the trees. He stared at Ramsy with hard eyes, but something in his face—a looseness around his jaw—made Ramsy call out, "What's your name?"

"JT," the boy called back, and from the way his voice sounded Ramsy knew it wasn't really his name.

"I'm Ramsy."

"I know who you are."

I know who you are. Hawk had said these same words to him the day Ramsy first showed up at the bar, nothing in his truck but a suitcase half-full of clothes and nothing on his face but an eye patch and rootless anger. *I'm Ramsy*, he'd said. *A buddy of mine said you could use some help around here*. Hawk had looked at him for a long minute. *I know who you are*, he'd said finally. *One of these days you'll get used to being a man who never needs to introduce himself again*. Ten minutes later Ramsy was behind the bar, uncapping beers for a crowd of strangers who couldn't stop staring. He couldn't remember Hawk ever giving his eye more than a second's glance, and soon the others followed his lead and stopped staring too.

"Hot coffee inside if you want it," Ramsy said, and then he went back into the bar. A few minutes later, the door opened, and the gypsy came in.

His hair was dark and thick and straight, cut in shaggy layers that ended just below his chin, his skin the color of river sand. He had the shadow of a beard on his face, and Ramsy could see the promise of it. He would grow into the kind of man who always looked in need of a shave. What Ramsy noticed most were his hands, slim and hairless and clean, the nails cut carefully square across. Looking at those hands, you'd think he was a good kid, a careful kid, not a hungry and reckless thief. There was a red scarf at his throat, looped over itself like something you'd see in a fashion magazine, but his coat was moth-eaten and too long in the arms.

He sat in the seat closest to the door and kept his coat on. He couldn't have been more than eighteen, but when he asked for a beer, Ramsy gave it to him. JT glanced at Ramsy's eye and looked away.

Ramsy twisted open a beer of his own. He wasn't afraid of the gypsy, but he wasn't a fool, either. He'd wait until he locked the door to take the cash from its drawer.

Finally JT looked up. "Got some things to sell," he said. "Thought someone here might be interested in buying."

"No one here this hour but me," Ramsy said.

JT met his eye then looked away again, a quick flash of unease on his face.

"I'll take a look."

JT reached into his coat pockets and scattered fistfuls of things onto the bar, earrings and cufflinks and necklaces and money clips, plain gold rings and rings with colored stones, a few odd cigars, keys on a ring, unmarked.

"Quite a collection," Ramsy said.

He took his time looking over the objects, feeling the weight of each one in his palm. Which were the earrings Mary Kolecik had loved? Where were the coins Frank Connell spent his whole life collecting? Ramsy had heard so much about the things people had lost. Now here they were, on a beer-sticky counter. In the dim light of the bar, they had no sparkle or shine. They looked like trinkets held in plastic bubbles in the machines outside the Shop N' Save.

"How much for the lot?" Ramsy asked.

"Asking two hundred."

"Don't have that kind of cash around."

"Fifty."

Ramsy counted out a small pile of fives and tens and pushed them over. JT folded them twice over, nodded at Ramsy, then stood.

"Appreciate the food," he said. "Was going through a rough patch. Should be okay without it now." Then he was gone.

Ramsy slid the locks in place then stared at the objects left behind. He shouldn't have bought them.

He should have spoken sharply, informed JT he was in the wrong place for a deal like that, called the police with a description of his face. This was what another man would do, what most men would. But the boy was hungry—Ramsy could see it in his eyes, in the way he'd said *fifty* as though it could have been any number at all.

At home he spread out the jewelry on the kitchen table and looked at each piece in the harsh kitchen light. Stolen goods. These were why the men in his bar triple-locked their doors and kept rifles by their beds. These were what the men referred to when they said the gypsies stole the only things they had worth anything. What would the men say if they knew he'd bought it all for less than the cost of his heating bill?

Ramsy would happily turn all of it over to the men, let them piece together what belonged to whom. They were honest men. They'd find the owners, make sure every ring and bracelet made it home. But there was no way to explain why he'd given the gypsy food, served him a beer, or why he'd cut a deal for stolen goods instead of calling the police. Thieving wasn't among the many sins Ramsy had committed in his life, yet here was evidence that argued otherwise.

Ramsy swept the jewelry into a shoebox and slid it under his bed. There'd be time enough in the morning to think it through.

*   *   *

In the morning, he woke with an unfamiliar hunger. He wanted strong coffee and a full stomach, so he headed to the Rowdy Buck for breakfast. Only a few cars were in the lot at ten o'clock—he'd missed the early rush and was in ahead of lunchtime—and Ramsy took a seat in a booth along the wall. A waitress poured coffee and took his order. Suddenly she looked at the door, and the diner went quiet for a moment.

"Lordy," she breathed. Standing in the doorway was Kitty Kurtz, pink-cheeked and blowsy with a puffy purple jacket and fuzzy white scarf, and behind Kitty Kurtz was a gypsy.

He was clearly a man accustomed to the cold. He wore a long brown leather coat that was well-worn at the hem and collar, and over his shoulders he'd slung what looked like cowhide, mottled brown and tan. A black knit hat pressed long black hair close to his neck. He was older than Kitty, though not old enough to have been in the war. Snowflakes were caught in the pelt, in the rough hair on his cheeks, and in the beard tied with a rubber band at his chin, and they melted into tiny glistening beads when he stepped inside.

The chatter started up again, tentatively, once Kitty and the gypsy sat down in a booth by the windows. As Ramsy ate his eggs and bacon, he watched them leaning toward each other over the table, all but holding hands around their plates of hotcakes and mugs of coffee. Ramsy looked around. No one else saw what he did.

When Ramsy raised his hand to signal for the bill, Kitty looked over. Her face paled, but this, too, was part of Kitty's theatrics. You didn't come to the Rowdy Buck and expect not to see anyone. You came to a place like this with the understanding that you would be seen. He left a few dollars for a tip and walked past Kitty's booth on his way to the door.

"Kitty," he said with a nod.

"Ramsy," Kitty said nervously. She gestured to the gypsy. "My cousin, Emilian." Even she seemed embarrassed by the lie, but she kept on talking. "He's visiting for a few days. He and Jack don't get along. Don't tell him you saw me, okay, Ramsy?"

Ramsy gave Kitty a long look and walked away. In his truck, he started the engine and let the cab warm up. It was for his sake as much as Jack's or Kitty's that he wouldn't say a word about hotcakes or coffee or gypsies in long leather coats. Getting in the middle of something like that—well, he could only imagine what Hawk would say. His days in town were numbered, and soon he wouldn't have reason to think of the Kurtzes at all.

*   *   *

That night, Charlie and Ash came into the bar together, talking in excited voices as they took their usual seats. Ramsy uncapped beers. "What's all this about?"

"Seems Jack Kurtz was right," said Ash. "Kitty's been playing around. Can't get Meg to talk about anything else. Said another waitress saw her with someone this morning at the Rowdy Buck. Probably family from out of state, is what I said at first." He paused. "Of course I could have sworn all Kitty's people are here."

"It's all over town," added Charlie. He exchanged a glance with Ash. "And it's not just anyone. Heard it's a gypsy she's been seeing. Foreign-looking, is what people are saying."

"People talk," said Ramsy. "Can't always believe what you hear."

"Sure, people talk," Charlie said. "But it's a crazy thing for someone to make up, ain't it? Too strange not to be true."

"Truth is stranger than fiction, is what they say," said Ash.

"Guess you never can tell who'll take a shine to a gypsy," Charlie said. Ramsy tensed, but Charlie didn't look at him and said nothing more.

Ramsy turned to the register while the men drifted on to other topics. Kitty Kurtz really was a piece of work. He remembered her from her Coal Queen days, her face showing up in the paper all the time as she made appearances at 4-H events, holiday parades, pageants all over southwestern PA. She'd been the kind of girl people expected would leave the area, smart enough, and pretty enough, to make a different sort of life. But she met Jack before she ever went anywhere and got married by twenty-one. Jack had been something too back then, a baseball player who'd made the All-State first team, and for a while they were as golden a couple as you could find in Shelk. Then Jack wrecked his rotator cuff in a boozy car crash, a death knell for his baseball career, and the years started marching along on Kitty's face. The attention she'd been used to dried up, and people turned their eyes to other, younger, women. Kitty had been fighting ever since to wrangle their gazes back to her.

This rumor about an affair wouldn't die easily—not least because it was true. If Kitty asked his advice, Ramsy would tell her to stay out of the mountains, cook some fancy dinners for Jack, and pray these strangers moved on soon. But Kitty Kurtz needed the spotlight, and Jack wasn't the kind to ignore whispers and speculation. Ramsy found it strange sometimes that he seemed to be the only one who knew when things would end badly. If anyone had asked him, he would have said, simply, *Just stop what you're doing, easy as that.*

In the days that followed, suddenly everyone had heard something about Kitty and her gypsy. Charlie's neighbor's son said he'd seen them outside the River Tavern, a bar by the railroad tracks. Harry Slavin had heard they'd bought hoagies at Sheetz. And Meg kept telling Ash about all the hotcakes Kitty and her gypsy were eating at the Rowdy Buck, even though she'd never seen them there herself.

They saved their stories for when Jack wasn't there, but one night, when conversation lagged, Jack said loudly, "Don't bother pretending you haven't seen her. Everyone has."

"You're wrong, Jack," Charlie spoke up. "We've heard things, sure. But we haven't seen her ourselves."

"Liar," Jack spat. "All of you, liars. You're all in on it. You'd love to see her leave me for a gypsy. Then you'd really have something to talk about."

"It's rumors," Ash said. "If we knew something, we'd tell you. Wouldn't let you be made a fool of, especially by a gypsy."

Jack snorted, but Ramsy knew this was true. There'd be hell to pay for any outsider who moved in on one of these men's wives.

"What about you, Ramsy?" Jack said. "You hiding something like these fools are?"

Ramsy imagined telling Jack about the gypsy with the long leather coat, his beard tied with a band at his chin. A word from him would send these men to the mountains. "Not my place to protect anyone," he said. "Not women, not gypsies, no matter what they do."

"But you will," Jack said. "Mark my words, Ramsy, Haggerty, all of you. You will. Not one of you has the balls to tell the truth to my face."

"Look," Harry Slavin said. "You say something to her, Jack? Talk to her about it instead of us? 'Cause if it was my wife being talked about like this—well, it wouldn't be."

Jack's face turned red. "'Course I've *said something*, asshole."

"There are other ways of saying it. Find one she'll listen to."

There was silence. Ramsy didn't look up from the glass he was polishing when he said, "Not the place for talk like that, Slavin."

"This is my *wife*," Jack said. He stood up angrily and hovered at Harry's shoulder, just long enough to make the other men shift on their stools, preparing to stand. Then something in Jack deflated, and he sat back down.

Ramsy had heard more than enough about Kitty Kurtz for one night, but an hour later, the bar door opened and Kitty stalked in, wearing a short black skirt and spiky blue heels with her bulky winter jacket. She stood for a moment in the doorway, and Ramsy knew immediately she'd come to make a scene. He could already see it rising in her flushed cheeks, her bright, wide eyes.

"Kitty?" Jack said. "What are you doing here?"

"You afraid I'll overhear something?" she said loudly. "Maybe I have, maybe I haven't."

Jack rubbed his eyes. "What do you want, Kitty?"

"I want you to know how upset I am," she said. "This rumor—everyone's heard it. Everyone's whispering behind my back. Janice at work has barely said two words to me, and you know I can never get her to shut up. And I just have to say I'm hurt, and surprised, that you wouldn't put a stop to this. Do you believe it, Jack? I'm sleeping with a gypsy? You believe this about your own wife?"

"Now, listen," Jack said tightly. He stood. "If there's gossip it's your own damn fault. Don't even have to make up rumors myself. You give them enough to talk about."

"Of course. Of course it's my fault. Right, guys? There goes Kitty again, stirring things up." She shot Ramsy a silencing glance.

"You think this is easy for me?" Jack said, his voice rising. "I have to hear it all day, every day. And everyone knows it's true. They've seen you, for Chrissake. You're not even trying to hide."

Kitty raised the toe of one blue shoe, spinning the stiletto heel. She looked around the room like she'd just noticed where she was. Her face softened. "Come on, Jack." She took a step toward him. "Let's not do this."

Jack stiffened and turned away, but Kitty grasped his shoulder with her long red nails. She pressed herself into his arm and spoke directly into his ear. "You know there's nobody else for me." Jack just shook his head, then drained his beer.

Kitty looked down the bar, keeping her hands on Jack. "You all know how much I love Jack," she said. She glanced at her reflection in the window and then turned her head, as though trying to catch a dimmer, more flattering light. "You all know I could never do something like this to him."

"You're so full of shit," Jack said. "All this talk—this is exactly why you started whoring around with those gypsies."

"Whoring?" Kitty took a step back, wobbling on the uneven floorboards. "Now I'm whoring?"

"I'm only saying what I know is true."

"You listen here." Her voice turned hard. "I'm a whore? You should hear what people say about you. They think you're pathetic. Pathetic!"

Jack slammed his fist against the bar. "If you weren't a woman—"

"That's enough," Ramsy said. "Take it out of here."

"Not going anywhere," Jack said. He crossed his arms and relaxed against the bar. "Heard my fill."

"I think they're right," Kitty said. "You're pathetic."

"That's enough," Ramsy said.

Kitty threw open the door, and cold air rushed inside. "If any of you were real men," she said over her shoulder, "you'd tell Jack he's letting a good woman get away." Then she left, slamming the door behind her.

Jack stayed where he was until he heard her car start up and drive away from the bar.

"Damn those gypsies," he spat, hurling his beer bottle against the wall behind the stools. Green shards scattered and beer pooled on the floor. No one spoke. Head down, Jack put on his coat. He crunched the glass with his boot at the door, and then he was gone.

"Anyone know what's really going on?" Charlie asked after a long, stunned silence. "This gypsy rumor true?"

"Jack seems convinced," Ash said. "But he's always been willing to think the worst of Kitty."

"This would be the worst," Charlie agreed. "Cheating, and with a gypsy—Jesus. Guess some folks will never get it, that the gypsies ain't our kind." He gave Ramsy a steady look that Ash and Harry didn't catch.

"Well. Can't blame the gypsies for everything," Ash said, but there was no conviction in his voice. Ramsy was glad again that he'd kept his secret to himself. He knew Kitty wasn't thinking about all this too deeply—the attention, and the reaction from Jack, were what she was after. But Ramsy knew that soon the whole thing would be out of Kitty's hands. She was going too far. An affair like this would demand action.

*   *   *

Late that night, just after Ramsy had emptied the register, he turned around to find JT sitting at the bar. Ramsy's heart accelerated, but he said steadily, "Didn't hear you come in." He didn't bother hiding the pouch of money, and when JT saw it, he shook his head.

"Didn't mean to scare you."

"What can I do for you? Not sure I'm interested in anything else you're selling."

"Just wanted to get out of the cold. Not many places someone like me can go around here."

"Drink?"

"What you're having," JT said. Ramsy poured some whiskey in a glass and put it down on the bar. JT touched the glass to his lips and then left it alone.

"You feel safe here," Ramsy said suddenly. "Why?"

"Someone with an eye like yours sees things differently," was all JT said.

Ramsy looked carefully at JT. He thought back to a cold, dark night, the sweep of flashlights over wrinkled paper bags, three boys with their palms on the roof the cruiser. He remembered his lie: *Unloaded their cart and paid like anyone else.* One of the boys had raised his head, stared hard at Ramsy, and when Ramsy remembered it now, he felt sure it was JT. That shaggy hair, that knotted red scarf—it was him, no doubt about it.

For a little while they drank in silence.

Then JT asked, "So what happened to it?" His voice held no revulsion, only curiosity, as though he were inquiring about where he'd been born.

"Vietnam," Ramsy said.

"You see a lot of combat?"

"I did," Ramsy said. "Had pretty good luck till I picked the wrong whore."

For a moment they stared at each other. Then JT said, "How old were you?"

"Twenty-two," said Ramsy. "Felt older after that."

JT nodded as though something made sense, though Ramsy didn't know what lesson he was taking from his words.

"Guess an eye isn't much, when you think of it," JT said finally. "Could've been worse."

"Was worse, before the eye."

After a while JT said, "They say we're gypsies."

"Aren't you?"

"No." He gave a brief laugh. "I mean, we travel around, but I'm from Indiana. People think what they want, though. We're strangers, and that's enough. Last town we stayed in—Owl Creek. We used to go into the stores just to see what happened."

"What did?"

"Everyone looked at us. Cashier, stockperson, whoever was there. Just stared until we paid and left. Or just left. All those eyes and sometimes they still couldn't see us."

"You stole from them."

"Eyes don't scare us." He lifted his chin and looked directly at Ramsy's face—challenging him to disagree. Then he snorted quietly. "If my old man could see me now."

Ramsy didn't look up from the glass he was washing, but he said, "You don't talk to him."

"Barely did even before I left."

Ramsy opened his mouth and then shut it. He wanted to say he understood how it was to live in a house where no one talked, where the only words spoken were sharp, disdainful, unkind. He wanted to say he understood what it was like to run, it didn't matter where, or what was at the end of the road— even if what was at the end was the last thing you thought you wanted. War. Disgrace. Night after night behind a bar, seeing into other people's lives until one day you found yourself behind their eyes, looking out.

He felt a sudden urge to say more, something to draw the boy out. He had no idea if he'd see JT again.

"Not easy leaving everything behind," Ramsy said. "Always something you regret."

"Or someone." JT paused. "Had a sister," he said. "She was in some trouble when I left—pregnant to the wrong guy—and our dad kicked her out. I shouldn't have left her."

"Why did you?"

"Wasn't thinking about her when I left. Besides— never thought it'd be forever."

"Is it?"

JT nodded, moved his drink between his hands. "Yeah," he said. "That life is gone for good."

They were quiet for a while. Then Ramsy said, "You ever miss it?"

"My sister," JT said. "Still wonder where she ended up, what the baby's like—it'd be five years old now. Talking, running. The rest—" he shrugged "—never felt like mine. I fit here," he said. "Traveling around, getting by. Like I was born for it."

"Not everyone finds that. You're lucky." Ramsy pushed JT's untouched whiskey aside, opened a beer, and set it in front of him.

"Lucky." He drank his beer in one drawn-out swallow. "Now I feel lucky," he said.

On the muted TV, a brown-suited man gestured to a cloudy mass moving jerkily across a map.

"Bet you're wondering why we came," JT said after a while. "Why your town and not some other. Why we left Owl Creek."

"I've heard the talk," Ramsy said. "Sounds like you found more than just petty cash out there."

"It wasn't us," JT said. "Not me, not my friends. It was Emilian, our leader." Ramsy remembered Kitty and her man, sitting in that booth at the Rowdy Buck. His quiet calm, his penetrating stare—Ramsy should have known he wasn't just another thief.

JT said that Emilian saw thieving as a way to get rich, not just get by. He'd always demanded the day's bounty, doling out allowances to the young thieves in his employ. In Owl Creek, he began bringing incredible sums back to the camp himself—five thousand, ten. This was cash in large bills from heavy safes, not ones and fives rolled up in sock drawers. Sums like this meant they couldn't stay in Owl Creek, though. A place you victimized like that couldn't be home for long.

The map showed no shortage of places they might go next, and they knew it wouldn't matter, in the end, which one they chose.

"Shelk has an ugly name," JT said. "So that's the one we picked."

"And you'll be here till Emilian gets his fill."

"He takes what he wants," JT said, "and we do what he says. Might not make sense to outsiders, but we're not all like him."

Ramsy felt a strange sadness stirring when JT walked out the door that night. Shelk was a new place, but as long as people like Emilian had their way, what awaited them here was the same as anywhere else. Fear, anger, suspicion, expulsion. And after Shelk would be another place, and another, and on and on until the faraway end of their lives.

*   *   *

At the end of October, close to Halloween, two for-tunetellers set up shop on Fair Street, in what had long ago been a dry cleaner. They didn't have a lease, had made no agreement to pay anyone for the space—no one in Shelk would have made a deal like that. But the girls had seen a lot of towns. They knew how to recognize a building that had been let go for so long that it would take some doing to determine who, if anyone, should be called if there was trouble.

Ramsy had gone out early to Pittsburgh Federal, and he pulled his truck off the road when he saw the sign in the dusty shop window. PSYCHIC, it said in cool neon blue. An eye flanked by two stars glowed underneath, and on a sheet of paper taped inside the window was written *Tarot $5*. Curtains were drawn, but Ramsy got up close to the glass, cupped his hands to the sliver of space between the fabric panels, and peered inside.

The dry cleaner closed years ago, but some of the equipment had been left behind. There was still a counter, and hanging racks looped behind it all the way to the back wall. But now those racks were draped with heavy red sheets and clustered strands of beads, flanking a low round table and two chairs in the middle of the space. A colorful tapestry covered the tabletop and pooled onto the floor. No light came in from outside, and the room was illuminated only by two papery lamps on the floor. All in all it was a hasty, makeshift arrangement, designed to be torn down and stashed away at a moment's notice.

The men came in to the bar that night with heightened color in their cheeks.

"They think we're idiots?" Ash said. They were self-righteous, certain the intruders had misjudged their mark. "I mean, who'd *go* to a place like that?" The men snickered into their beers.

When Stella came in, eyes lowered, Ramsy suspected, right away, that she had gone.

"How much did they take?" he asked quietly once the men had left.

"I only went to ask about the girl," Stella said. "I only wanted to know where she is, if the baby's okay."

"How much?"

Stella pressed her lips together. Her eyes shone. "I agreed to the five-dollar reading. I thought it was only fair. She said she didn't know anything about the girl or the baby, and then she just kept talking."

"She saw you had something at stake. Saw an opportunity."

"She told me I had an evil surrounding me—" She shook her head.

"How much?"

"A hundred. She asked for five. Don't say anything, Ramsy. People already think I've lost my mind. They'd say, Oh, of course she fell for it, she'll believe anything, Stella Vale—"

"Stella."

"I'm not stupid, Ramsy. I don't know why I believed."

Ramsy sighed. "Can't beat yourself up," he said. "These are professional thieves. They know what to say, what to look for. Sure you're not the only one." He poured himself a drink. "Hell, even I got fleeced," he said. "JT came in a week ago, sold me some jewelry they'd stolen. Tried to get what he could from me."

"You bought it?"

"Kid like that won't ask for a handout, and he needed the money. I'll get it all back to the men."

Stella seemed calmer after that, and soon she left for home. Ramsy had to remember that she'd been in Shelk her whole life, sheltered and sad. Her tragedy had given her a different perspective than most people, but these didn't translate into an understanding of how the world really worked. She had good reason to think the universe was against her without knowing anything of the universe at all.

CHAPTER 6

1219 Bittersweet Road

It was a house where children lived. He knew by the wagon propped outside on the stairs. He'd had good luck in houses like this—though parents might find themselves struggling, there seemed always to be piggy-banks, or toy safes, full of fives and tens from a generous grandma. He watched the house for two days, marking when the mother—roundly pregnant—and children went out for a walk, and on the third day, when they turned on their child-sized bicycles onto the neighboring street, he went around to the back door and went inside. Another bonus of houses with children was distracted mothers who forgot to lock doors.

He took his time. They'd be gone half an hour at least. He searched for silver in the cupboards, stamps and coins in the closets, jewelry in the dressers. There were a few crystal wineglasses on the top shelf in the kitchen, but they wouldn't survive a trip in his canvas sack. He found an engagement ring in a bowl on the bureau, as he suspected he might, the pregnant woman's finger grown too fat to wear it. Modest, but not nothing, set in a thick gold band. He took a handful of cufflinks and a man's leather-strapped watch, and then he went into the children's room.

Pink, all pink, so he looked for heart-shaped lockets and earrings with semiprecious birthstones. He found both in a jewelry box with a ballerina that danced when he opened it, spinning to a tinny whine. He also found a small red safe whose plastic combination lock didn't keep him from wedging open the door with a pen. Inside, a fifty-dollar bill folded in a narrow Christmas money card. He stuffed it in his pocket and put the safe back on the shelf with its little door closed.

Before he left, he looked around. Two small beds with flower-printed sheets, a closetful of girl-sized clothes. What he'd taken, they might never notice. It made him happy, in a way, though he hated them, too, for this.

On the first Sunday in November, Ramsy drove north to Liza's. "Sunday supper," she said when she made the invitation. "Can't imagine you having Sunday supper all alone."

"Just another meal," he said.

"No, it isn't. Come around two. And I have some things to show you, now that you'll be moving in." He felt foolish when Liza's words jolted him. Between JT's visits, the excitement over Kitty, and the constant stream of news about the thefts, days went by without his remembering that he was actually leaving Shelk. The feeling of isolation that had fueled his decision had lessened, but he felt it again when he set out for Liza's.

He guided his truck around the curving Shelk roads until he hit the highway, then drove with his window open. The day was bright, and the cold air stung his face. He felt alive, and light, like he was emerging from underneath a heavy flannel blanket. After an hour, he entered the Fort Pitt Tunnel that burrowed through Mount Washington. Yellow lights shimmered sickly on the dingy white-tiled walls as he steadied his truck in the narrow lane. For a long stretch the mouth at either end was not visible. The radio faded to static, and all Ramsy could hear was the fast grind of tires on pavement. But then there it was, daylight, Pittsburgh spread out before him just across the Monongahela River. Ramsy emerged feeling, as he always did, that he'd traversed some great distance, that what he'd passed into was somehow radically different from what he'd left behind.

"Come in, come in," Liza said. "Let me take your coat. There. Take your boots off if you want. Come into the kitchen." These first minutes were hard. Being cared for didn't come naturally for Ramsy.

He left his boots on but wiped them on the rug by the door, and followed Liza through the house. "You look well," he said. Her hair was longer than he remembered, the ends split into curls, and she'd gained a pound or two.

"Thank you," Liza said. "It's good to see you, Ramsy. And the babies are here!" The children, one on Mark's hip, the other holding his hand, gave Ramsy frightened glances then scrambled out of the kitchen, to freedom.

Mark shook Ramsy's hand. "Good to see you," he said.

"They've grown."

"Children will do that," Mark said, and he smiled.

It was a different house this time—bigger than the last, nicer. There was still clutter, but there was also space. He followed Liza into the living room, and then the dining room and kitchen, small rooms full of furniture and toys, as she proudly showed off her home.

"And down here's the basement," she said, opening a hollow-sounding door off the kitchen. Ramsy followed her down into a large open room with a low dropped ceiling and a beige linoleum floor. An old couch and armchair flanked a TV in the corner. On the other side of the room were a ping-pong table, a card table and chairs, a toy chest, and a teetering stack of board games.

"My favorite room," Liza announced. "All I've ever wanted is a big finished basement. This sold us the house right here."

Ramsy almost staggered. He barely heard the rest of Liza's chatter. The words *All I've ever wanted* throbbed in his ears. A finished basement—damp in summer, freezing in winter, home to centipedes who'd run across the TV screen. If this was all she'd ever wanted, then her father—Joe Pounds—had done a hell of a job. If Marcie had stayed with Ramsy, Liza's life would have been full of wants— much more serious and heartbreaking wants than a basement. Liza had everything she needed thanks to Pounds and, now, Mark. Ramsy had given her nothing, not so much as a cheap glass vase. He would bring something next time. Something nice. Wine, or video games for the children. But he knew anything he brought would be liable to get lost in a full house—a full *life*—like this.

Upstairs, the phone rang. "Be right back," Liza said.

Ramsy sat down on the couch. He could hear Liza talking in the room above, then a laugh. After another minute he heard footsteps on the stairs, and Liza's children crept into the room. They stared at Ramsy but kept their distance as they walked to the toy chest in the corner.

"Hello," Ramsy said. The children said nothing. Ramsy watched them as they dug in the chest. They were his grandchildren—his blood—yet he felt only uneasiness.

When they sat down for dinner, Liza served meat-loaf and mashed potatoes and lima beans—"Our favorite Sunday supper"—and coffee afterward with slices of banana cake. Liza talked too much as she always did, but Ramsy welcomed it. He found himself at peace despite the chaos of family life—the confusion of feeding and being fed, the constant needs of young children. And though he'd never wished for his solitary routine back home to be different, he remembered now that he hadn't chosen it. He'd gotten used to it over the years, but he hadn't chosen it.

"Well," Liza said, once the plates were cleared, "of course we wanted to visit with you, Ramsy, since you'll be making this your home, at least for a while." She smiled. "And it is yours, you know that, the extra room is all ready for you, for as long as you'd like it."

"Yes."

"Come upstairs. I'll show you."

He followed her upstairs, into a room at the end of the hall. "It's smaller than what you're probably used to," Liza said. "But still, I think, okay."

There was a bed and dresser and desk, all in the same light wood. Pillows were propped two-deep against the headboard, and there were candlesticks on the edge of the dresser. Though it was tastefully done, Ramsy could see that everything in the room had the sheen of a discount store. But when Liza urged him to sit, the bed was soft. He'd be able to sleep there.

"The room's a good size," Ramsy said.

Liza smiled. "We have something else we'd like to show you. Mark will stay with the kids."

So Ramsy buttoned the coat Liza retrieved from the hall closet, waited while she slid into loafers and her own coat, and followed her to her car. "It's not far," she said, backing out of the driveway and heading east.

"Where are we going?"

"You'll see."

They drove along the pretty streets in silence. Soon the houses spread out, and there were patches of trees and a few vacant buildings—nothing like Shelk, but dim in its own way. "Almost there," Liza said. She turned to him. "It really is good to see you, Ramsy."

"You, too."

"Here," she said, turning left into a small gravel lot. "No one's done much with this part of town. But Mark and I drove by this place and thought of you." She looked at him, hopeful. "We thought you might have a bar here, once you moved. You like your place so much we thought it might make it easier for you, to have one here."

In front of them was a small square building, with white siding and a low-sloped roof and a *For Sale* sign by the stoop. Two windows and a door stared like a face from the front, and there was a window on the left side and the right. It looked like a dentist's office.

"Well?" Liza said. "What do you think?"

He couldn't imagine serving a drink there, couldn't even imagine his hand on the cheap brass doorknob. But wasn't a place what you made it, and the company you kept there? It was cleaner than his old log cabin, certainly more modern and spacious. It wasn't what he would have chosen for himself, but perhaps that made it better, having been chosen for him by someone who cared. He wasn't in a position to know.

"Possibilities," he said to Liza. His smile wasn't forced.

"That's all I needed you to say." Liza was beaming, as though she'd brought home a report card with a line of pointy A's.

Traffic was thinning at that hour, and Ramsy tried to relax. He told himself it wouldn't be so bad, living with Liza. He'd get used to being catered to, and he'd learn to make conversation—with Mark about sports

and hunting, with Liza about the children and, perhaps, the past. He'd learn to live a different life.

"Come on outside," Mark said when they got back.
"Liza'll put the kids down and then we can say goodbye.
Bring your beer."

Ramsy followed Mark onto a small deck in back.
They stood at the railing, looking out at the yard. It
was cold, but the air felt good. Ramsy sipped his beer.

"Hope this isn't out of line," Mark said carefully. "The
kids've been asking about your eye. They don't need to
know much, but I wanted to be truthful if I could."

"Must be like a monster to them."

"They're curious, is all. They've never seen an eye
patch outside of Halloween."

Ramsy was quiet. "Lost it in the war," he said finally.
"Vietnam."

"Lot of men there worse off than me."

Mark nodded, waiting, but Ramsy had no more to
say. "I appreciate it, Ramsy," he said. "The kids hear
about war a lot. Might help them understand. And
Liza and I are certainly glad to know your story."

*   *   *

Only a few people had ever dared ask Ramsy about his
eye. When the rare person did ask what happened, he
said what he'd said to Mark: he'd lost his eye in Vietnam. It was easier just to conjure the images of war
and give himself the chance of being seen as a hero—
or, at least, as a regular man, an unlucky man, maybe,
but not a fool.

He'd gone to war. That was true. He'd gotten his
draft notice in 1967, two years after he graduated high
school in West Virginia. He was working nights at the
glass factory, sleeping with the shades drawn during
the bright afternoons, his father asleep after his own

shift down the short hallway of the trailer. Every evening, Ramsy got up and put food outside for the cats that lurked in the yard. He'd lost track of how many there were. They came from all over and found no reason to leave.

The draft letter didn't promise anything, but Ramsy told himself he was grateful. He knew without the war he'd die in this town, maybe even in this trailer, working shifts and putting food out for a herd of stray cats until he took his last breath. He saw the letter as a railroad switch like the one a hundred yards in front of the trailer, grinding and wheezing and clanking to put an oncoming train on a different path.

"They'll make a man of you," his father said. The morning Ramsy left for training in North Carolina, the farthest south—the farthest anywhere—he'd ever been, his father was at the factory. No one said goodbye.

He was posted to Dong Ha, north of Danang, with the 1st Battalion, 9th Marines. He realized right away he wasn't like the other men in his platoon. He had no worn pictures. He received no letters. In the jungle, waiting out the hours, the other men talked of home. There were girlfriends and mothers to miss, and, for some men, wives and children. Pictures were drawn out again and again. Calendars were kept and carefully marked. No one said *When the war is over...*They all said *When I get home.*

All the men had talismans—photos, charms, rabbit feet, socks or beads or coins that seemed to offer some protection. Ramsy had a stone, gray and jagged, the size of a quarter. It looked like a piece of gravel from a driveway, and maybe it was, carried in tire treads to the tarmac where Ramsy picked it up before boarding his plane to Vietnam.

He showed it to the men in his squad one night when they talked of things they'd brought.

"What's it mean?" asked a man named Colter.

"Don't mean anything," Ramsy said.

"Why'd you bring it, then?"

"Belongs where I got it. Want to bring it back there one day."

The men laughed at him for this, the soldier staying alive for a stone. But then Ramsy kept staying alive, when other men didn't, and no one laughed anymore. He was known as the lucky one, and the men became protective of the stone. The soldier who had nothing to lose led them safely across mined clearings, through sniper fire, down booby-trapped trails. He won a Bronze Star, once, for sprinting behind a hut and killing a sniper who'd taken out three men in his squad as they humped to a new lookout point. The other men had hit the ground, firing shots from behind thick growths of elephant grass. It was foolish, what he did, but it wasn't something he'd thought about. He saw his friends go down—one, two, and then, even though they realized what was happening, a third—and he ran.

With months still left in his tour, the fighting was getting more lethal. As casualties mounted—so many that his battalion would eventually be called the Walking Dead—Ramsy was tempted to step back and let whatever would happen, happen. It was a relief when they handed him his list of R&R choices—Bangkok, Sydney, Hong Kong, Taipei, Tokyo—and he chose Taipei. For Ramsy it seemed to promise the least amount of familiarity, the greatest distance from everything he knew. He wanted to find something different, something that would make him care about staying alive, and he wanted to be alone as he searched.

This wasn't easy in Taipei. Ramsy and the other men on his flight were surrounded by a crush of taxi drivers and hotel touts and would-be guides as soon as they stepped off the bus in the city. Ramsy got into a cab with two men from his platoon, Halinsky and Ruck, and they all got rooms at the New American Hotel. There was a stink of fish and grease in the room, and he could hear traffic and shouting on the street six floors below. Ramsy drew the blinds. The room was small but it was his, and he could breathe.

When he left the hotel the next day, he kept to side streets where he knew he wouldn't see other GIs, quiet streets where he could hear voices and clanking pots through open apartment windows. He heard his own footsteps on the ground and felt light without his gear, so light he felt he might float away and disappear.

He headed to the O.K. Bar, where he heard Jimmy Ruskin on the speakers, and found Halinsky and Ruck drunk with girls in short skirts on the stools next to theirs. Ramsy was greeted with cheers, and glasses of beer lined up in front of him. He drank quickly, realizing that being alone wasn't what he wanted at all; and in a place like this, if you were lonely it was your own damn fault. Soon another girl was on a stool next to his. She wore a short white dress and white high-heeled shoes, and her long dark hair was pinned up at the sides with barrettes shaped like butterflies. Her dark eyes were black-lined, her mouth a plump coral pillow. "You wait for someone, GI?"

"No."

"You wrong, GI. You wait for me."

He didn't crack jokes or regale her with stories about the war or try to feel her up like Halinsky and Ruck. He could barely bring himself to look her full in the face. But by the way she squeezed his arm she seemed to understand something—surely she'd heard a lot, this girl, more than he could ever tell—and a peace settled in him. She was curvy, and he wanted curvy. He wanted flesh he could hold in his hands.

He paid a brusque, unsmiling man what her bar contract required and took her home, to the hotel. That night a home was what it felt like, with his shoes on the floor of the closet and this girl in his bed. She stayed even after they'd done what he'd paid for. He watched her sleep on top of the sheet, the ceiling fan stirring the hair by her temples. The war seemed far away but his old life did, too, the messy room he had in his father's trailer, the fights with his father that marked each day. That wasn't home, and the jungle wasn't either. This was as close as he'd come in a very long time.

"Stay with me today," he said in the morning. When he offered her more money she agreed. Again he set out into the city, but with Nikki at his side, he saw slope-roofed temples and rickety market stalls, watched eels writhing in water-filled cauldrons, wandered in neighborhoods where other GIs never went. He took Nikki's arm to dodge bicycles. He choked on the smoke from roasting corncobs. And they kissed by the Danshui River and sat with their hands on each other's knees when they drank coffee at cafes, and it felt real and sudden. He would have given his arm to have her stay with him another night—but all he had to give was more money, paid once more to the stocky, unsmiling man at the bar.

In the morning, she was gone. But Ramsy's head was filled with images of his new life. The other men had women waiting at home—mothers, girlfriends, sisters, wives—and this was their reason for living. Ramsy understood it now. He'd never seen much of a future for himself, but here, now, was a chance to make it different. He would come back to Taipci after the war. He would start a little business with Nikki. They would vacation in the mountains, get up at dawn to watch sampans slicing Sun Moon Lake. The city offered so much noise that he would never again hear the sounds of the jungle, or the factory, or his father. He could look forward to that. He could *live* for that.

He didn't rush to the bar that night. He knew Nikki would be there. He went with Halinsky and Ruck to the Intercontinental for dinner, and they feasted on roast duck, noodle soup with oysters, dumplings whose fillings were a mystery, ordering more and more dishes, not caring what they spent and grateful for the hot food on their tongues.

Later, at the O.K. Bar, he didn't see Nikki. He sat at the bar and waited while Halinsky and Ruck gathered girls around them, in no hurry to choose. Then Ramsy saw her, parting the curtain over a door to the left of the bar. Ramsy waved, but Nikki didn't see him. She stood with another man, settling a bill. Ramsy got up and went over. "Let's get out of here," he said, taking her arm.

But the man shoved him backward. "Whoa, GI," he said. "Nikki's taken."

"There's been a mistake." Ramsy opened his wallet. "Tell him, Nikki. You're going with me." And he pushed the man, hard, out of the way.

The man shoved him again, into Nikki. She was knocked to her knees, a high heel skittering across the floor. Ramsy had no chance to help her up. In a flash, there was the stocky bar man with a knife, and Ramsy instinctively lunged, grabbing the man's arm and slamming him against the wall. He moved in for a punch, but a foot shot out, and Ramsy was down.

A Marine passed out cold on the floor of a bar rarely got anyone's attention. But when Ramsy let out an agonized scream, blood rushing through the fingers he held against his face, the bar emptied so fast Ramsy nearly felt a vacuum in his ears. Then he blacked out.

He woke up in a hospital bed, the world split between dark and light. A Marine sergeant from the R&R Center was standing by his bed. He told Ramsy two things. The half-light, half-dark world was his forever, and he was going home.

Ramsy protested. "I'll be fine," he said. "Let me get over this and I'll get back out there, Sergeant. Something like this won't stop me."

"Not the kind of thing you get over, Private. And we don't need no one-eyed men in Vietnam."

He was flown back to Saigon with men he did not know, and from there he flew home with the other men who were being evacuated out. Ramsy sat with his face to the window the entire flight. He couldn't look at the bandages, the crutches, the wounds that would become scars. They deserved to go home. He did not. He wished he'd died on the floor of that bar. The war had given him nothing, and he'd given nothing to the war. But it was in him, in his nostrils and ears, under his fingernails.

When they landed, he got off the plane and hurled his piece of gravel as far as he could. *Happy now?* he seethed to no one. *Happy now?*

He went home for two weeks, long enough for him to understand that few people in town would ever look at him again. A buddy had an uncle in Shelk who needed help with a bar, and this was as good a plan as any.

His father told him, "Better think twice before telling what happened to that eye. Hooker stories ain't good for the U.S. Marines."

Ramsy packed up his bag, turned his truck toward Shelk, and never saw his father again. He didn't bother telling him about the Bronze Star. Disappointment would be Ramsy's parting gift.

Hawk Porter, the owner of the bar, was in his eighties when Ramsy met him. He studied Ramsy for a long time, taking in the patch over his eye, the long hair already streaked with white.

"I'm too old to work all the time now," he said, years of mining and smoking in his voice. "I heard you were lucky in the war, but a patch like that says otherwise. No need to tell me your story. I don't want to know it. Heard too many already. But I need some help. Need an heir. This stack of sticks interest you?" Ramsy said it did.

Other men might have wanted choices, might have wanted to explore different paths. There wasn't much exploring a one-eyed man could do, so Ramsy was happy enough to take what he'd been given and settle in. He found he was glad to be alive when he drove that twisted mountain road after sundown, under tall witch-finger pines that blocked out the sky. He was glad to see the yellow windows of the bar when he made the final turn and to hear sticks and dirt and leaves under his tires as he steered up the unpaved drive. The yellow glow from those windows guided him inside.

"Ramsy," Hawk said with a nod, and Ramsy nodded back. Little else was ever said between them, which was how they both wanted it. In that bar, silent but not alone, Ramsy found a kind of peace. Two years later, Hawk died, and the bar was his.

All of this was how he lost his eye, and why he said "Vietnam" when the war was the least of it. The lie seemed beside the point. He went to war and lost his eye. That was what happened, the beginning and the end. The middle hardly mattered. When people whispered *one-eyed man*, it was like they'd whispered *quiet* or *tall*. Part of him, unchangeable, not exactly something to be grateful for but not something he'd want to lose. He barely noticed his half-dark world. And at night, in his dreams, he saw with both eyes open.

*   *   *

Just before the exit that would take him back to Shelk, Ramsy stopped at a diner, sat at the counter, and ordered coffee and apple pie. He needed to still his mind, come back to the present, before he turned his truck down familiar roads. He read the menu in front of him and tried not to notice the glances he got from the waitress and the short-order cooks. From speakers in the ceiling came Christmas music, though it was not yet Thanksgiving. The voices were familiar—Andy Williams singing "It's the Most Wonderful Time of the Year," Rosemary Clooney singing "White Christmas." In his chest rose up a kind of longing he'd never felt before. It wasn't sadness, or regret. It wasn't even love. Instead it felt like homesickness for a place he couldn't quite name, a place he might not have ever been. He pushed his pie away and left a few bills under his coffee mug.

The panic left him when he was back in his truck, and as home grew closer, he wished he'd finished the pie. In the dingy light of early winter evening, Shelk sat quiet and still, having gone on without him as though he'd never been there at all.

CHAPTER 7

40 Crown Vetch Street

It was a one-story red brick with three cat figurines in the front window and a real cat asleep on a chair on the porch. The boy peered in a window at the back of the house. From there he could see to the living room, where an old woman was asleep on the couch, her head thrown back. He tried the back door—unlocked—and slipped inside. He was in the kitchen, dim in the cloudy late afternoon. On the table was a heavy crystal bowl holding an orange and a few bananas. A dish on the floor by the sink was full of half-eaten cat food. He checked the freezer. He found an envelope at the back, between frozen peas and a box of ice-cream bars, and opened it—a half-inch stack of bills. He put the envelope in his jacket pocket without counting the money inside.

He saw now that to get to the bedroom he'd have to walk past the sleeping woman, but he wasn't afraid. If she heard him, what could she do? He'd be out the door before she could find her phone. He crept past, noting the stains on her sweatshirt, the knee-highs wrinkled around her ankles. A soap opera was on the TV, volume

*low. Two blonds with fat diamond necklaces faced off on
what looked like a pier. "This time you've gone too far,
Monica. How dare you?"*

*Before he reached the bedroom, he paused. He knew
already he'd find little in the way of jewelry, but a china
cabinet near the front door, ten feet behind the couch,
made him pause. He slid open the bottom drawer. It was
an old wooden cabinet, and the drawer stuck stubbornly
on rough runners. He crouched and held his breath, but
the woman remained asleep. The cat on the porch, however, peered at him through the window. Turning back
to the drawer, he found what he'd hoped to—a heavy
wooden box that held a set of silver. Family silver, he
knew, passed down two generations or more. He tucked
the box under his arm and didn't bother closing the
drawer. He wished the woman good rest and left once
again through the kitchen, taking an ice-cream bar on
his way.*

The next morning, Ramsy pulled boxes from the
crawlspace under the eaves in his bedroom and began
packing what he could. He wouldn't bother with all
of it, didn't plan on selling his house. He'd just close
it up till he got settled and decide later what to do.
He packed his books and pictures (not many, mostly
buddies from the war, not one photograph of someone living), and his collection of knives. He packed his
clothes and shoes and the blanket he liked from the
bed. He packed his alarm radio and his tapes of Willie
Nelson and Charlie Daniels. That was all. He didn't
want or didn't need the rest.

At the bar that night, he packed pint glasses and
tumblers. "You taking those with you?" Stella asked.
She was watching him over the rim of her wine glass.

"No," Ramsy said.

"Then why pack them?"

"Because it makes it more real," he said. But really he was thinking of Marcie, who left without a trace, her drawers and closets just as they had been with only a few dark gaps where there'd hung a favorite shirt, a worn pair of jeans. It had left him hoping, too long, that she'd come back. When a life was packed in boxes, there could be no mistake.

Stella finished her wine and stood to go. "Tired," she said. "Not in the mood tonight for company."

"You'll be back before I close?"

"When are you closing?"

"In the next couple of days."

"I'll come back," she said. Then she was gone.

When the men came in later, the first thing Charlie said was, "We're under siege." It was happening all over town, the men said, strange kids entering businesses alone or in pairs, asking for work. There weren't many places to go—the hardware store, Shop N' Save, Thrift Drug, a Goodwill, the old dress shop and sheet-music store barely anyone ever went into—and they sometimes showed up twice, even three times a day, as though the answer for one would be different for another. Some owners had started bringing guns to work, keeping a hand on the long handle under the counter when they said firmly they had no work to give.

"And they're panhandling," Ash added. "Two guys and a girl, corner of Fair and Main. Guitar, singing, the whole bit. Came at my car with a plastic bucket when I was stopped at the light. Like I'd roll down my window for a gypsy, for Chrissake. Shameless."

"Like rats," Harry said. His brother owned the hardware store. "Need a pied piper to get them outta here."

"Or just a lot of guns," Jack said.

"Works too," Harry agreed. "Soon enough they'll get the message."

For once, Ramsy agreed with the men. The message couldn't be clearer: these kids weren't welcome, and never would be. Even Ramsy himself wondered what they were thinking, descending on the town this way. They were thieves, was the main thing, and no matter what the reasons behind what they did, it was too late for them to change course now.

"Gotta have some admiration for those gypsies," Ash said after a while. His voice was angry, but there was truth in his words. "You ever wonder about all the places they've seen?'"

"I've heard they've been all over," Charlie said. "Out West, even. Probably hitchhiked in."

"Probably seen more than all of us put together," Ash said. "'Cept you, Ramsy." The others had been too young for the war.

"You imagine what it'd be like to up and go anywhere in the world?" Charlie said. "Don't even know where I'd go if I could go. Anywhere. Jesus. I'd kill to be free like that."

Ramsy wondered what JT and the rest must think of the people they robbed, stuck here as solid as the mountains. The light of the TV flickered, and for just that instant Ramsy was glad he was leaving. Then Jack said, "Guess we'd all run hell knows where if we were chased away at gunpoint"—and the feeling was gone.

*   *   *

On Tuesday, on his way back from Shop N' Save, Ramsy drove down Tansy Road and spotted JT shoveling snow outside eighty-year-old Edna Tally's beige-brick ranch. He pulled his truck over to the curb and rolled his window down. JT looked up. "Hey, Ramsy," he said and walked over to the truck. Ramsy noticed he wasn't wearing gloves, and his knuckles were mottled red and white where they gripped the handle of the shovel. His coat was hanging open. At least he had on a scarf and hat.

"You found work," Ramsy said. "Heard at the bar you'd all been having some trouble. People are talking about your friends, trying to find work in town."

"Told them they were batshit crazy. They wouldn't listen."

"Not the smartest place to go around asking favors. What's their plan?"

"They don't know what the hell they want. Some are getting tired, that's all. The crime, Emilian, living out of a car, all of it."

"And you?"

JT shrugged. "It's winter now. Not one of us wouldn't like to be someplace warm. Living like we do—in the winter you start wondering if there's a better way. Me, I could keep going forever. But not everybody can." JT was quiet for a moment, and Ramsy's mind went to the girl in the parking lot, and her baby. Not everybody could keep going through the cold.

A curtain moved at the front window, and then Edna came out onto the porch, arms crossed against the chill. "Is there a problem here?" she called.

"Not here to give trouble," Ramsy called back. "I know JT. Just wanted to say hello."

"He's doing a good job," she said. To JT she added, "Knock when you're done with the front walk. I have hot chocolate ready."

When she went back inside, JT said in a low voice, "It's not much, I know that. But it's something."

Ramsy nodded. "Alright then," he said. "See you."

Before he turned off Tansy, he glanced at JT again in the rearview mirror, methodically pushing and tossing snow, leaving a pathway good and clear. Ramsy felt a warmth as he watched, pride. Maybe he'd been wrong after all. Maybe JT and the others would find some acceptance, even forgiveness. It proved again how little he knew about Shelk, how distant he was from its people. Maybe he assumed these kids would never fit in just because he himself never really had. All the more reason to leave. People would do what they would do, and Ramsy would never be able to fully understand.

He drove to the corner of Fair and Main before heading to the bar. The musicians were there, with their guitar, bongo, and tambourine, and Ramsy pulled off and opened his window to listen. He didn't know about music, but he knew it was different from anything he'd heard before. The music was fast but keening and melancholy, crying out for something Ramsy couldn't name. It was the kind of music you'd expect to hear in dark faraway places where the mountains were full of wolves and fog and the stones in the cities and castles were older than Shelk itself by centuries, where no one spoke a language you could understand. Ramsy dropped a few bills into a bucket the drummer brought to his window.

That night, when the men came into the bar, they were talking agitatedly, and it didn't take long for Ramsy to realize they were talking about JT. "Junie and I were driving to her mother's," Charlie was telling Jack. "Scared the hell out of me to see it—a gypsy, out there by Edna's in broad daylight."

"How'd you know who it was?" Ramsy said.

Charlie looked at him oddly. "What do you mean, Ramsy? From looking, I don't know. You just know a gypsy."

"Charlie called me up, and we went back to let that gypsy know what's what," Ash said. "Gunned my truck over the curb and pushed a pile of snow back onto the sidewalk with my plow. Let him think twice before doing anything funny."

The men's beers remained untouched on the bar. "I don't like it," Jack said after a few moments. "They're moving in on us now. Saw two of them on the bridge yesterday. Had a dog with them—a Shepherd. Middle of town. They were laughing like they was just two regular kids. Walked real close to the curb." Jack let out a short, uncomfortable laugh as he and the others shrugged into their coats and stood to leave. "Let me tell you, it wouldn't've been a tragedy if a car'd veered over and nipped them."

When JT came in later, Ramsy said, "Heard the men gave you some trouble at Edna's."

"Like I told you, not easy finding an open door around here. But we need the money, you know? Something apart from what we hand over to Emilian."

"Something honest, then."

"Maybe." He leaned forward to take the beer Ramsy had left for him on the bar. "It's not right," he said. "Seeing inside people's lives like that. It gets to me. I don't want to know about all the things people keep hidden."

Ramsy thought back to standing in his own house after the break-in, surrounded by everything that made up his life. What had the thief thought of his home, when he'd found there was nothing to take but an old pistol? To an outsider, Ramsy's life would look empty. Tragic. Ramsy watched JT, slowing draining his beer. Of course, there were a lot of tragedies in a place like Shelk.

"Not easy to make a change like that," Ramsy said.

"More talk than anything," JT said. "The people here don't trust us. They never will."

"Haven't given them much reason to."

"We still gotta eat."

"Then it's not so easy, for folks to take you on faith."

"They're not just afraid of what we might steal," JT said. "They're afraid of *us*. They're afraid of what we've seen." JT looked up at him. "The old lady gave me a chance," he said. "Maybe someone else will, too. Like I said, be nice to get some money in my pocket, go my own way."

There was something between them then, a question unasked, and Ramsy felt his stomach roll. So this, then, was why no others had come to the bar to ask for work. JT had claimed it as his. Ramsy couldn't bring himself to offer or refuse, and he held his breath until the weighted moment passed.

"Listen," Ramsy said. "Not my place to give advice. But what your group's trying to do here won't work. Wish it wasn't this way, but I can't change it. And I have to tell you the anger's growing."

JT nodded, as though he understood that there was nothing for him in Shelk. "I know," he said. "We get it. But Emilian said he ain't ready to go."

"Doesn't seem sensible," Ramsy said. "We might not have much in the way of law around here, but the state police will track him down sooner than later."

"They won't get far with Emilian," JT said. "He only goes into the homes he thinks have big scores. So far, Shelk hasn't delivered."

"So the rest of you would get in trouble. He willing to take that risk?" Ramsy replaced JT's empty beer with another. The boy lifted the bottle, but he didn't drink right away.

"Emilian thinks he's got a good thing here," JT said. "He's got his cash from Owl Creek, he's got a girl, he's got that other lady. Why leave now?"

"I'll talk to him," Ramsy said. "Explain how it is."

"Emilian would never come here."

"Then I'll go to him."

Fear flashed in JT's eyes.

"As a concerned citizen," Ramsy said. "Not any connection to you."

"Okay," JT said, and there was relief in his voice. Someone would finally step in and make things right. Ramsy had forgotten how young JT was. Now, in comparison, Ramsy felt a million years old.

*   *   *

The next night he told Stella he was going to talk to Emilian. "Can only get worse," he said. "Harder they push this town, worse it'll get. Someone on the inside needs to explain how it is here."

"I'm going too."

"No."

"I have a stake in this, Ramsy. I helped JT, same as you. And maybe Emilian will listen to a woman. He won't think you're a threat if I'm there."

Ramsy busied himself at the register and then turned to face her. "It won't work, Stella. You won't find that girl and her baby."

"Why not? Where else would she be?"

"They're liable to be spread out. Some in the caves, some in cars, tents. We don't know what kind of setup they have."

"So I'll just go with you, then, to help."

Stella's voice told him it was decided, and he let the argument go. Once they got up there, she would see. Maybe that was the best thing after all. Maybe that was even what he himself wanted—reassurance that the girl wasn't there.

Stella was still at the bar with him when JT arrived. He stopped in the doorway when he saw her, but Ramsy nodded at him to come inside. "Stella," he said, introducing her with a tilt of his chin. He'd let JT give his own name if he wanted, but JT didn't offer it.

"She coming with us?" JT asked. Ramsy nodded.

They left the bar in silence and got into Ramsy's truck, Stella in the middle. JT didn't give any directions, so Ramsy headed into the mountains the way he knew.

After twenty minutes JT said, "Here." He pointed to the right. "Park off to the side."

Ramsy killed the engine. He waited while Stella pulled on a hat and gloves and looped her thick scarf once more around her throat. "Ready?" he asked, and they all went out into the snow. JT walked down a narrow path into the trees, and Ramsy and Stella followed. After five minutes, they came to a clearing. There was a fire in the middle, and a few cars and vans parked around it. Farther off was an old RV up on cinder blocks.

"There," JT said. They treaded carefully through the camp, stepping over crates and buckets, logs arranged as benches, propane tanks, a small soot-filled grill. A few dirty blankets and pillows were strewn around the fire along with an ice chest and a large cast-iron kettle. Empty jugs from a water cooler were half-buried in the snow. A rope was strung between two trees, but the only thing hanging there was a pillowcase with a large brown stain. No one was in sight, but they heard someone playing a guitar behind one of the vans. When they reached the RV, JT gave a light knock and led them inside.

"Wait here," he said, and he squeezed down a narrow hall. Ramsy heard him and a girl talking in low voices. "Come on back," JT said finally, loud enough for them to hear.

In the back of the RV was a tiny room with a low, small bed. And on the bed sat the girl, the palm reader, with the baby asleep beside her, her head on a pillow, a blanket wrapped sloppily around her body. Ramsy didn't look at Stella, but he heard her intake of breath. "It's you," Stella said.

JT said, "You know them, Adrienne?" and the girl gave a quick shake of her head.

She looked younger here than she had at the Shop N' Save. Her face and arms seemed slightly doughy, unformed, the bones and muscles not yet hardened under the skin. Dark blond hair hung in stringy clumps down to her shoulders. From her ears hung rows of small brown beads threaded on long leather laces. Dirt around short fingernails, chapped pink lips. In the poorly heated van she was wearing only a red milk-stained T-shirt and a colorful knitted scarf around her neck. JT hovered close by, his eyes never leaving her face.

"Emilian isn't here," Adrienne said.

"I need to talk to him," Ramsy said. "When will he be back?"

"Not sure." Her voice was hard, accustomed to distrust and suspicion.

"It's important. Concerns you, JT, everyone."

"I told you, he's not here."

"Happy to wait if I have to. Can wait here all night."

Fear flickered on Adrienne's face, and JT met Ramsy's eye and shook his head. Ramsy sighed and turned to go. "Stella, come on. Let's get out of here."

But Stella's eyes were trained on the mewling baby. There was a gray shadow of sweat and saliva and milk in the creases of her tiny neck. Large wet stains bloomed across Adrienne's chest. She looked down and sighed. "All I smell anymore is sour milk," she said.

Ramsy thought he might be sick. He wondered if he was the only one there who knew about Emilian and Kitty Kurtz. Maybe it was part of life among this group, the way it was for them in every town. He didn't know and didn't want to know. But he couldn't bear looking at the tired girl and that struggling baby any longer.

He reached for Stella's elbow, but she shook him off and asked Adrienne, "Can I hold her?" Every muscle in Ramsy's body screamed at him to grab Stella by the waist and pull her out of there, but the hopeful smile she gave Adrienne—as though they were in a warm, clean living room, and the girl was a happy but tired young friend—stopped him. When Adrienne nodded, Stella sat down and picked up the baby, who mewled again then resettled herself in the crook of Stella's arm. "What's her name?" Stella asked.

"Serena," Adrienne said.

"How lovely."

When Stella looked up at him, Ramsy saw two things on her face: what might have been, and what might be. "Let's go," he said. "Now."

Stella didn't release the baby, and Adrienne reached over and pulled her from Stella's arms. No one spoke. JT pushed past them. Ramsy heard a cupboard open, the kitchen faucet rush on, and then JT returned with a glass of water. Adrienne sipped it then lifted the bottom of her shirt, fumbling with a clasp on her bra strap.

"She needs to feed the baby," JT said, and he led them back through the RV and out into the snow.

"I'll see ya," he said at the edge of the clearing. Ramsy nodded.

"That baby," Stella said, but Ramsy put a hand on her arm and led her away.

"That baby," she said again when they were back in his truck. "It was all bones. That girl needs more food—she's not making enough milk, or the milk isn't rich enough, or—I don't know anything about it, Ramsy, only that a baby can't live like that, unwashed, in the back of a *car*. Is that *Emilian's* baby? JT was so protective, but he surely doesn't know anything about how to help. We need to—"

"We don't need to do anything. Not our place."

"Blankets, at least. And maybe some formula and a few bottles. Some baby soap and washcloths, but where would she have a bath? We could drive them to my house, let them stay for a few days—I wish you'd say something," she said.

Ramsy stared at the road. He clicked on the high beams, lighting the deep snow in the trees. "We can do those things," he said finally. He wasn't a monster. "Seems risky, but we can buy whatever you want, whatever you think will help. But I don't think you can take them home."

Stella sat back, agitation still raw on her face. And all Ramsy could think was that it was too bad about the baby—she didn't ask for this kind of life, was helpless to improve her lot—but it was time for these travelers to go.

*   *   *

When Stella came to the bar two days later, her face was pale, with dark-shadowed eyes. Ramsy thought he knew why. Adrienne's baby was right around the age Lucy was when she disappeared—she'd have the same weight and heft, the same bulk in Stella's arms; she'd have the same sleepy gaze, the same cries and coos. The image of Stella holding that baby chilled him, down to his bones. He felt unsettled even with Stella sitting right there before him, drinking her wine and listening to the men talk of new thefts. When he met Stella's eyes across the bar, he fumbled a glass in his hands and it cracked against the side of the sink.

"I'm not sleeping," Stella said as soon as they were alone. "When I close my eyes I hear Serena crying. I can feel how hungry she is. How cold." She sipped her wine. "And Adrienne—she needs clean clothes, clean sleepers for Serena. I want to ask JT what I can do."

They waited a long time for JT. He came in at midnight, coat once again open despite the cold, and this time Ramsy saw the zipper pull hanging loose at the middle of his chest, useless.

"That baby," Stella said once JT had taken a seat. She kept her voice even. "Emilian's?"

JT nodded. "Gotta feel sorry for her," he said.

Stella leaned forward. "I'd like to help."

"Emilian won't like it."

"Just buy a few things. Things she needs."

"I wouldn't do that if I were you. Emilian doesn't take well to people who get involved that way."

"Say you stole it—some baby blankets. Some formula."

JT shook his head. "I can't do that," he said. "Emilian says we take care of our own. But I'm the last person he wants stepping in to take care of Adrienne."

Stella threw Ramsy a frustrated glance and left without a word.

Once she was gone, JT asked, "Why's she care so much about someone else's baby?"

Fifteen years of looking and she's found something, Ramsy thought, but all he said was, "Seems to me you care, too."

JT's jaw tightened. "Adrienne went into labor the night after Emilian planned a major theft in Owl Creek. He wouldn't take her to the hospital—said it'd draw attention to us, showing up there. A couple of women Emilian knew said they'd help, and they locked themselves in the RV with Adrienne. I listened from outside—they just yelled at her to quit screaming. Twenty hours of this."

"Poor girl," Ramsy said.

"I had to break a window to get into the RV, but I got her. Carried her myself out to the car and drove her into town. She could have died, or the baby. Maybe both."

"Someone had to have sense."

"I told the hospital I was the father so I could stay. Emilian never even showed up to visit, but he'll never get over what I did."

"If not you, someone else would have stepped in. He must know that."

"Doesn't matter. It was me." He shrugged. "I don't blame her for choosing Emilian," he added. "Not exactly a fair contest, him or me."

"Can't be easy to see her with him."

"Not easy to see her out there with Serena at all. Sometimes I think I can still do something for her, you know? Like if I earn some money I can help get her out of there, away from Emilian. I could help get her settled, someplace safe for Serena." He took a last swallow of beer. "If your friend wants to help, she'll have to get past Emilian."

"Hope it won't come to that," Ramsy said. But he knew he'd say nothing to Stella, even if he had the chance. He knew already it wouldn't work.

*   *   *

Ramsy wasn't a sentimental man, but on nights like this, when shadows from the road swept over his walls as he lay awake in bed, he remembered the afternoon Liza had first called. He was having coffee in his kitchen, a few cups before he left for the bar, and he was looking out the window. It was September, and the sun was so bright it hurt his eye, made it water. He squinted and saw blurs of red and yellow trees, a smear of blue sky. Even on days like that he woke looking forward to night. The phone rang as he drank the last of his coffee.

"I'm looking for Zaccariah Ramsy," a girl said.

"This is Ramsy."

"This is Liza Pounds," she said. "I'm your daughter."

She'd been only twenty-one then, and her voice hadn't yet mellowed into a woman's voice. He'd always been thankful for whatever he'd said that morning, because after that she kept calling. First she called in the afternoons at his house, and then, once he could tell her he preferred it, at the bar at night. Their conversations were spare and short but warm, and over the years she'd been kind. But on nights when he lay awake it was that first conversation he remembered, those first words coming out of nowhere from the phone he held in his hand: *I'm your daughter.* Words he'd never expected or even hoped to hear.

Ramsy hadn't seen any pictures from the twenty years Liza had been away: not one picture from school, not one picture snapped at a birthday party or under a Christmas tree. Childhood pictures seemed like something he didn't deserve, part of a world he didn't belong to. He'd had to imagine Liza growing up: her limbs stretching out, her body changing shape, her face thinning in the cheeks and chin. Sometimes he imagined she looked like him. Sometimes he hoped she did. But when he met her and saw she looked like her mother, he wasn't surprised. Still, he'd tried to find himself. He could, but only barely: a shadow of his jawline in hers, and similar hands.

The pleasure he took in thinking of Liza always faded. He ended up thinking of Stella, and the phone call that never came for her: *We've found your baby. She's alive and well.* He'd lost Liza because he was lazy and didn't know the first thing about being a man. Marcie had been right to leave. Stella didn't deserve any of it, and she never got a chance to see whether her imagined pictures of Lucy were right or wrong. It wasn't fair. Yet whenever he voiced frustration over her tenuous grasp of reality, her relentless and wayward hope, he could almost read her thoughts: *What right do you have to ask me questions? Your daughter came home.*

CHAPTER 8

181 Arrowhead Road

She said they'd left her: her husband, her sons, the only people in her life who mattered. She said they'd decided life was better without her—or, at least, this was what their absence suggested. Divorce was common, these days, but to lose her sons—it seemed like unjust punishment for sins she'd spent years regretting.

This was what she told the girl who'd offered to read her cards and who'd conjured meaning from swords and cups and wands. "You're right," the woman said. "Who knew but you're right." After this she invited the girl to her home. Once. Twice. Each time the girl read the cards to enlighten the woman on some particular worry, and it became clear that the woman believed her problems were connected somehow, with some root cause she could eliminate if only she knew what it was. The woman had a wide-eyed gaze that suggested she'd spent her life believing what people told her. The girl knew she might not find herself the subject of such a gaze again for months, or years.

On her third visit, heart pounding, the girl said, "I feel your money's the problem. Your money's cursed." She'd heard how this was done from others she'd met once on the road.

The woman frowned. "I don't have much. Just some money my father left when he died."

The girl requested an egg, which the woman brought in on a dish from the kitchen. In her sleeve she fingered a tiny carved head she'd found once in the trough of a carnival game. Then she cracked the egg and slipped the head into the yolk as it slid onto the plate. The woman screamed, and the girl said quietly, "There's evil here. The money you have—I can help you, but I need to touch it with my own hands."

The woman, trembling, handed over a black leather purse. "It's there, all of it," she said. "Please help me." The purse held a thousand dollars.

When she left the woman that day, the girl tucked the small carved head safely into an inside pocket of her blouse. Her lungs pushed against it again and again as she ran.

Ramsy had gone too far, visiting the camp. Emilian had seen him at the Rowdy Buck, and it was clear Ramsy knew about him and Kitty. If Ramsy had to be honest, he'd say he must have been looking for trouble. What else could have come from confronting Emilian that way? There was anger in him, Ramsy realized. Not like the men's, but it was there. Anger at Emilian for pushing troubled kids into crimes they didn't want. Anger at Kitty for putting her needy, sorry soul on display for the town to see. Anger at the townspeople, too, for closing their doors against these strangers, even though Ramsy couldn't blame them. Who was he to try to make things different? Best to leave before he did something he'd truly regret.

He'd promised Stella he wouldn't leave without saying goodbye, and he waited two days for her to come in. He bruised his shins on the boxes he'd packed, had to unpack and repack every time the men asked for a drink. But Stella didn't come, and it was possible now that he might never see her again. He could go to her house—he could call her on the phone—but he knew he wouldn't. If Stella wanted to say goodbye, she knew where to find him. Her absence from the bar was a goodbye of its own.

The night Ramsy had chosen to close the bar, JT came in. He arrived coughing, a dry hack that hunched his shoulders and left his forehead tense and red.

"Should get that looked at," Ramsy said as he opened a beer.

"You really think a doctor in town would see a thief?" JT said. His voice was hard tonight, taunting, lower than usual with the cough and fatigue.

"These aren't bad people," Ramsy said evenly. "Can't see someone turning you away." But he frowned, unsure if what he'd said was true.

"Should say my goodbyes," Ramsy said eventually. "Been planning to close for a while now. It's finally time."

"Right," JT said. "That sign. *Closing.*"

"Tried to give fair warning. Good luck to you, now. Try to get Emilian to go your way."

JT looked at him for a long moment, and then he nodded. "I'll be seeing you, old man." When he finished his beer he coughed and stepped out the door, back into the cold night.

When he left, Ramsy shoved the boxes closer to the back wall, checked the lock on the window, and drew the curtains. He turned the water off, turned the heat off. Then he tucked the money pouch into his coat, turned off the lights, locked up the bar, and went out to his truck. The bar was closed. It was over.

*   *   *

He slept a lot in the days after closing the bar, slept and watched TV. He spoke to no one. He didn't call Liza—he wasn't ready to go to her just yet. He thought, now and then, of JT, his broken coat and hacking cough, but he did his best to push it away. *Worry'll undo you*, as Hawk said. *Always does.* And he thought about Stella, stopped himself over and over again from driving to her house. It had been only a few days since he'd seen her, but it felt like she'd been gone for a very long time.

One evening he ran into Ash Haggerty at the gas pumps outside Sheetz. Ash saw him first and called out—"Ramsy!"—and they shook hands by Ramsy's truck. Their breath formed cold clouds between them, and Ash rubbed his hands together to stay warm. Ramsy knew Ash wanted to tell him something by the way he wouldn't meet his eye.

"Something happened," Ash said. "It's Stella."

Ramsy jerked the gas pump out of the truck and fumbled it into its cradle.

"She's okay," Ash said, but Ramsy's heart didn't slow. "They found her husband."

"Seth disappeared fifteen years ago."

"Well, they found him," Ash said. "Dead, but they found him."

"And Lucy?"

"No trace of her. Searched his house, top to bottom, for clues. It's like she never even existed."

"She existed."

"I know," Ash said. "I'm just telling you what I heard. A reporter from Pittsburgh was snooping around in town today, asking questions, looking for Stella."

"They find her?"

"Probably. Everyone knows who Stella is."

He told Ramsy that Seth Kimmell was found dead in his living room, in a house on a quiet street in Ohio. He'd been living there for about a year, selling cars at a place in Dayton. At first people thought he'd been murdered—he had a reputation for making bad deals—but it turned out that a vein in his head had burst and killed him. Seth's live-in girlfriend had found him. The son of a gun had a girlfriend.

"He had a different name," Ash said. "Not like he changed it legally. Just something he was going by. The girlfriend found out his real name when she went through his stuff after he died, and then the cops got in on it. Everyone knew he'd been in some trouble, but no one knew about the baby till the cops started asking questions."

Ramsy knew Ash wanted him to say something, to lash out with violence or demand to know how Seth Kimmell could have been living a normal life just one state away. But all Ramsy could do was shake his head and raise a hand as he retreated into his truck. Life went on for some people and not for others—Ramsy had never understood it. Seth Kimmell had always been gone, but there had always been the chance that he might come back with answers and explanations, even the baby (a teenager now) in tow. Now, he was dead and always would be. He'd taken Lucy to his grave.

After he drove away, he imagined Stella alone at home without the lights on, her eyes damp, a wrinkled tissue clutched in her hand. Then there he was, stepping out of the kitchen with mugs and teabags on a tray, the teakettle just beginning to whistle. Her eyes were full of gratitude, and the drink he made calmed her, let her put the tissue down, relaxed her shoulders and her hands. Then he was upstairs, preparing her bed, lighting a lamp on her bedside table so she wouldn't have to enter a dark room. Then she was in the doorway, tired and weak with grief—

It was self-indulgent and insulting to imagine himself rescuing Stella. It wasn't like him, and Stella wouldn't want it.

At home he went to his bedroom closet and pulled out shoes and clutter until he found a brown shoebox in the back. He sat on the floor and took off the lid for the first time in over a decade. This was his Stella box, though Stella didn't know he had it. He'd barely remembered it himself until Ash told him the news about Seth. Stella's loss was something he thought of every day, but the details seemed distant, like a story he'd heard long ago.

When Stella started coming to his bar, he dug through stacks of old newspapers he'd piled by his shed until he found the ones carrying stories about what happened. For some reason, he clipped them. He didn't know why. At the time, he didn't know much more about Stella than the kind of wine she liked to drink, but the whispers he'd heard about her searches struck something in him. It wasn't pity. It was envy, if anything, envy of hope so raw and persistent that it would drive her out to the highway night after night even after all logic told her there was nothing to find.

He looked at one of the articles now. *Shelk pharmaceutical salesman Seth Kimmell was arrested last night for the kidnapping and disappearance of his six-week-old daughter. According to his wife, Stella Vale, an inebriated Kimmell came home at 2:00 a.m., screaming obscenities, and took the infant from her crib. State police found him unconscious at the wheel of his car at 3:00 a.m., but there was no sign of the baby. Kimmell claims he does not know what happened to her. Authorities are actively seeking information to help with their search. "A child doesn't disappear into thin air," said State Trooper Chris Petrowski.*

Alongside the article was a picture of Seth, wearing a suit, young and smiling.

There had been times when Ramsy wanted to kill Seth Kimmell. Long ago he'd told Stella he didn't know Seth, that he'd never heard his name in town. But he'd lied. Seth used to come into the bar, before he made it with his investments and started hanging around with the country-club set. Ramsy remembered Seth when he was trying to build a life that didn't revolve around the Polish social club and deer hunting, as so many lives in Shelk did. Ramsy wasn't sure what gave him his drive. There were plenty of good people in Shelk, plenty of nice-enough homes, and not many people wanted more.

When Seth made it, he let everyone know. He replaced his old drinking buddies with new golfing partners. He replaced his old hangouts—Ramsy's, the Elks—with the country club, the golf course, and small restaurants on the other side of the mountains. He kept himself clean-shaven and out of jeans and flannel shirts, and he drove a Honda sedan. Everyone tittered when he took up with Stella, a waitress, but since she was beautiful—even more beautiful after Seth dressed her up in new clothes and jewelry and stylish heels— they understood.

Ramsy had never trusted Seth. He didn't take to men who turned their backs on past lives, old friends, former selves. It was one thing to bury mistakes, turn over new leaves as life plodded on. But elbowing past those who'd stood by you just to get on to the next thing—that was no way to live, hurtling forward in time without anything to hold you back. Nothing but trouble came of a life like that.

Ramsy put the article back in the box and then scooped out the rest of the contents: an antique crystal drawer-pull, a water-filled pen from Niagara Falls, a faded photograph of a woman waving from a porch, a bracelet made of small blue beads. These were things Stella found on her searches and gave to Ramsy the nights she stopped in. *Gave* wasn't exactly right. On those nights, she came in after searching and sat, wild-haired, without saying a word. She never even asked what her wine cost. She just left a few bills, whatever she thought was enough. Ramsy never counted. And along with the money, she left one trinket or another, like offerings on some kind of altar. She never told him where they came from. Her searches weren't something she talked about. Ramsy couldn't imagine throwing the trinkets away, then or now. They still felt holy to him, charged with the feelings of that time, and he wiped them with the edge of his shirt.

From the box, Ramsy took out a folded paper and spread it on the floor. "Have You Seen Me?" it said at the top. Below the words was a large color photograph of Lucy in a pale pink sleeper, staring black-eyed at the camera, a tiny fist visible by her head. Below the picture were her height and weight, her full name, a number to call, a reward. Copies of this flyer were all over town the morning after the kidnapping—in store windows, on telephone poles, on bulletin boards, in the hallways of schools. Smaller tri-folded versions appeared on restaurant tables and checkout lanes all across southwestern PA. Ramsy hung one of the flyers on the door of his bar. After two months, Stella came in one night with the flyer in her hand. "I don't want to see this when I come here anymore," she said. Ramsy put it in his box.

Ramsy repacked the box. He wondered what Stella would say if she knew he had it, a kind of scrapbook of the dead. It was morbid. He should burn the whole thing. But it meant something to him to have it. He'd done something good—even if it was nothing more than keeping a bar door open, pouring a glass of wine. Someone had needed him, and he had been there. In a life like his, it mattered. He'd keep the box in his truck. Maybe he'd find a reason to show it to Stella someday.

He set out, without thinking, toward Stella's house, uninvited: something he'd long ago sworn he'd never do. A light was on in her downstairs window. When she answered his knock, her face said she'd expected him.

"You're afraid to look at me," she said when he stepped inside. "All my life someone's been afraid to look at me. What do they think they'll see?"

"They—"

"Pity me. I know." She took his coat and scarf.

"I heard about Seth."

"Everyone has. People came to the library today just to see if I'd lost my mind."

"Are you okay?"

She looked at him with her head tilted and smiled with her mouth closed, without her eyes. "The news."

It was the second story on the eight o'clock news. "New developments in a fifteen-year-old kidnapping case," said a young blond in a serious voice. "Former Shelk resident Seth Kimmell, who served a prison sentence for the kidnapping and subsequent disappearance of his baby daughter in 1988, was found dead yesterday in his home in Kettering, Ohio. Kimmell moved to Kettering in 1990 after his release from prison and worked under the name James Hansel. He died of an aneurism and was found by his live-in girlfriend, who claims she knows nothing about his past. Detectives hold little hope of finding any clues to the whereabouts of the missing child.

"In Moon Run today, a building collapsed…"

Stella turned off the TV and they sat in silence. Then she put her head in her hands. "I'm sorry," she said after a few minutes. "You must think I'm crazy, acting this way over a man like Seth."

"No."

"I don't love him."

"I know."

She shook her head, angry at herself. But Ramsy understood. She was grieving him, despite everything, because she'd cared about him once. She'd invested her future in him. He was part of her life no matter what he'd done or where he'd been, and now he was dead.

Stella stared at him. "Your eye," she said softly. "Sometimes I can't stop looking at it." He let her stare. "You're a handsome man, Ramsy," she said. "Everything about you is right there on your face." It was something she'd said to him years ago, on a moonlit night in her bed. She'd touched his smooth chin and cheek, his fine, straight nose. But then there was the red swash where the eye had been. It was a shame, Stella had said.

Now Ramsy wanted to put his palms on her cheeks, rub her shoulders, take her hand, but he stayed where he was at his end of the couch. It seemed as easy as reaching over and lifting one of her hands from the crook of her elbow, or stretching his own hand over and touching her face, just like that, as he might touch a doorframe or a soft flannel shirt. But there was a lot more to it than just the movement of his muscles and bones.

"Stay for a minute," she said. "I'll make some tea."

As she drank, her face tensed. She chewed her lip, already raw. Ramsy saw blood on her tongue.

"They could find something," she said. She wasn't looking at Ramsy. "When his girlfriend cleans out his stuff, they could find something. They said it's a different woman. Maybe this one knows more. Maybe she'll come forward with something she's suspected but couldn't say while he was alive."

"Seems unlikely after all this time," Ramsy said. He could see Stella's chest trembling under her thin cotton shirt.

"Does it?" she said. "He had nothing when they caught him. That seems more unlikely to me. There were never any clues, and I found that the most unlikely thing of all."

"Would've told you by now, I'd imagine."

"He just died. Anything there is to discover will be found in the days to come." Finally she turned her stricken face to him. "I've had a bad feeling for weeks. Didn't know why. And now I feel something's out there. What could it be, Ramsy? What do you think they might find? Would they even contact me if they do find something? Should I call someone in Ohio, a detective maybe, and—"

"Stella."

"I just want to know if something's found. It's been years. They might not think I'm here, waiting."

"They'll find you. Pretty hard to hide, these days."

Stella drank her tea—hard, long sips, right to the bottom. Her face was flushed from the steam, and when she spoke after a while her voice was under control. "So," she said. "You're closed?"

"Yes," Ramsy said. He knew she knew it, but she did this sometimes, pretended distance and indifference. "Almost time to leave."

"You ready?"

"Sure." He shrugged. He could do it, too.

"Guess I'll have to find someone else to talk to," she said. "Figure out what's next for me, now, too." She gave a humorless laugh through her nose. "Maybe I should join up with the gypsies."

"They're not gypsies," Ramsy said, "they're just kids. Runaways."

They were quiet for a long time. Ramsy tried half-heartedly to draw her out, but she refused to tell him anything more—"I'm fine," was all she said—and Ramsy didn't insist. She hadn't cried at all, but he didn't believe she was fine, especially when she pushed open a window and let winter air pour into the room.

Ramsy stood to go. "It's freezing, Stella," he said. "Close it."

"The cold air will do me good," she said firmly, and then she said it again: "The cold air will do me good." Ramsy shuddered as he finally walked out to his truck.

*　　　*　　　*

Alone now, Ramsy wound along the back roads to his house, and his mind reeled with the things Stella had said. He kept hearing her voice, kept seeing the flatness in her eyes. It hurt him to think about her, but he couldn't get her face out of his head. He turned left three miles before his house, onto the scantily paved road that led into the mountains. The bare branches of hemlocks and pines blocked most of the falling snow. Animals' eyes glinted in his headlights.

Ten miles farther in was where JT and the rest were staying, and Ramsy didn't want to go that far. He slowed the truck, the tires straining against the road, and scanned the woods to the left and the right, though he knew they were not there. This was madness. He didn't want to see them. He just wanted to put something in his head besides Stella. He should've gone home, poured some whiskey.

Finally he stopped the truck and, giving in to an urge pulling like rope on his throat and heart, he turned the headlights off. For a long moment he sat in darkness. There was no difference now when he opened or closed his eye. If he wanted to, he could fool himself into thinking his left eye wasn't gone, that the blackness was just the blackness of the night. He heard animals swishing through the dry brown woods, and his own breathing. Then he clicked the lights back on and turned the truck around.

Back home among his packed boxes and bags, Ramsy sat at his table without the lights on. His heart ached for Stella more than it had for years. The night after Marcie left, he'd sat at this same kitchen table, and the silence in the house sunk into his bones. Liza had been a quiet baby and Marcie, too, had valued silence, but the absence of even the slightest sounds of them—their breathing, their sighing, the brush of their skin against blankets and clothes—was loud in his ears. He could hear the night outside but that was all, and even that seemed far away.

That night, he'd wanted to call someone. He'd wanted to open the fridge for someone else's bottle of beer. There'd been no one, of course, and he'd made it through that night—and all the nights after that— alone. They weren't nights he chose to remember very often, but they came back to him now, as he thought about Stella. Was she sitting in the dark like he was, descending into memories? Or was she tucked into bed, accepting sleep? He hoped she was sleeping, but his chest felt warm and open when he pictured her sitting just like him.

Stella would need someone now—and he was leaving her. He'd known it since he put up the *Closing* sign, but hadn't let himself admit it. Who would she talk to in the evenings, without his bar to go to? She didn't tell him everything—didn't bare her soul to him—but he'd learned over the years that not saying everything was a kind of soul-baring, too.

Ramsy had seen something in Stella before they'd ever met. It happened in the weeks after Lucy disappeared, before Stella began coming to the bar. The searching, by that time, was over, left to hopeless police files. Neighbors had spent their pity and were left awkward and sorry.

But Stella kept searching for Lucy long after the official search had stopped. The first time Ramsy saw Stella on the road, he didn't know it was her. It was late, and he slowed when he saw her, as he would have slowed for anyone along the road at that hour. She was walking on the shoulder. He rolled his window down.

"Can I drive you somewhere?" he'd asked, but when she turned to him—wild-haired, blinking in the headlights' glare—he saw his mistake.

"No," she said, "but thank you." He drove away fast, feeling guilty and ashamed. In his rearview mirror, he saw her stoop for a bag, lift it, empty it, then move on. He told no one what he'd seen, and if others had seen her, they'd kept quiet too. Ramsy didn't stop when he saw her again, and after a month, she stopped searching bags, put that part of life behind her. But he'd never forgotten that fragile, unlikely hope in her eyes. People dealt in strange ways with grief, and their rituals were often grotesque, but his feelings toward Stella had never veered into pity. It was no wonder that Seth's reappearance in her life, even as a dead man, would dredge up her unlikely hope once more—and, just as Ramsy had done so many years ago, he was about to simply drive away.

Unless he didn't. Unless, just for a while, he stayed.

CHAPTER 9

13 Bellflower Street

It wasn't the nicest house on the block. The beige vinyl siding was faded unevenly, and the green plastic awning over the porch stairs was cracked. But care had been taken. Bright rugs had been set out over the porch's brown-and-beige outdoor carpet, and yellow mums in old half-barrels marked the end of the short walkway to the sidewalk. There was a wreath on the front door made of twigs and red berries, and the house number had been painted in white on a small wooden oval. There wouldn't be much here, but there would be some-thing: old, prized, carefully kept.

She went in the aluminum back door that opened onto a walkway leading to the garage. It wasn't locked, probably never was. Neighbors were probably used to poking their heads in and calling Hello? *The door led into a mudroom full of shoes, with coats hanging on hooks on the wall. The girl slipped from there to the steps off the living room. Anything she'd want would be upstairs. It would be with things that had no value to anyone—yellowed christening gowns, old lace—but it would be there.*

The stairs creaked. She stopped, not breathing but not nervous. There had been no car out front. She kept going. The top step creaked even more loudly, and when she quickly hopped into the hallway, she noticed a door was closed. Not a bedroom door. Not the door to the attic crawlspace—the bathroom door. She backed up slowly, slowly, placing each foot deliberately on the plush green carpet, until her left foot hit the creaky spot again, and a woman's fearful voice came from the bathroom: "Who's there?"

She ran. She took the stairs two at a time, losing her footing on the last couple and skidding to the bottom, hitting her knees. From upstairs came a scream, then another. She banged out the back door and ran through yards, not stopping until she'd made it to the main road. Then she took a deep breath and tried to walk normally. But her own heart was racing, as though she'd been the one surprised in the bath.

The next day, on the back of the sign that said *Closed*, he wrote in black marker, *Open November 19*. Big black letters, gone over several times with the wide part of the marker's tip. It was visible from the road, but since hardly anyone drove up that way unless they were coming to the bar, he didn't expect anyone to see it.

Inside, he took the stools down from the counter and unpacked a few glasses from a box. He felt like he'd returned from someplace far away, and he turned the TV on and sat down with a bottle of beer. He imagined what Charlie, Ash, and Jack were doing now: probably sitting with beers in their own kitchens, or watching TV while their wives cooked dinner. It was too soon to find a new place, but Ramsy knew they would, someplace small and dark near the railroad tracks on the river. The bartender might ask them questions at first, but he'd learn soon enough. There were men who liked to talk and men who didn't, and men who'd talk only when they felt absolutely safe to do so. The men from his bar were of the third group. It always took some time to figure out who was who, but their new bartender would learn soon enough.

Maybe their wives were happy to have them home, or maybe they wished for another hour, two hours, to themselves. Ramsy didn't know what their home lives were really like. He only knew what he heard in the bar, and those words were stained with alcohol. He'd put the word out in town tomorrow that he was open again, and he decided he'd call to tell Stella after a few days had gone by.

At eight o'clock, Charlie and Ash knocked on the door. He didn't answer it—it was unlocked—and eventually they pushed it open themselves.

"Says open," Ramsy said. "You don't have to knock."

"We were on our way home," Charlie said. "Thought we'd drive by, you know, just in case."

"In case what?"

"Case you changed your mind. And you did."

They were the only two in the bar that night. Charlie's oldest daughter, just eighteen, had gotten pregnant. "That son of a bitch," Charlie said sadly. "I don't care what she says. If I see him again, I'll kill him."

They spoke little, now and then calling out answers to *Jeopardy!* clues beaming silently from the old TV.

"Stella holding up okay?" Ash asked when they drew their coats on to leave.

"Seems so," Ramsy said. "Haven't seen her today, but I'd imagine so."

Ash's eyes were bloodshot with beer and fatigue, and he seemed to see right through him. "It's good you're open," he said. "It's good she has a place to go."

"Yes," Ramsy said. He wasn't surprised that the men knew Stella had something to do with his decision to stay.

"Listen," Charlie said. "I saw Stella today—walking into the pediatrician's office down on Main Street. Had a young girl and a baby with her. She have family in town?"

"Maybe so," Ramsy said, but he could barely speak the words. Seth had been as much family as Stella had ever had, and now he was dead. Charlie was watching him carefully, and Ramsy prayed he hadn't gotten too close a look at the girl. "I'll be seeing you, Charlie," he said, and he was relieved when Charlie walked out the door.

Maybe it wasn't what he thought. Maybe Stella did have someone, a young cousin Ramsy didn't know. Otherwise—Ramsy shook his head. Otherwise, maybe it was best he'd decided to stay after all.

He called Liza when the men left. "So when can we expect you?" she said.

"Turns out I can't leave just yet," Ramsy said. "Something's come up here. I need to stay."

Silence. "Is it the gypsies?"

"No." He would never worry her with JT and the rest.

"Did something happen? Are you okay?"

"I'm fine," Ramsy said. "But I need to be here. Want to be."

"I told you we'd stay out of your way, Ramsy, the bedroom's at the far end of the hallway and you'll have your own bathroom—"

"Liza," he said, "it's not that."

She wouldn't ask any more questions, had learned over the years to recognize the tone in his voice that meant he'd said all he was going to. Ramsy was always amazed at how quickly women could detect that tone, and how many of them ignored it—and he was grateful that Liza was one of the ones who understood to let it go.

"I'll talk to you soon," she said, and her voice was tired. Not angry. He hadn't thought she would be. "I'll get you to change your mind, Ramsy."

He waited at the bar another hour in case Stella, on a walk, saw the lights on. Then he closed up, got in his truck, and headed home. He slowed at the sign at the end of the drive. It wasn't November nineteenth anymore, and seemed silly for the sign to still say so. He reached into the glove compartment for his marker, then drew back. Could he say for certain that tomorrow he wouldn't be on his way to Liza's? Until this fall there'd never been a question of where he'd be the next day, and the next day after that. Now, he wasn't sure. He drove on. Tomorrow, if he was back, he'd change the sign.

*   *   *

The next morning he dialed Stella's number as soon as the coffee woke his nerves, but before he had time to think too much. "It's Ramsy," he said when she answered. Her "hello" had sounded suspicious.

"Ramsy," she said. "How are you?"

"I'm keeping the bar open for a little while," he said. "I wanted you to know."

"I'm glad." There was hesitation in her voice. "Was Liza disappointed you put off your move?"

Hearing her say Liza's name made Ramsy feel tentative and careful. "Yes," he said. "She doesn't understand why I'm staying on."

"What did you tell her?"

"I said there were some things here I had to take care of first."

"What things?"

"Things."

"I know you," Stella said. "You don't do things on a whim. You had a reason, or reasons. You don't have to answer now," she said. "But someday I would really like to know."

Ramsy heard a noise in the background—a high-pitched mewling, like a cat or a crow. It came again, a cry this time, unmistakably. "What's that sound?" he asked.

"What sound?"

"It's a baby, Stella. I hear it crying."

"I've got the TV on. Just needed some voices in the house this morning."

"You never watch TV." There it was again—a cry, and then a shushing.

"I should go," Stella said. "I'll see you later, Ramsy." The line went dead.

*   *   *

Ramsy wasn't sure how to spend the hours until opening his bar that night. He'd only been out of his regular schedule for a few days, but he could barely remember it. Much more than a week and a half seemed to have passed.

At noon, a hard gust of wind rattled the windows of his house, and an image of JT flashed into his head. He'd come back to the bar, Ramsy was sure of it, and when he did, Ramsy wanted to offer him something.

There was Christmas music in the parking lot at the mall in Lawrenceville. Tinny jingling bells greeted him at the department store entrance, and a young blond girl with gum in her mouth pushed a red paper coupon into his hands.

"Fifteen percent off anything but perfume," she said. Ramsy folded the coupon into his pocket.

He hadn't been to the mall in years. He did what shopping he had to do at the Shop N' Save or the Walmart over in Moon Run when he needed new shirts or socks or jeans. And he hadn't bought a new coat in over a decade. Would he find coats here, the right kind for a young boy?

Ramsy knew what would matter most to him in a coat: warmth. He bypassed slim jackets made of thin material and found what he wanted: a heavy black coat lined with red-plaid flannel and filled with down. It was a plain coat with a boxy cut, a plain silver zipper, and two side pockets. There was a hood, too, that buttoned at the throat. It was the kind of coat that would go on warm and stay that way, through long snowy nights around a fire. Ramsy hesitated over the size before finally choosing medium.

With the coat in his arms, he glanced around the floor. There were men's clothes and shoes, and a display of luggage. Around him, people were lifting clothing from racks, carefully eyeing each piece, searching for something. Ramsy walked to a table piled with neatly folded sweaters. He touched a blue one, then the neckline of a soft brown v-neck, both made of thick wool. Did JT have a sweater like this? Ramsy had never bought clothes for another person—not even for Liza when she was a baby—and he found it uncomfortable to stand there and try to imagine those clothes on someone else's body. He drew himself straight and went to the checkout with just the coat, where he presented his coupon when prompted.

He passed the children's clothing department on his way out of the store and stopped short. Near the aisle, examining a rack of small pink sleepers, was Stella. Other clothes were draped over her arm—pink-dotted onesies, a fleece hoodie, a thick, plush sack for sleeping—the hangers tangled at her elbow. When she lifted a sleeper from the rack and held it up, her eyes met Ramsy's.

Guilt flickered on her face, but she recovered. "Well look at us, Ramsy, out shopping. How long's it been—a year? Five?"

"Ten, since I've been here."

Stella shifted the clothes on her arm nervously, but her laugh was genuine. "Guess no one can stay away from the mall forever."

"What'cha got there, Stella?" he asked. It was a useless question—clearly, she had baby clothes—but Ramsy wanted to see what she would say.

"An old friend had a baby," she said. "No one you know. Lives out in Pittsburgh. Just got the announcement in the mail."

He nodded. And when Stella said, "And you?" and gestured to his bag, he said, "Needed a couple new shirts" and left it at that. For a moment they stood there, holding their clothes for the runaways, and then Ramsy said, "Well. I'll be seeing you."

When he exited into the mall, he looked back. Stella was holding up a white sleeper now, checking something on the tag at the neck. She looked peaceful. Happy. Ramsy suspected there was more to this than just buying new clothes for a cold, skinny baby—the cry he'd heard on the phone told him that much—but Stella could do as she wanted. She didn't owe him any explanations. He'd stayed in Shelk because of her—but he stopped himself there. She'd never asked him to do it, owed him nothing for his choice. If he wanted or expected something in return, he should have told her up front why he'd stayed. Well, Stella would tell him if she wanted, or wouldn't, if she didn't. Bag in hand, he left the overheated mall and let himself be serenaded by dreamy carols as he walked to his truck.

He started the engine and waited for the defroster to clear fog from the windows. As he sat, he wondered if he'd gone overboard, if JT would be offended, if he'd think Ramsy was being—what? Too concerned, too protective, too involved?

He shook his head. *Watch yourself, Ramsy.* He could hear Hawk's voice gusting in through the vents.

Worry'll undo you. Always does. But it was Hawk who'd given Ramsy a place at the bar, who'd helped him get his first apartment in Shelk, who'd given him a reason to get out of bed every single day. And what had Hawk known of Ramsy aside from the missing eye, aside from that he'd been in the war? Barely more than his name. What had he been back then but a runaway himself?

The truck was warm now, the windows clear, and Ramsy shifted gears and pulled back onto the road toward home.

*   *   *

That night, it was like nothing had changed: the men sat drinking in their usual spots, and Stella sat in her seat farthest from the door. Ramsy stacked the three packed boxes behind the bar. Soon he stepped around them automatically, and stopped hitting his shins.

Eventually, everyone left but Stella. She kept her face turned to the window, and Ramsy knew by now there were all kinds of reasons why people wouldn't meet his eye. He wanted to ask about Adrienne and the baby, but instead he said, "Heard any more about Seth?"

"It's over," she said. "It never happened." Her voice broke almost imperceptibly in the last few syllables, and no one possibly could have heard it but him. For one quick moment, Ramsy felt light. She did need him, after all. She could pretend it never happened—any of it, all of it—but it did happen, was happening. And Ramsy would be there when it finally sunk in.

At that moment, the door opened and JT stepped in. "Knew I'd see you again," he said. "Knew you wouldn't stay gone."

"Have a few more things to deal with," he said. "A few days, a few weeks, then I'll close for good."

JT drank his beer. Now and then he coughed, not bothering to cover his mouth with his hand. He looked colder than he had before, and Ramsy wondered if he should start bringing food again.

JT looked over at Stella a few times, but when it became clear she wasn't leaving, he began to talk. "You didn't miss much, if you were wondering," he said. "We're still here. Obviously. Emilian's still not ready to go."

There was a long silence. Ramsy didn't look at Stella when he finally said, "Got something for you." The coat hung on a wall hook next to Ramsy's own, and he took it down and held it out to JT. "Thought you could use something warmer than what you've got."

JT gave Ramsy a hard stare before taking the coat. "Don't want to owe anyone any favors," he said. "Not the reason I've been coming here."

"Nothing's owed," Ramsy said. "If I can keep a man from freezing to death, I'm happy to do it." He meant to sound casual, but instead it sounded sarcastic, gruff. Still, JT nodded, and he put on the coat. He kept it on as he finished his beer, and Ramsy was pleased at the coat's good fit, the precise corners of the pocket flaps, the good strong stitching along the zipper. It would last.

"There's this, too," Ramsy said when JT stood up to leave. He dug in his wallet for two twenties and a ten. "See a doctor about that cough. There's a clinic over in Moon Run that takes walk-ins—this should cover it."

JT shoved the money in his coat pocket and stood. "Not used to having someone watching out for me."

Ramsy sensed Stella looking at him. "Just thought you could use it," Ramsy said. "That's all."

Before JT left, he turned to Stella. "Adrienne said she saw you at the library."

Stella glanced at Ramsy. "Yes."

"Came back with formula and diapers. She showed me, but she didn't tell Emilian."

"Was glad to see her," Stella said. "She can stop in anytime she wants, like I told her. Library's not the warmest place in the world, but at least they're out of the cold."

JT looked at her for a long moment, unsmiling. "You're taking a risk," he said. "It's risky for Adrienne, too. Dangerous, even." He kept his gaze steady on Stella. "Wish I could do what you're doing," he said. "Just glad someone is."

They were quiet for a long time after JT left. Then Stella said, "Adrienne and Serena came to the library a few days ago. Was going to tell you. But."

"She come for books?"

"She came to see me," Stella said. "I know you don't trust me to handle this the right way. I'm sorry I can't change your mind."

"I think this is a mistake," Ramsy said.

"You don't feel that way about JT."

"That's different."

"Is it? Food, a coat, the money—what's this all about, Ramsy?"

"Not about anything."

"People have needed help before."

"Not like this," Ramsy said. "Not like this." But he couldn't explain what made it different, why he felt compelled to make these offerings.

"You're kind, Ramsy," Stella said. Her voice sounded far away. "It means something, you know? Someone, somewhere, is hoping a stranger will be kind to one of those kids. After a while that's all you can hope for. That's all I have to hold onto anymore—that someone will be kind to Lucy if she needs it, wherever she is."

As Ramsy locked his bar that night and drove down to the road, he thought of the other time, long ago, when he and Stella shared something no one else could possibly understand. Now different kids brought them together. Stella was of Shelk as much as Charlie or Ash or any of the others, but tonight Ramsy remembered what had drawn him to her, and what drew him to her still: she thought like an outsider, acted like one, too. They both lived day in, day out, in a place they'd never truly belonged.

*   *   *

Every evening when he got to the bar he stopped his truck at the end of the drive and took down the last day's *Open* sign. He stood with a piece of cardboard he'd brought from home and the black marker from the glovebox, balanced the cardboard on his raised knee, and carefully wrote out *Open* with the new date underneath. *Open November 21. Open November 22.*

That day, the men came to the bar in an excited group, Charlie and Ash together straight from the mine, Harry Slavin in a truck close behind the others. Ramsy heard their voices—loud, firm—before they came inside. When they opened the door, they stopped talking.

"Jack here?" Charlie asked.

"Haven't seen him," Ramsy said, and the talk resumed as the men shed hats and coats.

"Probably heard it already," Ash said to Ramsy. "Kitty's leaving Jack for the gypsy."

"It's all over town," Charlie added. "Junie heard her on her cell phone at the Shop N' Save."

"Meg's sister works at Walmart and saw her buying a suitcase," Ash said.

Harry said, "Not surprised Kurtz ain't here. Probably loading up his gun."

Ramsy frowned but said nothing. He didn't like the sound of this rumor. It had the ring of desperate ultimatums, last straws. Half a second's thinking would be enough to know it wasn't true. A woman like Kitty would never give up her creature comforts for a rootless life on the road. Jack had complained countless times about Kitty's expensive maintenance: manicures, highlights, enough store credit cards to fill an empty Altoids tin. Then again, this was Kitty Kurtz, only happy if someone, somewhere, was talking about her. No telling what she might get it into her head to say, as long as it got Jack into a froth.

Eventually, Jack did come in, and the bar fell silent. The men looked at him wide-eyed, then at each other, and they left so quickly Ramsy wondered if they thought Jack might actually have a gun on him. Without a word, he poured Jack a whiskey and water and refilled it, twice, before opening him a beer. Jack shook his head and pushed it away. "Whiskey," he said. "Should be no surprise to you that tonight I don't want to think too much."

For nearly an hour he drank that way, slowing down but still steadily emptying glass after glass. He looked stricken, not angry. Ramsy had no great sympathy for Jack, but he couldn't picture him without Kitty. By the way Jack swallowed with a grimace, it seemed this was exactly what Jack was imagining.

Finally Jack held up a hand. "I'm done," he said. He was drunk enough now to stare at Ramsy without flinching, and without hiding genuine feeling behind threatening words. "You see me?" He spread his arms wide. "Kitty makes me like this. But this is how I'd be without Kitty every single goddamn night." He looked at Ramsy, angry, helpless, a weary confusion on his face. "Maybe I would be better off without her. That's what everyone always says. But it's too late, Ramsy. I'd be ruined."

"Ain't the first time you and Kitty've gone down this road."

"This is different," Jack argued. "She's gotten carried away before, but she always runs back once she's gotten some attention. This thing with the gypsy—it's too much. She's pushing me, Ramsy, trying to get me to leave her."

"Not sure what Kitty would get from that."

"She'd get everything," Jack said. "She'd be the tragic divorcee. She'd feast on that the rest of her life." He sighed, tired now.

"It didn't have to turn out this way," he said quietly. "Kitty wasn't the only woman I could have married. Things could have been different. There's a woman I still think about," he said, and when Ramsy started to say he should keep this to himself, Jack held up a hand. "No, I want to say this. There was a woman years back, when things started getting bad with Kitty. Didn't last long. I saw Kitty's face every time I was with her. But it meant something. And every day—sometimes when I'm going to bed, sometimes when I wake up, sometimes when I'm taking a piss, sometimes when I'm just going about my business on a regular goddamn afternoon—I think, well, maybe in another life, who knows. But I'll never find out. It's the dangedest thing. This whole life I might've had—I ain't never going to have it. I'll never know what's behind that door."

"Far as I know," Ramsy said, "no one's ever been able to go back and do it all over again."

Jack's face was flushed, but instead of taking off his coat, he glanced at his watch. "Should be going," he said. "Kitty'll start to wonder." The dark look in his eyes said what Ramsy was thinking: *If she's even at home.* Then he said, "My worst fear is ending up like you, Ramsy." He swayed a little on his barstool when he said it, the force of his words catching him off balance. "So alone you don't even know it anymore." Jack swallowed, hung his head.

All Ramsy said to Jack was, "Easy, now. We all have our troubles," and soon Jack stumbled out the door. After a minute, Ramsy heard car keys fall to the ground.

"Goddammit," Ramsy muttered, and he hurried out after him. "Wait," he called. "I'll drive you."

They drove in silence, Jack dozing in his seat. When they arrived at Jack's, Ramsy got out of his truck and took Jack's arm. He steadied Jack as they walked slowly up the snowy walk. No one had shoveled in a long time, Ramsy could tell. There was thick hard-packed snow underneath the powdery fresh. He waited while Jack searched his pockets for his key.

"Goodnight, Ramsy," Jack said softly when he pushed the door open. He didn't have to speak quietly—the house was dark, and Ramsy knew from the hollowness of the silence that Kitty wasn't just asleep in bed.

"Goodnight," he said. He walked back to his truck and got inside but didn't start the engine. He waited. A moment passed, and a light went on in a window at the side of the house. Ramsy got out of his truck and walked through the yard, his boots sinking into the snow, until he reached the window. The window was curtained only with thin nylon fabric. Three beer cans were lined up on the sill—probably one of Kitty's many improvised alarms. Ramsy put his nose to the glass and peered inside. Jack sat at the kitchen table, his coat still on, his head in his hands. In the harsh overhead light, Ramsy could see the shiny worn elbows of the coat, the threads at the cuffs. He'd taken off his ball cap, and his hair was thin and flat against his skull. For a quick, heart-stopping moment, Ramsy saw himself sitting at that table—as a younger man, confused and newly alone.

Ramsy climbed into his truck and sat for a minute while the engine warmed. His jaw was tight, and he clenched the wheel. Damn that Kitty. Damn the Kurtzes, too, both of them, but damn that Kitty.

There were only so many places Kitty could be this late at night, and Ramsy set out with a kind of resolve he hadn't felt in a good long while. First he drove past the Laurel Motel, its neon-orange sign glowing VACANCY without the V or final C, and scanned the cars in the lot. Kitty's wasn't there. He drove out of town a couple of miles and checked the lot of the White Tail Motor Lodge too. No Kitty. She could be in the mountains, but Ramsy thought she was unlikely to venture up there in the snow. He remembered the men mentioning the River Tavern, so he drove there next. In the nearly empty parking lot, he spotted Kitty's beat-up silver Nissan, and he pulled in beside it then climbed out of the truck.

Kitty was at the bar alone, the heels of her purple boots hooked over the rung of the bar stool, a strip of white skin visible between the top of her jeans and the bottom of her short black sweater. She was applying lipstick then staring at herself in the small mirror at the top of the lipstick tube. On the stool next to hers was draped a heavy brown and white hide. She jerked her head up when Ramsy approached.

"Jesus Christ, you scared me," she said. She glanced nervously toward the bathroom door. "Done at the bar for tonight?"

"What're you doing, Kitty?"

"What's it look like?"

Ramsy stared hard at Kitty and said nothing.

"I don't have to explain anything to you," she said. "You have no idea what it's like for me, staying with a man like Jack all these years. He doesn't even see me anymore. I could've done something with my life. I could've left this town."

The bathroom door opened, and Kitty and Ramsy both watched Emilian walk toward them. "Trouble?" Emilian said.

"Ramsy was just leaving."

Ramsy ignored her. "I drove Jack home tonight," he said. "So drunk he could barely walk."

Kitty looked down angrily. "Yeah? So?"

"Jack doesn't say it but he wants things to be different. Not saying he's an easy man. But he's your husband. That means something."

"No one can force me to be unhappy," Kitty said. "So what if other men think I'm beautiful? Will it get me back all the time I've wasted? Will it?"

Ramsy had to take a breath before he finished what he'd come to say. "Not my way to get involved," he said. "But you need to know Jack's angry. They all are. I'm telling you to be careful, Kitty. Think about what you're doing. And you—" he lifted his chin toward Emilian "—you should know things are not going your way. Makes no difference to me when your group goes. But not everyone would say that. Some might be ready soon to force your hand."

"This a threat?" Emilian said. His eyes were hard.

"A warning, is all. Take it as a kindness. You won't find much around here."

Ramsy turned to go, but Emilian's voice stopped him.

"Let me give you a friendly warning too," he said. "You tell that woman to stay away from the baby. She's going too far now. I take care of my own."

"Baby?" Ramsy heard Kitty say, her voice bright but confused. "What baby?"

Ramsy left the bar without looking at either of them and walked back to his truck. He turned on the engine and took a few deep breaths to thin the anger in his chest. He knew Stella. If he relayed Emilian's warning, she'd only take it as more proof that the baby needed her help. She was as stubborn as Kitty was, in her way, refusing to see the consequences left behind her like roadkill.

All he could see was Jack at that table. Ramsy gritted his teeth as he drove away from the river and the
railroad tracks. He hadn't broken the window at Jack's
house, hadn't scattered beer cans or ransacked dresser
drawers, but he still felt as though his pockets were full
of someone else's money and much-loved, much-pro-
tected things.

CHAPTER 10

1445 Mayapple Avenue

The house was promising. Two stories, red brick, a front porch with dry mums in pots and a porch swing with quilted cushions. The back door was locked, but the intruder easily broke a small paned window, and reached in to undo the doorknob lock and chain.

He stepped inside onto hardwood floors and wondered where to start. No cash in a house like this—these people would have accounts at the bank and would know better than to keep a lot of money around. So he went upstairs to the bedrooms and started in the one with shoes kicked off by the doorway. There were treasures in that dresser. He could feel it. Years of entering houses like this had given him a feeling about drawers and closets, feelings that turned to images as vivid as dreams. He wasn't always right, but he was right enough of the time to be a kind of hero to the others. They brought back a few gold charms while he brought back watches and diamond rings.

For a moment he sat on the bed and listened. The wind rustled a drift of dead leaves that had gathered beside the house, but that was all. Barely any sounds this time of year. Then he got up and opened the top dresser drawer. Black and white bras, socks, a pile of satin panties. He opened the top of the bureau—handkerchiefs, men's socks, a small tray with two bottles of old cologne. He closed the drawer and went to the closet, where on a shelf he found a small gray safe with a U-shaped lock. On the dresser was a palm-sized clam shell holding safety pins and pennies—and a silver key. He unlocked the safe and filled a bag with the velvet pouches and boxes.

When he emerged from the closet, he heard their voices. They were coming up the stairs. The intruder quickly unsheathed his knife and waited by the door. When he jumped them, the woman screamed, and the man shoved her away. The intruder said nothing, his blood pounding like ocean waves. He brandished the knife as though fending off wild creatures and fled down the stairs.

It was Thanksgiving: most of the men had spent the day with families where love was sometimes indistinguishable from battle. And being so close to Christmas, it was always a weary time of year. Ramsy knew the men's minds were far away, on gifts they wanted for their families but couldn't afford. By eleven, the men took home the silence they'd come with. It wasn't a night to stay out late.

Ramsy cleaned the bar and set out two wineglasses and a couple of forks and plates he kept behind the counter. Soon Stella came in carrying a large cloth bag. "Happy Thanksgiving," she said. She unloaded plastic containers foggy with steam: mashed potatoes, green beans with slivered almonds, gravy, baked chicken legs and thighs. The bar filled with food smells, and Ramsy's stomach growled in response. He pushed out of the swinging gate, sat on a stool beside Stella, and began to eat.

It had started years ago, after their affair had ended but before the frost between them had thawed completely. Stella had come in late Thanksgiving night with a dinner for Ramsy in an aluminum pan. She'd cooked for herself—always had—and knew Ramsy would go home to plain pasta or a few slices of toast, holiday or not. For a few years she'd brought him dinner this way. And then she'd started bringing dinner for them both.

Ramsy was struck, as he was every Thanksgiving, by the pleasure he took—on this one day only—in not eating alone. He wasn't a ritualistic man, and hadn't had a family long enough to build traditions, but he was grateful for the continuity of this meal, year after year, Stella's good cooking and kindness, those plastic containers with the steam. Next to him, Stella's face was calm in a way that Ramsy saw only when she'd had too much to drink, and the glass in front of her—her first—was still half full.

"It's delicious," he said. "Thank you."

"It's as much for me as for you."

On ordinary days, Ramsy sometimes felt that he had no appetite at all, and he ate because it was time to and because he knew it was something he had to do. But on this night he felt ravenous, allowing Stella to serve him again from the containers, and eating until barely any food was left.

When the bar was clean and the containers were rinsed and repacked into their bag, Stella climbed into the truck with Ramsy. A storm had blown up, and the snow was so thick in the air he had to drive looking out his side window to stay on the road. It took them a long time, and he drove tensely, without speaking. When they reached her house he walked her to the door and held her elbow—pointy under her coat—on the slippery porch stairs. "Would you come in tonight?"

she said. Not *would he like to*—just *would he*. It was as close as Stella ever got to admitting she didn't want to be alone. It didn't happen often.

"Okay," said Ramsy, and his heart beat deeply. This was different from letting him check the locks on her windows and doors or look for thieves in the closets. He was glad to go in, and relieved, too. Surely Stella would tell him now what she was doing with Adrienne and Serena. Maybe they'd even be there at the house, and he'd be able to pass on Emilian's warning and explain why this contact had to stop.

Stella's house was warm as it always was. Stella turned every lamp on, so that light from the windows spilled out onto the snow. Ramsy sat down in the living room while Stella drew the curtains and made tea. He looked around at her walls and shelves. On her bookshelf were castoffs from the library, their spines sun-bleached, their call numbers still visible on white stickers. They were books no one in Shelk ever read: biographies of artists and actors, a history of western Pennsylvania, and unpopular novels.

The closet door, near the stairs, was ajar, and Ramsy peered closer. He saw a stack of pale yellow and pink blankets, a large paper shopping bag with diapers peeking out, a pacifier and wrinkled burp cloth hastily laid on top. The bottom of a faded bouncy chair was what kept the door from closing. So the baby had not just been here. She had played here, maybe even napped here.

When Stella brought in their tea, her cheeks were red from the steam. "Careful," she said when Ramsy went to sip. "It's hot."

Ramsy stirred in a spoon's tip of sugar, then kept stirring to cool the tea.

"Well, here," she said when she'd finished her cup. "I want you to see something. I'm not sure why. Maybe it was hearing the news about Seth. Will you stay just a little while longer?"

"Long as you want."

He expected Stella to point to the bouncy chair, but instead she disappeared upstairs and returned with an album, white-covered and plain. "We never got a real wedding album," Stella said. "I made this one myself." A wedding album—this was what Stella wanted him to see? "Go on, open it. I look at it every so often, just to remember I'm not crazy. I was happy, Ramsy, you see that?"

Ramsy forced himself to focus. It was true. He saw her happiness in every picture on every page. She'd worn a plain dress, and her hair was dark and straight, parted in the middle. She wore a veil that puffed in the back and hung to her shoulders. Stella had been more than happy. She'd been beautiful. He'd known it before, but it was different to see it there on the page, to be able to stare at her as long as he wanted. He closed the album.

"You were young," Ramsy agreed. "You were happy."

Stella was staring dreamily into the distance now, as though the pacifier and the blankets and all the rest of it didn't even exist. She turned on the TV, and they watched reports of the storm. After a while, Stella fell asleep. Ramsy could see the shape of her legs under the navy blue soft-knit pants. There was a sliver of pale skin where her wool sock ended. Underneath that sock, he remembered, were small, white feet with thin ankles and perfectly rounded toes. If Ramsy were a praying man, he might have prayed for peace in her life, but instead he began gathering his coat and boots.

Stella opened her eyes and sat up sleepily. "You should stay," she said. "It's terrible out, Ramsy."

"I'll be fine," he said. "Not that far to home."

"Too far for this storm."

"I'll wait out the worst of it."

She got up and moved to the stairs. "Well, good-night," she said. "You know your way around. Blankets are near the sofa—take whatever you need."

"I will. Goodnight, Stella."

Halfway up the stairs, Stella turned. "You change your *Open* sign every day, like every day you decide whether to stay or not. Am I going to show up one day and find you gone?"

"I don't know," he said.

"Every time I go there I hold my breath," she said. "Until I see the sign I hold my breath."

"I wouldn't leave without telling you," he said.

"You almost did, once."

"That was a long time ago." When he first went out to meet Liza, Stella had to hear the bar was closed from someone in town.

"Decent men say goodbye, Ramsy. I don't want to feel like that again."

"You won't have to."

She nodded. "Goodnight," she said. "I'm glad you're not driving."

"Me too," he said. "Goodnight."

Alone downstairs, Ramsy turned off the light. He felt strange walking around in his socks and unbutton-ing his shirt while Stella undressed one floor above. For a while, he lay on his back, awake, listening for Stella's footsteps on the stairs or his name whispered from her bedroom doorway. But Stella didn't come. He hadn't really expected she would, but there was still that feel-ing—left over from so many years ago—that she might. And that he wouldn't mind if she did.

*   *   *

Ramsy was at the bar early the next day when the phone rang. It was a woman's voice, familiar, but he couldn't place it. "You don't know me, I don't think. I'm Junie Snyder, Charlie's wife."

"Met you once years ago. I remember."

"Well, I'm calling with a favor to ask," she said. "A few of the other women and I are wondering if we can talk to you."

"Talking to me now."

"I mean in person. At my house. Can you come by this afternoon?"

"Charlie okay?"

"Oh, fine. But Charlie doesn't know about this. None of the men do. Will you come, Ramsy? It's important. I know this is strange, but we need your help."

"I'll be there."

At three o'clock, he knocked on the front door of the Snyders' white-sided ranch. It only took a minute for Junie to open it up. "Come on in, Ramsy. Sorry for the mess—my route just ended." She was still in jeans and a heavy blue shirt with her name over the pocket, the kind all the school bus drivers wore.

He followed Junie into a living room with bare white walls and a sagging blue couch. He didn't know all the women in the room, but he knew Meg Haggerty, Pam Slavin, and Betty Wyatt. Meg was in her brown and orange uniform from the Rowdy Buck, probably on her way home from her shift. He was surprised to see Kitty Kurtz at the edge of the group. He knew the other women usually kept their distance. But there she was, in tight blue jeans and a blue-plaid blouse that barely reached her waist. If Kitty was included, things must really be bad. She didn't look at Ramsy.

"This is Ramsy," Junie announced, but it was only formality. In a flash Ramsy saw he held a place in these women's lives, that his name was part of their married conversations—*I'll be at Ramsy's. You're always at Ramsy's. Call me at Ramsy's once you calm down.* By the way the women murmured hello, he knew they believed their lives and their marriages would be better if his bar—hell, maybe he, too—didn't exist.

Junie brought over a cup of coffee in a Pittsburgh Steelers mug. "Cream or sugar?"

"Black is fine."

"So I guess we should tell you what this is all about." The women glanced at one another, and then Junie continued. "Meg, why don't you start? What happened to you is what got all this going."

Meg glanced at Ramsy then looked away. "There was a gypsy in the house last night," she began. "Ash was out, and I came home from the Rowdy Buck and ran a bath like I always do after my shift. Ash has been telling me to lock the door when I'm in the tub, but sometimes I forget. I forgot this time, too. I heard the back door open and shut, and then there were footsteps on the stairs." She took a long breath. "I started screaming, and whoever it was took off running. I jumped out of the tub and called the police." She stared at Ramsy, fearful and helpless, pulling at the sleeves of her tightly crossed arms. "They were in my house," she said. "*In my house.*"

No one said a word. "You know the weirdest thing? I could swear it was a girl. Could tell by the footsteps. Young, like one of the girls who works at the diner before school. Whoever heard of girls getting caught up in stuff like this?"

She shifted in her chair, the story over. The women looked at Ramsy. He wasn't sure what this had to do with him, but he gave Meg a long look. "An awful thing to go through," he said. "My house was robbed, too. Got home just in time to see the thief run out." He couldn't bring himself to say *gypsy*. He remembered that primal shock, the unmooring he'd felt after the intrusion, and he didn't even have a wife to worry about protecting. He'd frowned at the men's anger, their reflexive fear. But now he imagined Ash's pale, worried face, the way his stomach must have cratered when Meg called, hysterical, still in her bathrobe, the police on their way, and he thought he was beginning to understand.

"You're wondering why we called you," Junie said. "It's because of the men. We've been hearing talk for a while now. They'd never tell us directly, but we hear things."

"This has pushed them over the edge," Meg added. "Ash has been tense lately anyway, standing at the window at night like he's waiting for something. I can never tell whether he wants it to happen, or dreads it. Now his own house—it's too much. I'm scared, but Ash is angry. They all are."

"Heard Charlie say he was tired of waiting for the gypsies to move on," Junie said. "Announced it was time to take action. We're scared. Scared of the gypsies and scared of what our men might do. We want the gypsies gone as much as they do, but not if it means making things worse."

"Scared Harry'll get Jimmy involved," said Pam Slavin. Jimmy was her son, known in Shelk as a high-school football hero.

Kitty jumped in. "Look," she said, "we've all heard that I'm supposedly having an affair with a gypsy." She fluttered her hands, dismissing it, avoiding Ramsy's eye. "Jack's angrier than I've ever seen him, and he's looking for a fight. I'm worried what he might do." The other women rolled their eyes at one another. "I didn't do anything," Kitty said loudly. "Believe me, I'd never do something like that."

Ramsy knew better than anyone that Kitty was lying, but that didn't change the point she was trying to make: Jack was angry. All the men were, and something dangerous was brewing. Kitty was afraid, Ramsy could see it. She hadn't expected her little adventure to lead to all of this. Ramsy looked at Junie. "What do you want from me?"

"We want you to stop them."

"Stop them from what?"

"From whatever it is they're planning to do. We don't know what it is, but you can find out. They trust you, Ramsy. They'll listen."

If there was any line to cross, Ramsy had crossed it long ago, the moment he lied to the cops, left food for JT, paid for stolen jewels. He didn't want to see the men take risky action any more than the women did. Except for Kitty, they were good women, doing their best. Just by coming to this house he'd made a decision, and after a minute, he nodded.

There was nothing to do now that the women had said their piece. Junie glanced at her watch. "Charlie'll be home soon," she said, and this was Ramsy's cue to stand. He put his coffee mug on an end table and raised a hand in goodbye. Then he paused.

"Anyone you know lose jewelry?" he asked.

"Linda Clemson," said Junie.

"Duckie Williams."

"Kitty, didn't you say the gypsies got Deirdre Scott?"

"And Kathleen Bell."

"They got my grandmother's rings," said Pam Slavin. "Think we were one of the first places hit."

"Have something to give you," Ramsy said. "Be right back." He went out to his truck and retrieved the shoe-box of jewelry. He'd put it in his truck before leaving home, thinking this might be his chance to pass it on. Back inside, he handed it to Pam. "Think your rings will be in here," he said. "Not sure any of the rest of it belongs to you," he said, "but I know you'll get them back where they belong."

Pam opened the box and drew a sharp breath. "Where'd you get this, Ramsy?"

"Pam, what is it?" asked Junie. The women crowded close.

"Stolen goods, is what it is," Pam said. "Ramsy?"

"Came my way," was all Ramsy said. "Just want to see it all back where it's supposed to be." Pam frowned. The other women looked at him with wrinkled brows and leaned away.

"The gypsies took these from us," Junie said. She suddenly looked wary, as though she'd made a mistake inviting Ramsy into her house. "They broke into our homes."

"I don't even feel right touching them," Pam added, though she peered into the box closely for her rings. "Doesn't even look like ours anymore, now that it's been with them."

"You a gypsy or something, Ramsy?" Kitty said. There was nervous laughter, but no one was smiling. With the support of the women momentarily behind her, she added, "Maybe Jack and them better think about watching you along with all those gypsies."

Ramsy just raised a hand and slipped away.

*   *   *

As Ramsy expected, the men started talking again a few days later. "It's getting worse," Ash said. "The gypsies have weapons."

"Always assumed they did," Ramsy said. He put a beer down before Ash and wondered if anyone had been seen with his .45.

"Well, then, they've been keeping them out of sight, until now."

Twice now, Ash explained, an intruder was caught in the middle of a robbery, and twice the intruder flashed a knife to escape. "Messed up Benny Potter pretty good," he added. "Near broke his nose. But he didn't use the knife."

"It's the cornered ones get violent," Ramsy said, thinking of Jack Kurtz.

"You standing up for them?" Charlie asked.

Ramsy backed down. "Just trying to understand."

Jack shook his head. "They're out of control. Gotten too comfortable. Only a matter of time before someone gets knifed in the gut. You hear me? Only a matter of time." The other men murmured. "Well, we have to do *something*." And though no one responded, their eyes agreed with Jack.

Jack was the last to leave, zipping his coat as the others nodded their last goodbyes and closed the door. Ramsy gritted his teeth. He'd given his promise to the women, but still the words stuck in his throat. Where the men saw malice, Ramsy saw desperation, though he knew those might wind up the same way in the end.

"Night," Jack said.

Ramsy nodded and turned away, busying himself at the register until the door closed.

JT slipped in not much later. "Glad you came in tonight," Ramsy said when JT sat down. "Gotta tell you the anger's growing. The men've seen weapons, or think they have."

"Do the same thing if you were in our shoes."

"Every man in this town has a gun. It's part of life here. Emilian give any sign of being ready to move on?"

"Said he's got it all figured out." JT shrugged, and Ramsy wondered if the warning he'd given Emilian at the River Tavern had had any effect. Maybe he should have said more, been more forceful. He didn't think he'd be exaggerating if he told him their lives were at stake.

"What's he waiting for?" Ramsy said when JT stood to leave. "He's got as good a chance of striking it rich around here as he does winning the Powerball. Or maybe he thinks he has a chance at a house with a white picket fence?"

At this, a laugh rose in JT's throat. "We've been to a lot of towns," he said, "and I've never seen one place, not one goddamn place, where any of us had a chance in hell of getting anything like that."

*   *   *

It was December. The signs of fall—the scarlet maples, the crisp blue sky, the smell of burning leaves in the air—had been gone for weeks. Blue twilight had just settled over Shelk when someone knocked on the door of Ramsy's house. He was heating bread and cheese on the stove, and he transferred the sandwich to a plate and turned off the burner before answering the door. On his stoop was Kitty Kurtz, a large cardboard box in her arms. It wasn't more than twenty degrees outside. Her cheeks and nose were red, but still Ramsy could see that her face was deathly pale.

"I'm in some trouble," she said.

Ramsy held the door open, and she came inside.

"Feels good to get out of the cold," she said. She squeezed the cardboard box tighter to her chest. "I know you don't want me here. If you ask me to, I'll leave." She took a deep breath. "But what I'd really like is to sit in your kitchen. Just for a few minutes. Please, Ramsy."

"Alright," Ramsy said, because there was a lost look on her face that told him she had nowhere else to go. At another time in his life he'd have turned her out anyway, but not now. He led her to the kitchen and put water on for tea. He laid out two spoons and two teabags. When the kettle whistled he poured water into two mismatched mugs and sat down.

"So. Everything is a big, big, big mess," she said. "I didn't have anyone else to talk to." She took a dramatic breath. "I've been—seeing someone. Emilian. Which you know. Anyway, Jack found out and went crazy. See this?" She angled her chin toward the harsh overhead light. Ramsy picked out the shadow of a bruise. "Only hit me once," she said. "Then he started with the dishes." Kitty's eyes were bright. "I brought the pieces," she said. "I didn't know what to do."

Ramsy pushed the box under the table with his foot. "You need something more than a trash can?" he asked.

"I need you to talk to him," she said. "He's out of his mind. He doesn't even care about me right now. He hates these people, Ramsy."

"Might just blow over."

"Not this time," Kitty said. "He's trying to get a group to go up there, where they camp. I can't have it on my conscience if something happens. I can't. He was calling the others every night, even before this happened. Said they were cowards." Kitty adjusted her blouse. "He's trying to get them ready for a fight."

"No promises," Ramsy said.

"I just want you to know something," she said after a moment. "I didn't know, when I met him, what he was doing here. It just didn't register. Anyway, when I found out, it was exciting. And I needed excitement. I needed *something*."

"Don't need your reasons," Ramsy said.

Kitty exhaled. "When we went out, people looked at me like I was with a kind of mythical creature. A kind of dangerous *god*. It was all part of it." She sipped her tea. She hadn't taken the teabag out and the tea was nearly black. "Then I found out he had that baby." She put the mug down.

"Those thefts in Owl Creek," she said, "the big ones—thousands of dollars at a time. Emilian was the one who did it." She twisted her hair again and again around her fingers. "He doesn't feel bad, even though it's all some people have in the world. He says it's just their bad luck, like they got caught in the rain. It's not right." Kitty stood. "No one listens to me, but I'm scared. Do you understand me? I'm scared for my life, Ramsy. Someone needs to do something." She waited for a response, but Ramsy had none to give. He kept his head down as she walked away.

After she was gone, he opened the box she'd left. No telling how many dishes had fallen victim to Jack's fury. The destruction was so total, so crushingly absolute, that simply throwing the dishes could never have produced it. He must have thrown them, then picked up the pieces and thrown them again, then stomped on the survivors with his work boots until he could feel the kitchen floor under his heels. Despite himself, Ramsy shuddered.

CHAPTER 11

401 Ivy Road

The girls who rang the doorbell were pretty and young, their dark hair bound back in thick braids that passed their shoulders. They wore jeans, with brown boots over their calves, and they each wore several sweaters buttoned one to the other in a tangle down their chests. They looked cold, and harmless, and when they said they had something they'd like to give the man, he opened the door and invited them inside.

The taller girl drew a folded, pink-flowered sheet from her large woven bag. "Here it is," she said, and she snapped the sheet open, raising it high over her head and pushing it close to the man's face.

"Hey, now!" The man batted it back, but it was like pushing a living creature, and he struggled with the sheet until his arms and head were draped in it, and he was as good as blind.

It lasted only a minute. "Got it. Let's go," he heard the other girl say, and suddenly the sheet was pulled free, gathered in a heap in her arms. He made a grab for the sheet but she turned, and he found his fist wrapped around the girl's coarse, heavy braid. She reached back and struck his arm. With a cry, he let the girl go. Blood had already soaked the sleeve of his thin white shirt and was dripping onto his shoe and the floor.

The girls took the long way back to the mountains, figuring the town was the least likely place the police would search. They stopped at a traffic light, standing fifteen feet away from a distracted mother with a stroller and a toddler. Suddenly the toddler darted into the street. A car was speeding past, and without thinking, one of the girls ran up and yanked him sharply by the arm back to the sidewalk. The boy began to cry.

The mother snatched the boy from the girl's grasp and whacked him on the behind. "Your daddy's gonna whup ya," she yelled. She said nothing to the girl. The light changed, and the mother herded the boy and stroller across. When she reached the other side of the street, she turned around. She looked at the girl and lifted the fingers of her right hand in an almost imperceptible wave. The girls hurried away. Their woven bag was still stuffed with the pink-flowered sheet, the blood-smeared knife, and the money the man had stashed in a safe upstairs, but it felt lighter than it had before.

Ramsy heard people talking at the gas station that morning about Adam Pozel's run-in with the girls and their flowered sheet, the gash left behind on his arm. It wasn't the first time the intruders had caused physical harm, but it shook Shelk. The existence of weapons was confirmed now.

They called it a neighborhood watch, but Ramsy knew it was just an excuse to bring their guns into the nighttime streets like they'd been itching to do all along. "Happened to Adam Pozel," they told one another, and as they talked Adam's two-inch surface wound grew into a lethal injury. "Could happen to you." By December third, fifteen men had signed on, enough to cover the main residential streets of Shelk in five groups of three.

Jack asked Ramsy to join in the watch.

"That's something for younger men," Ramsy said and left it at that. He wanted to tell Jack that they should leave the kids alone instead of hunting for them in the streets at night. That's what it was, after all: hunting.

The kids weren't stupid. They knew to keep their distance now. He'd given them enough warnings, said his piece. He didn't like where this was headed, but he wanted to stay out of it. A group of men, a dark Shelk street, a stranger in sight—Ramsy would never be able to do what the men wanted, and he knew it would take little more than a suggestion of the wrong alliance for them to turn their guns on him.

The first night of the watch, the men came in with rifles slung over their shoulders, as comfortable around one another's Remingtons and Rugers as they were among their own children and wives. A celebratory spirit hovered over the bar. Gone were the fearful faces, the hardened, downturned eyes, the weary rumors of thefts and knives. The men were finally taking action.

Jack had brought copies of an intricate schedule of routes and times, which changed among the groups each day so no man went two nights with interrupted sleep. The plan, such as it was, was simple: walk, look around, run off any intruders you see.

"They'll know we won't stand for it anymore," Jack vowed, and the men clapped and hooted. Boots on the pavement, shoulder to shoulder with other men—this was what mattered. Hunter and hunted was what it came down to. Rescuing their town from its siege.

Ramsy said nothing when Charlie, Ash, or Jack came to the bar on nights they didn't have their routes. It made him uneasy to imagine the armed clumps of men plodding through the streets. He wasn't their target, but he still felt a persistent, nerve-jangling alertness that made it difficult to sleep.

Ramsy saw the watch himself one night when he was driving Stella home. When Ramsy turned onto Walnut, five blocks from Stella's house, his sweeping headlights revealed a group of three men along the roadside. They looked over their shoulders at the sound of the truck, and Ramsy recognized Ash and Jack. In the dark, from that distance, Ramsy and Stella were invisible behind the windshield, and the men turned back around without acknowledgment.

"The watch," Ramsy said in a low voice. "You see them pass by your place at night?"

"I have," Stella said. "I hear their footsteps." She shook her head. "They're together, Ramsy, the people in this town. It may not be right, what they're doing, but it's something, isn't it? Banding together like that, believing in the same thing?"

"Can't say there's anything about this I like."

"Of course not. That's not what I mean." She turned to the window, and suddenly Ramsy realized: she was talking about the search for Lucy.

"These aren't bad men," Ramsy said.

Stella nodded. "I haven't felt like part of this town for a good long time. Not like that." Ramsy pulled alongside the curb in front of Stella's house. "Goodnight," she said.

As Ramsy drove away, he thought about what Stella had said. He'd never had the town behind him, but he'd had Stella, and this had been enough. He looked for the men as he drove home, wanting to see them as Stella had. But the streets were empty.

*　　　*　　　*

Then one night the men got what they wanted. Three members of the neighborhood watch were walking along Horsetail Road when a lone boy appeared fifty feet ahead, holding a plastic bag. "Stop right there, gypsy," Leo Ralosky shouted, and before the boy could run, the men were on him. Sam Franklin tackled him, binding his arms behind him while the other men pummeled his face and chest. When the bloodied boy slumped in Sam's arms, Sam released him.

Leo grabbed the plastic bag and looked inside: a bag of chips and a bottle of Coke from the twenty-four-hour Lynn's Market at the top of the road. "Guess this gypsy was hungry," he said.

The truth came out the next day: Ethan Foley of Owl Creek, in town to visit a cousin, was beaten and robbed by three men on Horsetail Road. Attacked without provocation. The kind of thing you never used to worry about in a town like Shelk.

For the moment, at least, the neighborhood watch was on hold. The men seemed abashed but also angrier, somehow, their desire for vengeance stronger than ever.

*   *   *

For a few days, the men rode out the last trickles of outrage and inquiry over the Owl Creek victim, so it took some time before people started to talk about Stella. Finally it got to be too much to keep quiet. It was Pam Slavin who saw it first: Adrienne and Serena climbing the steps of the library. Then she heard from a neighbor who'd gone to the library to use the computer that Adrienne was sitting in a frayed armchair in the reference room, nursing her baby, a steaming mug next to her. It was the mailman who turned it into something to talk about.

"Nearly every day she's there," he told anyone who would listen, and most would. Stella's tragedy, though long in the past, had marked her as a permanent person of interest and speculation. "The girl's never said a word to me," he added. "But I've heard her singing to the baby. Couldn't understand the words, but I've heard it a few times now. Last time I was in, Stella was humming along with her."

The men knew better than to bring gossip about Stella to the bar, so it took a while for the news to reach Ramsy. Ash finally brought it up one night when he arrived earlier than the rest.

"Don't mean no disrespect," he began. "Thought you should know about Stella and the gypsy girl." And he told Ramsy what he knew.

Hurt, not surprise, burned his throat. So she would keep it from him, but allow the whole town to see. The hurt gave way to anger as he poured drinks for the men. She didn't care what people thought, and that was fine. But helping this girl so publicly while the men were grasping for any excuse to go after anyone—reckless, was what it was.

He needed to see it. That evening he parked behind her house, where he could see her kitchen window. Stella's car was there, parked in the space by the backyard gate, and the lights in the kitchen were on. Movement—Stella, setting the teakettle onto the stove. Her hair was loose, and she'd pushed the sleeves of her gray turtleneck up to her elbows. He couldn't see her face at that distance, but he saw the occasional flutter of her hands and knew she was talking to someone.

Then Adrienne appeared with Serena cupped at her shoulder, no bigger than a bag of oranges. She bounced in place, swaying from side to side, and then followed Stella out of the kitchen.

Ramsy had seen enough.

*   *   *

When Stella came in the next night, she made a few comments about the weather then sat in silence, drinking her wine.

"Things okay at the library?" he asked.

"Fine," she said. "Cold today, though." She laughed a little. "Old heating. And encyclopedias from 1982."

Stella drank her wine. Finally, Ramsy couldn't take it anymore.

"'Fine' isn't what I've been hearing," he said, his voice hard. The anger had rushed up all at once, and now his heart was pounding. He put both hands on the bar and leaned forward.

"And what have you been hearing?" Stella said. He saw that she'd been ready for this. Her face was set, her voice defiant, her message clear even without being spoken: *You can't stop me. I won't be stopped.*

"You know damn well. People've seen you, Stella. I've seen you, out at the mall. There're baby things all over your house. It wasn't just a bag or two left at the library, was it, or a few things sent up with JT."

"You're leaping to conclusions, Ramsy," Stella said. "So I had some baby things in the closet. It doesn't mean Adrienne's been to my house."

"I saw her," he said. "Last night, in your kitchen."

"You were spying on me," she said. "Unbelievable. You couldn't have asked me, could you, like a regular person. You listen to the gossip and then you decide to spy through my window. Fine. She's been to my house. She needs a place to go. That man—Emilian—he's not good to her, Ramsy. And I don't need your permission. For this or anything else."

"Not saying you do." She wouldn't listen now, he knew it. "But you don't know what you're doing. The men are angry, Stella. They'll turn on you, turn on Adrienne. It won't take much. You'll cross them at the wrong time, just like that Owl Creek kid they assaulted."

"So you're afraid," she said. "I'm not."

"It's too much, Stella. Letting her into the library, into your house—you might not care what lines she crosses, but understand: others do."

"You think I'm not aware of this?" Her voice was quiet now, though Ramsy heard no weakening resolve, no second-guessing. "They come to look at me. The women. Every day it's one or two of them at the library. They look at her and then look at me, but not one of them has the nerve to say anything." She sipped her wine. "I got a call from Judy Ferris, too."

"Judy Ferris?"

"Head of the library board, as much a boss as I have there. She said she'd gotten some calls about the kids hanging around. 'I don't know what you're doing there,' she said, 'but I'll be keeping my eye on you.'" Stella shook her head. "I just don't understand," she said. "I don't understand this at all."

Ramsy scoffed. "It'll end badly," he said. "Didn't tell you before, but Emilian sent you a warning. He wants you to stay away from Adrienne." He held up a hand when Stella started to protest. "Not saying he's someone you should obey," he said. "But maybe you've helped enough. Maybe what you've done has helped already."

"It's unlike you, Ramsy, caring what the town thinks. You're helping JT. I thought you'd understand." She sighed. "You're leaving. So don't talk to me about what's going to happen when you might not even be around to see it."

"It's not like that," he said, but she was already on her way out the door.

*   *   *

A night of snow had left the *Open December 9* sign wet and soft, and pieces of it tore loose in Ramsy's hand the next day when he took it down. He tossed what was left of it in the back of his truck and took out a fresh piece of cardboard he'd ripped from a box at home. *Open December 10*, he wrote. He went over the words again to make sure the ink had set, then went inside the cabin.

Later that evening, when his back was turned, he heard Liza's voice at the bar. He hadn't expected her there, and it took a second to realize it was her. When he turned around, she flinched when she saw his eye.

Ramsy lowered his head. "Have the patch at home," he said. "People are used to it here."

"I'm sorry," Liza said. "It startled me, that's all. I just didn't—I just didn't know it was like that." She looked at him and forced a smile. "You don't have to hide it from me at my house. Not if you don't want to."

"Better that way, there," Ramsy said.

"I hope it's okay I'm here," she said. "I wanted to see the place you're so attached to. I want to understand why you don't want to leave." Her smile was tentative, hopeful.

"Just surprised to see you," Ramsy said. "Of course it's fine."

Ramsy uncapped a beer and set it in front of her. "Take your coat off," he said. "Make yourself comfortable." She shrugged out of her coat and put it over her purse, then took a sip.

"How'd you find me?" Ramsy asked.

"I asked at the Sheetz on 119," she said. "The man couldn't figure out why I was asking. Told me it wasn't the kind of place I should be going to."

The men would be arriving soon, and Ramsy watched the door. For the first time, the silence in the bar unnerved him. It wasn't unusual for a man to come in alone, before the regulars had arrived, and sit in silence with a beer or two before counting out his bills and leaving. Staying quiet then felt as natural as breathing. With Liza, it felt like breathing underwater.

But Liza said, "It's nice here. I don't get much quiet at home."

Where did Liza's devotion come from? She had his blood in her—that would be part of it—and though blood created obligation, not love, he didn't doubt that Liza loved him. If he tried to define *love*, it would have to include the things she did: the calling, the worrying, the invitations, the plans made on his behalf. But how did it begin? Marcie was never one to hold a grudge, and Ramsy couldn't imagine her wasting life with curses and condemnation. But she wouldn't have forgiven him entirely. He imagined he probably hovered some-where in the back of her mind, willfully—but not actually—forgotten. So what did Liza think of him all those years, and what did she think of him now? She was in his bar. If she was trying to understand him, here it was. Here it all was.

"What did Marcie tell you about me, all these years?" Ramsy asked—because the answer to that might explain the rest.

"Not too much," she said. "Was a long time before I knew Joe wasn't my real father. I was fifteen. I found a picture." Liza sighed. "She told me no one could get inside you and she didn't want to die trying. She always felt guilty, Ramsy. It wasn't easy for her."

"Does she know you're here?"

"No."

"Does she know I might move out by you?"

"I'll tell her." She took a breath. "Don't worry about what Mom thinks, Ramsy. This has nothing to do with her."

The men came in around eight o'clock, and not long after that, Stella. Stella sat in her usual seat, and the men adjusted their patterns around Liza. Everyone looked at her, and she at them, and finally Ramsy said, "This is Liza." He was going to say *my daughter*, but the words pooled on his tongue and trickled back inside. Nods and hellos from the men. A nod from Stella.

"Open again," Stella said. "Just like you told me." She kept her voice neutral, but Ramsy heard the testiness underneath.

He wished he had a minute to tell Stella this visit was a surprise, that he didn't know what to make of it, either. But the way Stella was looking at Liza said she didn't want explanations—she just wanted to stare, take in every detail, drink them like the wine in her glass.

"Real nice of you to come out here," Charlie said to Liza.

"Wasn't hard," Liza said. "It's time I got to know this place."

The men nodded, because that was the expected response, but Ramsy could see their doubt. They had no reason to dislike Liza—they knew nothing about her. Ramsy kept her to himself. But she was, to them, an outsider, one who laid claim to something in town, and they left after only one drink.

"You don't want to go so soon," Ramsy said, but they smiled apologetically and said goodbye.

Now it was only him and Stella and Liza. They were positioned like points of a triangle, with Ramsy at the top. He poured more wine for Stella and hoped someone would think of something to say. Finally Liza said, "Any news about the gypsies?"

"They're still here," Ramsy said.

"Have you seen them?"

"No," he said. He hoped Stella knew not to tell Liza what had been happening this fall—being robbed, being swindled, taking care of JT and Adrienne.

Stella added, "Ramsy checks my closets sometimes to make sure I don't see them either."

"Really," Liza said.

"They'll go on their own time," Ramsy said. "Nothing to be too worried about."

Liza didn't ask any more questions, and when she finished her beer, she stood. "I'll talk to you soon," she said. "Thanks for letting me stay a while."

"Wait," Ramsy said. "Before you go." He went out to his truck and opened the glovebox. The white teddy bear and the photo album of baby pictures were there as they'd always been, waiting.

He brought them into the bar. "Been carrying these around," he said. He couldn't look at her face. "They belong to you, if you want them." Liza reached for them. "Never took many pictures, but there's a few. And the bear's something I bought the day you were born. You used to sleep with it," he said. His voice was so gruff it sounded mocking, or angry. But he saw her smile.

"I'm really glad to have these," she said. "Thank you." She turned to Stella. "Nice to meet you," she said, and then she was gone.

A long time passed before Stella spoke. "She looks like you," she said. "You are everywhere on her face."

"No. She's Marcie."

"She's you," Stella said. "God, I'm shaking. Feel my hands, Ramsy—ice-cold." She wrapped her hands around Ramsy's arm and held on. "I feel like I've seen a ghost," she said.

She was shaken, as Ramsy was. Liza was a voice on the phone, a fixture in a city far away—it was different when she was right there, in his bar, in his life.

"I didn't ask her to come," Ramsy said. "She surprised me, too."

"Are you saying you didn't want her here?"

"I'm just saying it was strange."

"She came all the way out here, tracked you down—and you wish she hadn't?"

"That's not what I'm saying. She's part of a different life—that's what I'm saying."

"God, Ramsy, you are a fool." Her eyes were hard, and the harsh words of the day before hovered between them again. "Don't you think she'll get tired of chasing you, one of these days? She loves you, Ramsy, and thinks if she just pulls hard enough—but that won't last forever. Count on that."

"You don't even know her."

"I don't have to."

"What are you suggesting I do?"

"I don't know." Stella shook her head. "She wants you in her life. Are you sure you want to pass that up?"

"I haven't," he said.

"That's right. You could be gone tomorrow." She shook her head again. "Even you don't know what you want."

Before he closed the bar that night, Liza called. "I'm home, and I know it's late," she began, "but I had to say just one more thing." She took a breath. "I know you're not coming."

"Of course I am."

"You said you needed to stay for a while. But I know you're staying for good."

"I never said that."

"But I can tell."

Another woman was asking him why he would or would not leave, if or when he planned to go. He'd spent his whole life making up answers to those questions, and not once had the answers been true. He waited for her to go on.

"When I was at the bar tonight, I knew," she said. "It's so obvious you're in love with her, Ramsy. Why won't you admit that's why you're staying?"

"I don't know what you're talking about."

"Please," she said. "Checking her closets for gypsies? You love her. I could see it in your face."

"I'm staying for a lot of reasons."

"One of which is her."

Ramsy didn't understand why he felt ashamed. He'd gone through life without admitting to anyone his attachments or his needs, assuming they'd know.

"Yes," he said, though he wasn't sure what he was accepting.

Before she hung up, Liza said, "What happened to her, Ramsy? There was something in her face when she looked at me—gave me goosebumps."

It wasn't his story to tell. Besides: if he told her about Lucy, Liza would understand his connection to Stella—and she'd understand that her return must have changed everything. There was no reason to burden her with that. So all he said was, "Her ex-husband died recently."

"That's terrible." There was a pause. "It's good you're there," she said. "For both of you."

CHAPTER 12

25 Milkweed Street

 The smell of the place said he'd made a mistake. The kitchen was full of soiled cat litter, and the living room was full of lilies. White lilies, and white carnations, wreaths and vases of them, some set on triangular wire stands on the floor. Small cards stuck out, affixed to white plastic picks. The centers of bows tied from white satin ribbon were damp now, fallen. There was the smell of warmed casseroles and coffee, and stale ashtrays filled to overflowing. By the sink was a seven-day pill case, three of the wells still crammed with pink and blue and beige-colored pills. He shivered. Death had been here.

 Others would celebrate stumbling into such a house. Deaths brought donations, offerings, Mass cards, baskets full of envelopes very likely containing cash. Deaths brought people too tired and sad to hide anything away, and too distracted to realize what was missing.

 It was a small house, with just one bedroom down a narrow hall. Nailed by the doorframe was a small pink plastic bust of an angel, a shell-shaped bowl of holy water under its chin. Without thinking, he wet a finger then flicked the water away.

On the bed were two suits, laid out on hangers. An empty hanger hung on the closet doorknob. On the dresser were two sets of gold cufflinks and a white hand-kerchief folded into a square. They were his, then—the dead man's. These were not what he wore to his grave. The suits looked alike, dark and worn. Had the chosen one been newer, lighter? Had it always been the one that fit best?

He quietly left the house, taking nothing but a near-black banana from the top of the toaster. He was a thief, but he'd seen death in his life, and he believed there were things that no one should touch.

The knock on his door early the next evening was insistent. Ramsy was asleep when he heard it, resting up before heading out to the bar. It jolted him awake, and he lay for a moment, heart pounding, until the knock came again—five hard raps—and he went to the door.

It was Stella. In the fifteen years he'd known her, she'd never been to his house. Whether or not Stella had thought of this before coming was unclear.

"They found a blanket," she said breathlessly. "In Seth's house. Lucy's blanket."

He stepped aside and let her in. They stood together in the middle of the living room.

"It's what I said, isn't it? I knew they'd find something. Her blanket, Ramsy—the one wrapped around her the night she disappeared." She grabbed Ramsy's wrists as she spoke—her hands were clammy. Her grip was strong as an animal's jaw.

"Let me get coffee," Ramsy said. "Sit down for a minute."

Stella ignored him. "And maybe there are other things," she said. "Things to prove she's alive. Do you think so, Ramsy? It wouldn't just be this?" She wasn't really looking for an answer, and Ramsy gave none.

Finally she sat down, tense, her back straight. "They've asked me to come to Ohio," she said. "Said the blanket is mine to claim."

"Will you go?"

"Yes," she said. She paused, long enough for Ramsy to bring her a mug of coffee from the kitchen. He put it on the tray table by the couch, where it remained untouched.

"I'm here to ask you something. Will you go with me? I've never made that long a drive alone."

It would be the longest time they'd spent together in years. "I'll go if you need me," he said.

"Tomorrow, if you can."

"Forecast is snow."

"Please, Ramsy." And Ramsy understood they'd be making the trip even if they had to drive through a blizzard.

She seemed calmer after this, and drank her coffee and then another. "Some of the kids came into the library today. Not too long after I found out about the blanket." She hesitated only a second before saying, "Adrienne wasn't there."

"They take anything?"

"Weren't there for that. Wouldn't care if they did, really. They just came up to the desk and asked if they could use the bathroom and maybe get a drink of water. I filled two paper cups at the fountain and had them waiting when they came out. They stood there and drank and then refilled the cups and drank again."

For a few minutes she said nothing. Then she said, "I asked them about Lucy." Ramsy's stomach dropped. "I asked them if Adrienne's real name was Lucy. They didn't think so."

"Jesus, Stella. Probably thought you were accusing them."

"I didn't make it sound like that." She paused. "I told them that I lost a baby fifteen years ago. Was wondering if they heard anything. They looked at me like I was crazy." She gave a small, dry laugh. "Maybe I finally am. It's strange, though, isn't it, Ramsy? These kids show up, and Adrienne and Serena, and now the blanket appears?"

She left with distracted thanks, and a promise that he'd pick her up early. Ramsy took out a duffel bag he hadn't used in years, and he put in a change of clothes and his few things from the bathroom. It was an easy trip to do in a day, down in the morning and back by dinner, but the heavy gray sky promised snow, a lot of it. A trip like this was impossible to prepare for. Preparing for the weather was the least he could do.

*   *   *

Early Friday morning, he drove to the bar and changed the *Open December 11* sign to *Closed*. No date this time, no explanation. He picked Stella up at seven, and they hit I-70 just as the sky began to lighten.

"Thanks for doing this," Stella said. But the words sounded forced, part of a world of favors and graciousness among solicitous strangers to which neither of them belonged, and Ramsy did nothing more than nod. He couldn't imagine Stella making this journey alone, and he knew it meant something that this was the way it had to be.

Ramsy was tense as he drove. Worry over Stella and what awaited them in Dayton was part of it, and he couldn't get the men out of his head. The watch had failed, but that wouldn't be the end of their anger. Ramsy knew full well that whatever was going to happen would happen whether he was there or not. He wouldn't fool himself into thinking he had any kind of power to stop it, despite what the women seemed to think. He gripped the wheel, worrying about those he'd left behind.

Right now, Stella needed him more. They passed exits for St. Clairsville, Quaker City, Zanesville. Two hours of highway disappeared under their wheels, and eventually Ramsy's dark thoughts steadied and calmed. Here they were, just the two of them, the world beyond the truck's warm cab no more than a gray, snow-scarred blur. There seemed to be little need for speaking, as though anything there was to say was known already, even the cadence of their quiet breathing somehow understood. He glanced over at Stella, her profile sharp in the morning light. And he let himself believe for a moment that there weren't any secrets, that the two of them were sitting here, side by side, with nothing between them but grief and dread and bone.

"They came back last night," Stella said, breaking the silence. "Same two as the first time."

The car lurched as Ramsy pressed down on the gas in surprise. "What were you doing at the library so late?"

"I went to print out directions," she said, rattling the paper in her lap. "They must have seen the light."

"You should lock the door if you're there at night."

"It was locked. I let them in. They came up to the desk and told me they knew where Lucy was. They said she was using a different name. They'd just found out about it. I asked where she was, but they didn't seem to know exactly. They said they told her about me. She wants to come home, but she needs money to get here. I asked how much, and they said five hundred dollars. That's what they thought they could get from me. Five hundred dollars to see my daughter. If they'd said five thousand, ten, I might have believed them."

"What did you do?"

"I asked them to leave. And I went home and stayed up all night, wondering if I'd made a mistake."

"You know you didn't. You know they're thieves, trying to get what they can."

"When you've been through what I have, you don't know anything."

They reached Dayton at noon and drove into the downtown, toward the police headquarters. "Want to stop before we go in?" Ramsy asked. "Get something to eat?"

Stella shook her head. "I want to get this over with."

Snow was falling when Ramsy parked the truck and fed a few quarters into the meter. Stella had pulled up the hood of her coat and tied a scarf around her neck. With the bulky hood around her face, she looked young and scared. She crossed her arms tightly and walked toward the entrance. Ramsy wanted to put a hand on her back but shoved them deep into the pockets of his coat instead.

The police station was garishly lit, with black slush puddled on the floor from the entrance all the way down the door-lined corridor. Stella approached a woman slouched at the front desk.

"I'm here to see Detective Rushkin," she said. "I'm Stella Vale."

The woman tapped a few numbers on her phone with a long orange fingernail and said, "Sign in here. Your husband, too." Stella wrote their names down on a clipboard without correcting her.

Eventually a heavyset man in a suit appeared in the corridor and approached them. They followed him into a large, cluttered office where two chairs were squeezed before one of the metal desks. The detective began explaining what had happened in the weeks since Seth's death, but it didn't matter what he said, or that he said anything at all. On the desk in front of him was a bag, and in that bag was Lucy's blanket. It looked small in the bag, small and thin and faded. It was white, with pink flowers and a thin band of pale pink satin around the edge. When the detective handed it to Stella, she stood to reach for it, and a heavy silence fell. Stella reached in and pulled out the blanket. She held it for a moment, rubbing the edges between her fingertips, then lifted it to her face. She kept it there for several long seconds. When she lowered it, her face was gray, her mouth slack, and Ramsy grabbed her arm.

"Put her head between her legs," the detective said. Ramsy gently pushed Stella forward and kept his hand on her back, feeling her breaths move in, out, so evenly he knew she was telling herself, each time, to breathe.

After a minute more she raised her head, looked around, sipped the water the detective offered.

"I assume you recognize the blanket," the detective said.

Stella nodded. "How did you find it?"

"The girlfriend brought it in."

"And what does it prove?" Stella asked, looking up at the detective with the blanket still clutched to her chest. "Where is my baby?"

The detective looked down. "Unfortunately there were no other clues."

"But if he had the blanket."

"It might have fallen off in his car. He might have kept it for reasons we don't know. It doesn't prove he had the baby after that night. Doesn't prove he didn't, either, but the dead can't speak. Wish they could, you know. Me as much as anybody."

Stella turned to Ramsy. "The palm reading was right. I got something back."

The detective raised his eyebrows.

"It didn't mean anything, Stella," Ramsy said. "A coincidence, is all. Nothing more."

She was pale when they got into Ramsy's truck. "We'll see if we can beat the worst of the snow," Ramsy said, but his words summoned snowflakes so fast and thick he had to slow to a crawl on the highway. "We should get off the road. Snow's getting worse. Driving this way will be seven or eight hard hours home." He looked over at Stella. "Okay?"

"Whatever you think," she said. Her eyes were closed.

At Lake Choctaw, he pulled off the highway and followed signs to a motel. The room was small and smelled of cigarettes. Holes were burned in the bed-spread and a worn footpath stretched through the dusty pink carpet from door to bed to bathroom. But the lamp by the bed made the room not quite so gloomy, and it was warm once Ramsy shut the door, protecting them from the snow and the icy road. Ramsy set down their bags, one for each of them. Lucy's blanket, in a plastic police bag, rested on top of Stella's.

She lifted the bundle but didn't remove the blanket from the bag. "I had a feeling as soon as she was born," she said. "I wanted to put her back in the womb. She looked—afraid. Her little red face, those tiny kicking feet. It was better for her inside."

"No controlling how you'll feel after something like that."

But Stella shook her head. "This was different. It wasn't hormones. It was dread." Ramsy couldn't bring himself to argue, and Stella wasn't waiting for him to respond. "You know she was kidnapped as a newborn," she said. "She was nursing all the time. She'd close her eyes and put one hand on my breast, and she'd nurse until she fell asleep. She nursed herself to sleep the night she was taken. I would have nursed her that night, two or three times, but she was gone. Do you know what it was like to be left like that, without my child, my breasts full of milk?"

"Stella—"

"I could tell you stories that would break your heart. But I won't. It's too dangerous to talk about, even after fifteen years."

"No one expects you to get over something like this."

"Good. Because I never will."

Stella wiped her eyes, took off her shoes, and lay down on the bed, facing away from him. Almost instantly, she was asleep. Ramsy switched off the lamp. The room turned blue-gray in the light edging around the curtains, and he knew she'd sleep for a good long while.

Ramsy put on his boots and coat and went quietly outside. He'd seen a diner not far from the motel, and he wanted coffee. It wasn't so bad plodding through the fresh snow, the sharp cold air on his face. And when he reached the diner, it felt good to sit in a booth by himself and order coffee and pecan pie, listening to the quietly playing soft rock and the murmur of other stranded travelers. Life had gone on here. While they were standing in the detective's office, while Stella was receiving the bag with Lucy's blanket, coffee was being poured here, eggs were being fried. And when he left tonight and returned to the motel, to whatever reckoning awaited Stella now that this final piece of the puzzle had been fitted, however imperfectly, into place, coffee would still be poured here. Eggs would still be fried.

The certainty of this made him think of Marcie and the peace he'd found in her diner all those years ago, eating pie while his buddies were still being blown to bits on the other side of the world, unable to go back even if he'd wanted to. He could never have known, when their love affair started, that it would leave his heart pulpy. He thought it was a shame that the beginnings of things never revealed their middles or endings, even though he knew it had to be this way. Stella would never have blushed and smiled at Seth's flirting at the country club if she'd known where it would all end up, in a brightly lit detective's office, her hands clutching what amounted to a body bag. Living life really meant taking constant leaps of faith, and Ramsy wasn't a faithful man. He ate his pie down to the crumbs and then trudged through even more new-fallen snow back to the motel.

*   *   *

Stella was in the shower when Ramsy returned to the room. Her bag was on the bed, unzipped. He saw a small open case with lipstick and a compact, a blue nightgown, a gray sweater. Finally Stella emerged, barefoot, wearing her flannel robe from home. Her face was moist and pink from the shower, but her eyes were still glassy and dull.

Stella didn't acknowledge Ramsy in the chair by the door. He wondered if she'd even seen him.

But then she said, "I don't think about what she'd be like. Over all these years I never wondered. Oh, of course I did, sometimes. But the Lucy I dream about is the baby Lucy I lost. I've always believed a baby stolen from her mother could never be properly grown." Stella neatened the clothes in her bag and then set it on the floor. She moved around the bed until she could sit down close to Ramsy. "I guess that means to me she's always been dead. I never thought of it like that before. I put her down to sleep that night and I never saw her again."

Something swelled in Ramsy's throat, just below his Adam's apple, and he thought for a moment he might gag, or cry out, and his legs tensed, readying him to flee. But he swallowed and stayed where he was.

For a while after Marcie took Liza, he thought about how the baby was growing. He even bought a book and kept track of months, milestones, changes. But after a few months, he stopped checking the book, and eventually he put it in the trash. The toddler in the pictures wasn't a baby he recognized, and soon he realized he wouldn't know Liza if he saw her on the street. Ramsy had spent most of his life like Stella had, with no idea of what his own child looked like. The difference was that Ramsy had always known Liza was alive. After a minute, he got up and moved beside Stella on the bed.

"Ramsy," she said. Her eyes were heavy. "I'm never going to find her now, am I?"

Ramsy's chest was tight when he answered, "No."

"I was never going to, even if Seth hadn't died."

"No."

"I knew it all along. I just know it more, now."

"Maybe it's better this way."

"Maybe it is."

Her eyes were red-rimmed, and for the first time, the hope in them was gone. That scared Ramsy more than intruders ever could. He wanted to say something to put the hope back in them, but he couldn't say what he didn't believe, and he didn't believe she'd ever find Lucy. He'd never believed it.

They sat in silence for several long minutes.

"You just going to sit there, Ramsy? If you can't see me now then there's no use your having any eyes at all."

Ramsy clicked off the lamp, plunging the room into the blue-black of winter twilight. The wall heater gusted, sending warm air billowing around them. Stella looked straight ahead, seemingly at nothing at all. Her long hair was still damp, and the flaps of her robe were crossed tightly at her throat. Her feet were flat on the floor, her hands clasped in her lap. She was waiting. Ramsy reached over and tucked her hair behind her ear. Then he cupped her head in his palm, pulled her to him, and kissed her.

He remembered, clearly, the first night they ever spent together. It was late summer, the time of year when the crickets' chirping seemed louder, more insistent, in the heavy evening heat, when the decadent blooms of climbing roses and honeysuckle stood out against parched brown grass and dusty earth. They'd driven home from the bar with their windows down, their skin sticky with sweat dried in the rushing air. He turned off the truck when they reached her house, and they sat in wicker chairs on her front porch and drank glasses of cold lemonade. From the porch, Ramsy could pick out late-summer constellations—the Southern Crown, the Shield, the Archer, the Harp—and he pointed them out to Stella.

"Look," he said, "that star, there, above the treeline, and that one, just above the chimney."

"I don't see it, Ramsy," she kept saying, until finally she did.

The house was hot when they went inside, and Stella didn't turn on any lights. Ramsy could hear a fan going in a room upstairs. He carried their glasses through the dark house into the kitchen and put them in the sink.

"You could stay," Stella said from the doorway. And he did. From her open bedroom window, he saw trees, their leaves unmoving in the hot night, stars between the branches, a different life from the one he'd accepted would be his.

They were miles and years away from any of it, but it was there between them just as it always had been. They lay together afterward under the sheet and comforter, the room overly warm now, wind softly blowing snow against the window. Ramsy thought Stella was asleep, but eventually she turned toward him.

"I knew about Seth's other life," she said. "Not long after we got married I found a few documents with his other wife's name. I didn't know the whole story, but I pieced most of it together. The wife called me once, and I didn't even tell Seth. I just hoped it would all go away. Then after we had Lucy she called Seth directly, and everything fell apart."

"Why didn't you confront him?"

"I was happy. It was the life I wanted. She was like—a phantom. I thought she'd disappear."

Ramsy moved his pillow closer to Stella's and took her hand, pulling it to his chest.

"So I'm to blame," she said. "If I'd confronted him when I first knew, none of it would have ever happened."

"You wouldn't have had Lucy."

"I don't have her now. I barely ever did."

Bottomless sadness threatened to drown them, but Stella took a breath and kept talking.

"She rarely cried," Stella said. "But the night she was taken, she screamed inhumanly. I still hear those screams, sometimes—unfamiliar and relentless, like an animal, not a baby. I've always wondered if that screaming might have driven Seth to do what he did." Ramsy tightened his hold on her hand.

"You know, I never thought of killing myself," she said. "Isn't that strange? Maybe because I was never entirely sure Lucy was dead."

Ramsy's blood ran cold. He wanted to think she was long past thoughts like that. Over a decade she'd been living with her loss.

"I'm glad you're here tonight, Ramsy," she said.

Stella's breathing soon evened out, but Ramsy lay awake all night. At three, the snow stopped, and the world was white and quiet. It would take some time for the plows to fan out, but the highway would be clear by six. It would be an easy drive home, and their lives would resume the pattern of an ordinary day. Ramsy would have his sidewalk to shovel, and the road up to

his bar. He'd have to hook the plow onto his truck for
that. And Stella—who knew what Stella would do. He
hoped, for the first time, that she'd spend some time
with Adrienne, just so she wouldn't be alone. Ramsy
wished for the snow to start up again. But instead the
dawn came, bright and clear and cold.

*   *   *

The roads had been plowed, but there were patches
of ice, and the driving was slow. When they were two
hours outside of Shelk, Stella said, "Let's stop, Ramsy. I
need to eat something."

They ordered hot roast beef sandwiches and fries
at a Howard Johnson's off the interstate. A few other
tables were filled, each one with a person eating
alone, staring at their undersalted food as though it
had secrets to tell. Ramsy knew to anyone else, he and
Stella were the lucky ones. Anyone looking on would
think they had each other, which was more than most
other people had.

The gravy on their sandwiches was cold now, con-
gealed to a jelly around crusts of bread and bits of
knifed-off fat. Ramsy was about to signal for the check,
but Stella held out her mug when the waitress came by
with the coffeepot. Then she asked, "How did it happen? Your eye. You've never told me, except to say it
was the war."

"Not something I talk about," he said. Exhaustion
and too much coffee made him feel outside himself, looking on from somewhere just to the left of
where he sat. "It wasn't the war," he said. "Happened
while I served, but in a bar in Taipei. Made a mistake.
Thought I'd found something, but it wasn't really
mine. The girl's pimp left me for dead with a knife
in my eye."

Stella looked away. It was a story no one could respond to. But Ramsy suddenly wanted to make Stella understand.

"Changed everything," he said. "Before the war, I didn't have anything, and I would have gone right back to it, to nothing. But I couldn't go home with an eye like this, a story like this. Had no place there anymore. Wouldn't have the life I do if things hadn't happened this way."

"So you believe in fate," she said.

"Not sure what I believe. All I know is what happened."

Stella waited in the car while Ramsy went over the edges of the windshield with the scraper. The ice was stubborn on a day like this. When he got in the car, he took off his gloves and started the engine. The cuffs of his coat were damp, and he turned on the heater, letting the car warm before shifting into gear.

"Wait," she said. "I can't drive anymore."

"Not much farther now, once we get going. Two hours, at most."

"I don't want to go home, Ramsy. Where do I put it?"

"I don't understand."

"Where do I put the blanket when I get back home?"

"You'll put it in a drawer, Stella. In a room you don't go into very often so you never have to see it. Or put it in your own bureau so you'll always have it close."

"I don't know which is worse."

"Neither do I."

"I'd forgotten this about you," she said. "Until now I'd forgotten. You never try to make me see the bright side, never try to cheer me up. I always loved that about you. Still do." She put a hand on his knee. "Thank you for that." She smoothed her hair, unzipped her coat. Ramsy shifted into gear, and they merged back onto the road toward home.

Shelk seemed different when they returned—famil-iar the way dreams were familiar, but so snow-covered that the shapes of walls and fences and street signs and rooftops were smudged out, left to the imagination. The streets were plowed, but badly, and Ramsy had to swerve around piles of snow.

They reached Stella's house. "Let me shovel your walk," Ramsy said.

"Thanks, but one of JT's friends will come later on."

She zipped her coat and lifted her bag from the floor. "I'll see you at the bar later," she said. "If not tonight, then tomorrow. If you're still open."

If he was open. Ramsy turned his head away. She was waiting, and he felt her waiting, giving him a chance to say what he should have said from the first moment he changed his *Closing* sign to *Open*—that he was staying for her. Of course he was, and finding him gone one day was no longer something she had to fear. He felt her waiting for other words, too, some recognition or confirmation, the kinds of things all women wanted, and which he'd never been able to give. He looked at her face. But all he could say was, "I'll be open," as though he didn't owe her anything, as though nothing had changed.

Without saying anything else, Stella got out of the truck and walked away, stamping through the snow to her front door. When she went inside she flashed the porch light, once. The trip was over.

*   *   *

Overnight a cold spell settled over the mountains, freezing the wet roads into treacherous sheets of ice so that only chain-wrapped tires could even attempt the steep grade. Uncovered skin grew tingly, then numb. It was the kind of cold—record-setting, historic—that made everybody forget that anything else was happening in Shelk.

Ramsy hadn't seen Stella since Ohio. After three days passed, he found himself on edge, glancing up at the door every few minutes as though he might catch her looking in. On the third day, late in the afternoon, Ramsy was passing time in the bar when JT came in, his cheeks shiny and red. The coat Ramsy had given him was zipped to the neck.

"Cold out there," JT said.

"Unusual to get cold like this so early," Ramsy said. "Used to be February, March. And nothing like this." He opened a beer and then, without asking, poured coffee into a mug. "Your camp getting by?"

"We've seen worse." He sipped the beer then wrapped his hands around the hot mug. "Probably best Adrienne and Serena are out of it, though. Even criminals like us wouldn't want a baby to freeze. Course, Emilian doesn't know about it. He's going crazy wondering where they are."

Out of it. So where were they? Ramsy's gut told him the answer, but he let a few minutes pass before he decided to speak. "You said they're out of it. Where'd they go?"

JT looked suddenly nervous. "Someplace warm, just for a few days. They'll be back soon as the cold breaks. Least that's what Adrienne said."

"Where are they?" No answer. Ramsy sighed. "Forget it. I already know."

"I tried to talk your friend out of it when she came up three days ago," he said. "She seemed nervous, but she was firm. She wasn't going to leave there without the baby at least."

"Jesus Christ," Ramsy said softly.

"He'll find out," JT said. "No one gets away that easy. Stella isn't the only one who's tried to protect her. It's only a matter of time before Emilian gets them back."

JT sipped his coffee. "She does what she wants, doesn't she, your friend," he said.

"Been this way long as I can remember. Time was she would have told me. Things change."

"When Adrienne joined up with us she was quieter, just did what she was told. Didn't take much for Emilian to get his way. He liked that. But something changed when she had the baby." He paused. "I miss her," he said. "This whole thing's crazy. Going off like this, leaving the group—it's not done. We might talk about it, but no one'll ever do it. Too hard to start all over." He paused. "I don't want her to come back. She deserves more than this, more than Emilian. She's where she should be. At least until the cold spell passes."

When JT left the bar that night, Ramsy called Stella. "It's Ramsy," he said. "I just talked to JT."

Stella sighed. "Well, you'd better come on over."

He locked the bar and drove to Stella's. She opened the door before he could knock and put a finger to her lips.

"Before you say anything," she whispered, "come see."

She led him upstairs to the room with the window overlooking the yard. The door was ajar, and Stella nodded at Ramsy to look in. On the bed was Adrienne, asleep, a crocheted blanket pulled to her waist. In the crook of her arm slept Serena, her cheeks pink and warm. Ramsy watched them for a long moment, then he and Stella went back downstairs.

"It's just until the cold spell passes," Stella said. "She didn't bring anything but extra clothes for Serena."

"This is what you wanted all along," Ramsy said.

"So what if it is?" Stella said. "What's so wrong about wanting to help this girl? You know yourself they're mostly just kids. You're the one who's been saying they're misunderstood."

"You've got it wrong," Ramsy said. "People are angry. You took a risk, going up there."

"But what do I have to risk? It doesn't matter what happens to me, what people think. And there was no danger. JT saw my car and stayed with me so they knew."

"No danger? Emilian's a criminal, Stella. He won't just let that girl go. He'll find out she's with you, and then what?"

"You talk to me like I haven't thought of all this a hundred times."

"You should've told me you were going up there."

"Why? So you could drive me yourself?"

"I could've done—something."

"You might have, once. You might have been right with me—trusted me—but now? You're leaving—you see things differently."

"You're wrong."

"Maybe. But I don't need to explain myself to you, Ramsy. I just don't. Not anymore."

She was tired. Ramsy saw it in her face. There was a slump to her shoulders, a weak tilt to her head, and violet shadows cupped her eyes.

"What happens next?" he asked.

"When the cold eases, they'll go, like I told you."

"I mean today. When they come downstairs."

"I imagine I'll give Adrienne food, some formula for Serena if she'll take it. I got some clothes, some bottles. You saw the diapers, the bouncy chair, all the rest of it. It's not so hard, Ramsy, understanding what people need."

He glanced into her kitchen. A package of chicken was thawing on the counter, next to a bowl of red-green apples and a few potatoes and carrots, celery, onions.

"Supper is chicken soup," she said. "You're welcome to stay."

Ramsy could taste that soup: the silky rounds of carrots, chicken pieces plump with broth, chunks of potato so soft a baby could eat them. Buttered toast. Hot salty broth sipped from the bottom of the bowl. But he shook his head, unable to see himself at that table of women, Serena sucking milk from a bottle with her pursed pink mouth, Stella pouring tea and keeping her watchful eyes on the girl and baby for any sign of want. He didn't deserve it and couldn't bear it if Stella turned that nurturing gaze to him.

"They don't belong to you," Ramsy said as he turned for the door. He knew that this, in the end, was what he'd come here to say.

"Oh, Ramsy," Stella sighed. "It's food and a warm place to sleep. That's all."

CHAPTER 13

153 Larkspur Road

The house was comfortable, and the boy was foolish. He'd known going in it would be a good one. It was one of Shelk's nicer houses, in a part of town they usually stayed away from. There was more likely to be an alarm, or a wife at home. But they needed something good today, so he slipped off from the others and came here. The doors were locked, but he broke a side window and climbed over the sill. Inside he found hardwood floors and framed photographs on the walls, matching tins on the kitchen counters and chocolate cookies plastic-wrapped on a plate. There was cash in the desk downstairs, paper-clipped to a checkbook, and ten fat rolls of quarters. He put these into his bag, but it was heavy, so he left it on the couch by the door.

In the rooms upstairs were beds with puffy quilts tucked under the pillows, curtains tied back with ribbons, glass jars on the bathroom counter holding cotton balls, hairpins, tubes of lipstick. Almost as an afterthought, he swept jewelry from the dressers into his pockets. Then he sat down on a bed. He lay back against the pillows.

And then, because the room was dim and warm and last night he'd been cold and hungry, he fell asleep.

He woke to voices, a woman's and a man's. He heard window, police, hurry, stay here. *He jumped up and stood by the doorframe, peering out. No one had come upstairs. He ran to the window. There was a roof, and from there he could jump—but the money was downstairs, the cash and quarters, too much to simply leave behind. If he made a run for it, he could grab the bag and be out the front door before anyone could stop him.*

He ran, quietly, but his footsteps were clear on the wood floors and the woman downstairs screamed. At the bottom of the stairs, he turned to grab his satchel but the man caught him by the arm and punched him in the gut, yelling, "The police, Irene, call the police!" The boy swung for his face and made contact, his knuckles white with pain. He yanked his arm free, grabbed the bag, and ran out the door. He ran and kept running and when he stopped he sank to his knees and vomited in a ditch. Then he ran until he was far from the house, far from the woman he'd frightened and the man he'd struck, far from the bed where he'd slept.

A big day in Shelk dawned a week after Ramsy got back from Ohio. The men had found a way to channel their frustrations—the pigeon shoot scheduled for Saturday, late afternoon. Pigeons had taken over the once-luxurious bank building on Main Street, which had been little but broken windows and crumbling bricks for three decades. The birds had squeezed through cracks in the boarded-up windows and ignored the *Condemned* sign on the door, making their home where heavy wooden desks and smartly dressed tellers once stood. To rid the building of pigeons, Shelk's mayor had made a plan: men would startle the pigeons out of the building with shots from the street. Ramsy wanted to stay home, but he also welcomed having something to think about besides Stella and her grief.

At four o'clock on December twentieth, fifty of the town's hunters—including the men from the bar—lined up on Main Street and pointed their shotguns. Crowds gathered down the block, where they had a good view of the building. The hunters' wives stood with thermoses of coffee and plastic-wrapped sandwiches, as though this were a battle that required fortification. Ramsy looked around for Stella, hoping she would be there. The library wasn't far from Main Street. She'd be able to hear the shots, even with the windows closed.

The first shots drew smoky clouds of pigeons from the ghost-blank windows, and the crowds cheered. The mayor, with a megaphone, shouted, "That's the way, hunters, that's the way!" The birds scattered into the sky, and then, after a spray of bullets, several fell like heavy stars onto the pavement.

Ramsy stood at the end of the street, watching the men with guns on their shoulders. He saw the men from the bar and a few others he recognized from town. A few wore camouflage and bright orange vests as though they were on a hunting trip.

It was a strange, calm afternoon. From the line of men, someone shouted, and a few others laughed. They kept shooting.

"Pretend they're gypsies!" someone screamed, and a roar went up from the crowd. Shots were fired at the building, and a new flock of birds rose into the sky. The men took aim with renewed purpose.

Soon the pigeons were gone, escaped or dead. For a while everyone just stood there. "Get a load of that," one man said, sipping the coffee held out by his wife. He pointed at the carcasses they'd kicked to the curb.

Then everyone left for the Lions Club spaghetti dinner, planned in honor of the day. A few men piled the birds in the bed of a pickup. A man sat sideways in the truck, his legs hanging out the door, smoking a cigarette.

"One hundred twenty-three of these suckers," Ramsy heard him say. "Too bad they ain't gypsies."

Ramsy walked past the old bank to get to his truck. He'd let the dinner go on without him. It was almost six by then, and the smell of gunpowder still hung in the air. Ramsy turned and looked behind him, where the bank building stood tall against the sky. The building was set to be torn down, broken into piles of bricks and pieces of wood. Then there would be a hole in the street, like a missing front tooth. Ramsy wondered what the men and women would tell their children when they asked where the birds had gone. He knew, later, what the blustery talk would be at the bar: *Twenty of those dead birds was mine.* Maybe the men would be calmer, their urge to fire their guns satisfied, their anger at the outsiders assuaged. But Ramsy knew he was wrong. Soon enough, the pigeons would be all but forgotten.

*   *   *

That night, JT and some friends went to the Lions' spaghetti dinner, held in the banquet room of the gray-stone Protestant church. Ramsy heard about it later, from Ash and Charlie. Both of them were Lions, and their wives cooked the spaghetti and took money at the door. They told Ramsy the story.

The banquet room had filled quickly in the early evening. People in Shelk looked forward to a spaghetti dinner. It was a way to get together, to get a good meal cheap, to celebrate something—like the pigeon shoot—that had the whole town talking.

By six-thirty the paper-covered tables were nearly full. Ones and fives were stuffed in a jumble in Junie Snyder's zippered pouch. In the kitchen, homemade sauce bubbled in cafeteria-sized pots on the stove, and steaming spaghetti was dumped into colanders in the sink. Plate after plastic plate of spaghetti—a meatball on the side—made its way out to the tables. People talked of the last spaghetti dinner, held at the Sons of Italy, and the fish fries the Catholic church by the river would put on during Lent. A different group of women was planning them this year, and there was some worry that things would be unfamiliar, changed for the sake of change. The din rose. Late arrivals waved greetings. Junie pointed out empty seats. And then, at quarter to seven, they walked in.

There were four of them, boys, in ragged jeans and ill-fitting coats. They walked in defiantly, Ash said, with challenge in their eyes, and they produced some wrinkled bills, enough for a dinner each. Junie looked around frantically for Charlie, but he was joking with friends. So she took their money and led them herself to an empty table far in the corner. They didn't say anything as they took off their coats and sat down.

The room had quieted as Junie led the procession, and she slipped back to the front table with her head down. For several minutes, no one spoke. Everyone had their eyes on the boys. In the kitchen, panicked whispers: Who would bring out the spaghetti? Should they bring it out at all? Betty Wyatt finally said, "I'll do it," and carried out the plates two in each hand. The other women watched from the doorway as Betty strode over and set the spaghetti down. It was so quiet, Charlie said, you could hear the tap of their plastic forks against the plastic plates.

When it became clear that the boys were going to sit there and eat their meals—enjoying the homemade sauce and meatballs as if they were as entitled to them as anyone else—the whispers began. And grew. Soon phrases stood out against the hissing: *Don't belong here. Have no right.* Then Harry Slavin stood. Harry was a big man, a former linebacker for the high school who'd kept his bulk. His football-star son, Jimmy, stood, too.

"Not your place," Harry said loudly, looking right at the boys. "Got no right to be here."

By now the boys' plates were empty. Their five dollars bought them coffee and a piece of vanilla sheet cake, too, but no one moved to bring it over.

"Sitting there like you're part of this town," Harry went on. "We're watching you, hear me?"

Still the boys did not move. Finally Kitty Kurtz crept out with the coffeepot and sloshed coffee into four Styrofoam cups, her hand shaking so violently the coffee splashed onto the table. A murmur rose up.

"It's just coffee," she said loudly. "Just pouring coffee, that's all." The boys sipped the coffee. No one brought out any cake.

At this point in the story, Ramsy turned away. He needed a moment to get past the image in his head: JT and the others, hungry and cold, paying their way for a bland church supper and waiting for cake that never came.

Harry had been standing for a while now. He looked, Ash said, like he might take a swing at the boys any second.

"Seems we treated you damn good," Harry said. "Now you best be gettin on."

The boys stood and put on their coats. A few other men stood with Harry as they made their way out of the hall, but no one moved. When the heavy church door slammed shut, there was pandemonium. Above the rest, Jack could be heard shouting, "What the *hell* you give them coffee for? You invited them here, I'm goddamn sure of it. Hell, Kitty, which one is he?"

"Can you believe it, Ramsy?" Charlie said. "Coming in like that, to our spaghetti dinner?"

"After tonight seems like they'll never leave," Ash added. "They think they got it good here."

Not so good, Ramsy thought, when anger greeted them wherever they went and cold open air was their home. But he said nothing to the men.

Not much later, Harry Slavin and Jimmy came in to the bar. Jimmy had visited Ramsy's before, but only in the summer when he and Harry were out riding quads on the trails. The men stood and shook hands.

Charlie clapped Jimmy on the back. "Good as raised you from a pup," he said. He turned to Ramsy. "Used to come over for Junie's chocolate-chip cookies after school when his dad worked a double." He winked. "Taught the boy everything he knows."

"They tell you what happened tonight?" Harry asked Ramsy. He nodded. "They've got some balls, I'll tell you that. Thinking it might be time to start up the neighborhood watch again. Do it right this time. Get closer to that gypsy camp, make sure they know we're serious. Tell Kurtz we're in if he gets a group together," he said to Charlie and Ash. "Gone on long enough. Too long."

The men agreed, and Harry and Jimmy soon left. For a while, the other men were quiet, drinking their beers. Jack arrived, and he sulked with his beer away from the other men.

"Were you at the shoot, Ramsy?" Charlie asked.

"He was. I saw him there," Ash said. He turned to Ramsy. "Didn't want to join in?"

"Haven't shot a gun in years," Ramsy said. "Not my sport."

"Got fifteen of the damn things," Jack spoke up.

"Ten, for me."

"Twelve here."

The men toasted with beer bottles, something Ramsy had never before seen them do.

"Maybe the gypsies will take this as a warning," Ash said, "if any of them were there."

"Even if they heard about it," Charlie agreed. "Not the sort of thing you can't know was happening. Seems like a message to them, somehow, especially after Harry said his piece at the dinner." The men murmured assent.

Ramsy frowned. "You were shooting birds," he said.

They all looked at him. "Not so different from shooting anything else," Jack said. "You take aim, you pull the trigger. Hell, you know, Ramsy. You was in the war."

*   *   *

As soon as JT came in that night, Ramsy told him, "Showing up at that dinner was a mistake. People around here don't take something like that lightly. This is their home—understand that. They don't have much, but they'll fight for what's theirs."

"We just wanted a hot meal."

"Not that simple. You had to know that."

"We know it more, now."

Again Ramsy remembered how young JT was, how young they all were. "Just want you to know there's been talk," Ramsy said. "A few men want to drive up your way. Nothing's planned yet, but if it happens it's liable not to end like anyone thinks it will, or wants it to. Don't want anyone to get hurt," Ramsy said. "Has Emilian said anything more about moving on?"

JT shook his head.

"I could come up again, try to talk to him. Explain how it is."

"Won't matter."

"Doesn't make sense, what he's doing," Ramsy said. "You pack up, you move on. Gotta be easier than what you're going through here. It's what you do, your group. Staying on no matter how bad things get—that's what other people do. Shelk isn't a place anyone wants to be if they had a choice about it. You have the chance for something different, anywhere in the world. So why the hell you risking everything for this, for overcooked spaghetti in a church hall, for Chrissake? Tell Emilian to go to hell. Just go, now, before someone decides to stop you."

He'd raised his voice, but JT didn't cower. He stared boldly back at Ramsy, and when he answered his voice, too, was angry.

"Think you know so much about us," he said. "Any day now you'll be closing, or so you say, so no one better count on you—isn't that it? You think leaving's so easy, but you've never done it. But you'll spend the rest of your life saying you will. That sign," he said. "Every day you change that fucking sign."

"Planning to move out near my daughter. Told you that."

"You know something, Ramsy? I come back in ten years, you'll still be changing that sign. So don't talk to me about packing up, moving on. We will. We have to. Like you said, it's what we do." He took a breath. "You found your place. You know yourself how hard that is. So don't act like all that is easy to throw away."

There was a long silence. Ramsy's heart pounded, but he didn't feel angry anymore. He opened another beer. When he slid it over to JT, JT held up a hand.

"Gotta go," he said. He slipped on his coat and then looked once more at Ramsy. "You can tell the men we're going," he said. "You don't have to worry about us."

Ramsy nodded. When JT opened the door, Ramsy said, "JT." JT turned around. "Watch yourself out there."

"See you," he said.

Then Ramsy was alone. He walked out from behind the bar, sat in JT's seat, and drank the beer he'd opened. He was nearly finished when Liza called.

"Can't talk long," she said, "but I've been thinking, and it's okay you're not coming. I was upset at first, but I think I understand now."

"Never meant to hurt anyone," Ramsy said.

"I know," she said. "You didn't. What I mean is, you don't have to be here with us. It can work like this, visiting. This is how it is with other people, right?"

"Hard to compare us to anyone else," Ramsy said.

"True." She laughed.

"Every day I feel lucky just to know where you are."

"It's something, isn't it?" Liza said.

"Yes," Ramsy said. "Feels like everything, sometimes."

They were quiet for a breath or two. "Maybe you can come out here to my place one day," Ramsy said. "Sunday supper. Mark, the kids."

"I'd like that."

Ramsy went outside to his truck and steered over ice to the end of the drive. He usually changed the sign the next day, but tonight he stopped and took a new piece of cardboard from the truck bed and the marker from the glovebox. *Open*, he wrote, steadying the cardboard against the hood. Before he could write *December 22*, he hesitated. Stella's words from the end of the Ohio trip ran through his head: *If you're open*. Finally, Ramsy hung the sign but left it as it was, without a date. *Open*. It could hang there till January, later, even, if the snow didn't sog it down. It was a small change, but Stella would notice, and maybe that was all that mattered.

For a moment he stood by the truck and listened. The cold had made the world brittle. He heard branches snap and fall from the weight of the ice. In the distance, a deer sprinted through the woods, its hooves cracking hard-frozen snow. The sky was clear, and in the open space above his bar, between the trees, he saw stars sharp as needlepoints. He took a breath and, for a moment, closed his eye. Cold air rushed into his throat, his lungs, scraping away what had been there and leaving only clean skin and muscle. And for a moment all of it—the men's anger, Stella's baby, the dread he felt when he thought of JT—disappeared, and he found himself thinking, *This is a beautiful place.* He took a few more deep, cold breaths. Then he got in his truck and drove home.

CHAPTER 14

37 Nightshade Street

It was a bright cold morning when Emilian parked his van in the driveway of Ed and Alice Jasinski's home in the nicest part of Shelk. If he'd paused for a moment, he would have seen the overgrown hedges by the side of the house, the shutters with paint in flakes the size of quarters. He might have noticed how the sun showed streaks on the windows, how dead weeds were matted down where snow had melted at the edge of the lawn. It was a home where two old people were barely getting by. Wealth, if there had ever been any, had long been spent or passed into others' hands.

Ed was outside with a snow blower, clearing off the walk. He straightened when Emilian stepped out of the van.

"Afternoon," Emilian said. "Gas company. I need to check the line. Just be a few minutes if you show me the cellar."

Ed laid down his blower and stood up. He was a big man, tall, with long thick arms and a wide chest that had held onto its strength, but at ninety years old he stooped a little, and his steps were measured and slow as he began edging toward the house. As a longtime homeowner he was used to all manner of people coming by—lawn care, pavers, meter readers, roofers—but something about this man set off a warning.

"We use electric heat here," he said. "Must be some mistake."

"Just gotta check," he said. "New gas line coming in nearby."

"You'll have to come back," Ed said. This time he turned and all but ran to the door. It didn't matter. Emilian was faster, and he came up behind Ed and shoved him inside. Ed tripped over the threshold and fell.

"Ed?" called Alice, who'd been lying upstairs with a headache. "Are you okay?"

He kicked Ed again to keep him from responding. When Alice appeared at the kitchen doorway, dark-toed pantyhose under black slacks and a soft powder-blue robe, he knocked her down before she could scream. He sat the couple back to back, binding their wrists and ankles and then looping a long band of tape around their waists and chests, securing them together. Then he ran upstairs.

A few minutes passed before he reappeared in the kitchen doorway. "Where is it?" he said. He slapped Ed across the face. "Tell me where it is."

"I don't know what you're looking for," Ed said. Behind him, Alice was sobbing. Emilian punched him in the gut, and she screamed. Each blow to Ed's body jolted Alice's too.

"Cash. Jewelry. Whatever. Don't waste my time."

He grabbed Ed's right pinky finger and twisted until he screamed. Ed had the large, calloused hands of a former heavy machinery operator, and though the knuckle cracked, Emilian could not break the bone.

"There's nothing," Ed choked out. "We don't have anything. Please."

Emilian produced a knife and stabbed Ed twice in the thigh. Then he grabbed Ed's face and pressed his thumbs into his eye sockets. Ed kept panting, "Please. Please," and Alice kept on screaming until she went silent.

When he'd beaten Ed into unconsciousness, he turned to her. But she was dead.

This was it, then. They had done exactly what the men had feared: killed one of their own. Accidental, intentional—it wouldn't matter to the men. The intruders had caused the death, and this was the point. Robberies, a cheating wife, showing up at the spaghetti dinner—and now an old woman was dead. Ramsy gritted his teeth. He knew it wasn't JT or the other kids who'd tied that old woman back to back with her husband, who'd scared her to death as her husband was beaten senseless. It was Emilian, he was sure. But he and Stella were the only ones who understood the difference. And whoever hadn't fled already would be the ones to pay the price.

Ramsy spent the whole day at the bar, hoping JT would come in—they'd be scared, those kids, and Ramsy hoped they knew his bar was a place they could go. But none appeared. He knew they still had to be up in the mountains—people would have noticed a caravan coming down—and Ramsy prayed they'd leave by nightfall. They were up there, then, waiting. Ramsy drank a beer, but it did nothing to calm the pounding in his chest.

The men didn't come to the bar that night, which was just what Ramsy feared. At eleven thirty, when the moon had finished its ascent and hung at the top of the sky, hooked and crooked, like a beckoning finger or a sideways grin, Charlie Snyder called.

"Listen, Ramsy," Charlie said. "I need you to do something for us. If anyone calls the bar tonight—Meg,

Junie, any of the women—could you tell them we were there? Tell them we were there and just left and were going to have a beer at someone's house. Could you do that for us, Ramsy?"

"Charlie. You don't want to do this."

"Like hell we don't," Charlie said. His voice was hard. "And I'd think twice before warning the gypsies we're coming. Don't think I've forgotten."

Ramsy grabbed his coat and locked the bar without bothering to empty the register. He hoped someone would rob him tonight—it would mean they weren't in the mountains. He climbed into his truck and gunned the engine. His truck heaved and protested up the steep grade, refusing to go above thirty even as he gave it more gas. He changed gears, cursing. No point burning out the transmission before he got there, but he was aware every second of the clock on the dash, flashing each minute away.

He relaxed on the pedal once he neared the caves. It was pitch black—every bit of moon and stars was blotted out, inked over with clouds. He turned the defrost on, as much for the noise as the cleared windshield.

When his headlights caught the red of Ash's truck in a clearing, he pulled in behind it. Snow clouds blocked the moon and starlight. Harry had deer-spotting lights on top of his truck, washing the woods in watery light. Ramsy jumped down and slammed his door. The cold air felt electric—different from the flat dark quiet of the mountains.

He heard voices, gruff and loud. Still time to step in, help reason this out. He ran toward the voices, through the trees, and stopped short of a clearing lit by a weak fire, built with only a few thin branches. Crouched around the fire were three young boys in jeans and worn coats, smoking cigarettes, and two girls with bright hats over their hair. Other faces appeared in tents and cars not far from the fire. He saw JT sitting with the rest.

The men stood in an uneven line thirty feet away.

"Stay where you are," Harry Slavin said. "We just wanna talk to you. It's time you moved on out of Shelk. You have what you came for. We want you to leave."

Harry was bigger than the other men by a good fifty pounds.

JT stood up, his arms crossed against his coat. "Maybe we don't want to leave," he called out. His voice was clear like glass. "Maybe we like it here."

Harry snorted. "Are you fucking crazy?"

"Lowlifes," Jack Kurtz shouted. "You rob our houses, you take our women, and now you kill an old lady?"

"We should've come up here weeks ago," Charlie spat. "Should've run you off the minute you came to Shelk."

"Not us you want," JT said. "We're not the ones who killed that woman."

"Yeah?" Jack sneered. "You the one who's fucking my wife?"

"It's not us," JT said.

A few men drew their rifles from slings on their shoulders and aimed them at the kids. Ramsy stepped out from the shadows, into the space between them.

"Wait," he said. All eyes turned to Ramsy. "These aren't the ones you want. They're kids, that's all." Ramsy kept his voice steady and firm. He didn't look at JT, just kept his face turned to the men.

"He's not one of us," Charlie called out. "He gave them food. I saw him. He's been with them all along."

"Now hold on," Ramsy said. He held his hands up. "Listen to me. These aren't the ones you want. You've said your piece. Time to walk away. Slavin, Kurtz, let's go now."

The men didn't move. Then Jack stepped closer to Ramsy and leveled his gun at Ramsy's chest. "You part of this, Ramsy?" he said. "You help rob our houses? You help kill that woman? What do we know about you, anyway?"

"He had our jewelry," called Charlie. "Gave it to the women, remember?"

Ramsy didn't move. Behind him he heard JT say, "Leave the old man alone," but it was too late. Ramsy heard a rainfall of clicks as the men released the safeties and pointed their rifles at him and JT.

Suddenly a piercing shriek drowned out the rest. "No!" screamed Kitty Kurtz, emerging at a sprint from the edge of the woods. She gestured wildly at Jack. "Put the gun down—put it down, damn it! Listen to me—he isn't the one you want—please, I can help you find him, just put it down—"

"Get out of the way, Kitty," Jack shouted. "This ain't about you anymore."

"No!" she shrieked again. She made a grab for Jack's gun. "Someone stop him—help me, please, someone stop him—"

There was a startling clang as someone kicked over a bucket of water onto the fire, plunging the camp into darkness shadowed by the distant light from their cars. Kitty screamed, and then four shots rang out. Ramsy saw JT collapse. Ramsy instinctively hit the ground, hands on his head, heart pounding, his face in the dirt. Then he heard the sound of the kids running away from the clearing.

"Cease fire. Cease fire," the men yelled. Flashlights swept the ground. Ramsy popped his head up. Kitty was crumpled at Jack's feet, a gaping, gushing wound on her neck. The men crowded close around her for a moment then took off running.

"Wait! Someone help me carry her," Jack screamed, and Charlie doubled back and lifted Kitty's feet while Jack took her shoulders. Blood ran from her neck to the ground. They rushed her to the trucks as quickly as they could. Engines roared, tires spun on sticks and snow. The men backed out, slamming on the gas toward the main road.

Then Ramsy was alone. He stood up and scanned the darkness. JT's body lay by the soggy fire. The silence was absolute, cotton in his ears. JT was twisted like a deer, and there was blood all over the ground. Ramsy knelt and put his fingers to his throat. Waited. Pressed harder, deeper, kneading the skin for pulse. He shook him, slapped his cheek. But there was no response. He was motionless underneath the coat Ramsy had bought, and Ramsy gently pulled the boy into his arms. His .45 sat on the ground by JT's hand. Ramsy picked it up. The safety was still on; it hadn't been fired. He tucked it into his coat.

A twig cracked. At the edge of the trees was a figure, half hidden, watching him. Ramsy stood, raised his hands. The boy took a step backward, and Ramsy remembered what he looked like: an old man with his eye gone, some kind of monster.

"He's dead," he said. "Don't just leave him." Ramsy waited. "I said, don't just leave him."

"I won't," said the boy.

"That's the worst of it, dying alone," Ramsy said, and the boy melted into the woods.

*   *   *

He would come to take the baby. This was what flashed into Ramsy's mind as he drove down the mountain. Emilian would come for Adrienne and Serena, grabbing the baby by whatever means necessary if there was any hint of protest from Stella.

The time for all the pretending had come to an end. These kids were not their sons or daughters, and there had never been a fragile peace. Their entanglements had never been meant to last. He'd done what he could; he said it over and over as he drove. He couldn't have stopped the men from going, couldn't have saved JT's life. He'd done what he could. If JT was lucky, his friends would bury him, mark the grave with a stone.

He sped down the mountain, braking desperately around the curves. He'd kill himself if he kept driving this way—but he thought only of Stella, sitting peacefully in her living room while Adrienne and Serena slept upstairs, feeling finally that the world was right. He had to get there.

At Stella's, he pulled up to the curb without bothering to straighten out the truck before he shut off the engine. A thin band of light glowed around an upstairs window shade. She was awake. He pushed the truck's door closed and hurried up the path to the porch, icy snow cracking under his boots. He knocked loudly on the windowless wooden door. His knock echoed then faded. He knocked again. This time he could sense the stirrings inside, could hear the creak in the ceiling and on the stairs. A light came on in the living room.

"Who is it?" came Stella's voice through the door—fearful but steady.

"Ramsy," he said.

There were two heavy clicks and a rattle—the knob lock, the dead bolt, and the chain. She pulled open the door. She had scissors in her hand but put them down once the light shone on Ramsy's face.

"You scared me to death," she said. "You look terrible." Her nightgown was open at the throat, and a narrow vein pulsed in the scooped-out hollow of her neck. She put her fingers there as though to quiet it.

"Stella," he said. "JT's dead. Kitty Kurtz, too."

"What? My God, what happened?"

"They were shot. Stella—"

"By who? Who killed them?"

"I don't know for sure. But, Stella, Emilian's coming."

For a moment Stella said nothing. Then she grabbed Ramsy's arm and pulled him into the room. She locked the door then ran through the house in her bunchy wool socks, turning off all the lights. Ramsy stayed where he was. He could see nothing in the pitch-black room, but he heard Stella's voice from the stairway.

"He won't get her," she said. "Not this time."

"This isn't the same," Ramsy began, but then a car door slammed. There were quick footsteps on the walk, and then a knock at the door. And then, a second later, another knock that turned to pounding.

"No," Stella said. Ramsy's stomach lurched. He'd wished so many times he'd been there to stop Seth before he took Lucy, and surely in Stella's dreams she was back there too, with a gun aimed squarely at Seth's chest and the courage to pull the trigger. But this time was different. The baby was not hers to keep.

The pounding got louder.

"Stella," Ramsy said, "you have to let him in."

"No," she said.

There was a crash, and glass from the window overlooking the porch clattered to the floor. Cold air rushed into the room, and through the broken window Ramsy saw Emilian's face looking in. A broom handle was in his hand. Ramsy gave a slight lift of his chin and unlocked the door. He turned on a small lamp when Emilian stepped inside.

Ramsy realized then that Stella was crying. She clutched her bathrobe, shaking so badly she could barely keep her balance on the bottom step. For a moment, Emilian paused, and he put the broomstick he was still holding on the floor. He looked at Stella without malice or pity. It was, instead, recognition—of a desperate kind of wanting that colored everything. Ramsy knew he would take what he'd come for.

"No," Stella said, and, wobbling, she spread her arms to block the stairs. "You won't take her from me. This won't happen."

Emilian approached slowly as Stella's voice rose. She attempted to widen her stance.

"Ramsy, do something! Do something, Ramsy, please, Ramsy—"

There was no such thing as second chances. History didn't repeat itself for people who deserved to make things right. Ramsy walked over to Stella and wrapped his arms around her from behind. She struggled, kicking, her voice a strangled gasp now.

"No, Ramsy, no—" When Emilian squeezed past them to go upstairs, Stella kicked again then slumped in Ramsy's arms. They stood there, like that, until Emilian came back downstairs, Adrienne and Serena behind him.

Emilian strode past Stella and Ramsy without turning his head, but Adrienne stopped in front of them. Emilian was at the door before he realized Adrienne wasn't following.

"Adrienne," he said. "Come."

Above the blanket, Serena's eyes were darting and bright. She'd woken up from a deep sleep, but she did not cry. Adrienne gazed at the baby, touched her nose. "No," she said.

"Adrienne." Emilian's voice was steady, and Ramsy saw the tension in his jaw, his legs poised for flight.

"I'm staying," Adrienne said.

"This isn't your choice," Emilian said. "That's my child. Don't make this ugly. You're coming with me."

He took only one step toward Adrienne before Ramsy said, "She's staying with us."

The gun he'd taken back from JT was steady and straight in his hand, pointed at Emilian. Emilian stopped. He stared at Ramsy's face. He'd seen the missing eye before but Ramsy knew he saw something else tonight: that Ramsy knew what he wanted, what was right. Things that had taken him a long time to understand. "Leave the girl," he said again. "Get out of here before they catch you."

"They're mine," Emilian said. But then, with a last grim look at Adrienne, he turned for the door.

Ramsy lowered the gun. Stella rubbed Adrienne's back. Adrienne closed her eyes then carried the baby upstairs to bed. It was over.

*　　　*　　　*

They were alone. Ramsy led Stella to the couch, and she curled limply onto her side, her head in Ramsy's lap. She stayed that way for a long time. Ramsy thought she was asleep, but when he looked at her face, her eyes were open. When she spoke her voice was hollow, but it was once again the Stella he knew.

"I miss her," she said. "Every day, every minute. You don't understand that. You can't, and you never will."

"I know." In her words he heard a jealous claim: *This grief is mine.*

After a while she said, "You saw JT die?"

"I tried to stop the men. If it hadn't been for Kitty Kurtz, it might have been me."

"Oh, Ramsy. They're really gone, then. I guess they have to be, now."

They were quiet. "You were awake when I got here," Ramsy said.

"Couldn't sleep. Had a funny feeling in my stomach, like I get sometimes. Usually nothing. But tonight"— she gestured to him—"I was right."

Her socked feet were tucked under her, and she held a pillow against her chest. She was still shaken.

"I'll make some tea," he said.

"There's water already warm on the stove."

He went to the kitchen, found teabags and mugs in the cupboard by the sink, and poured in still-steaming water from the kettle. The warmth of Stella's house—the softness of it—unsettled him after his trip to the caves. She'd cleaned that day. Ramsy could see the gleam where she'd dusted the shelves. The house smelled like tea and lemons.

Cold drafts swept in through the broken window. Ramsy drank his tea. Stella was waiting for him to say something.

Marcie had waited, too, the night before she left. He'd come home late, but she'd rolled on her side toward him when he got into bed. He could smell her shampoo and the lotion she used on her skin, and he put his hand on her hip. After, she said, *I love you*. He nodded in the dark. But her head was on her own pillow, too far to feel it. *I love you*, she said again.

I heard you, Ramsy said. *Didn't you feel me nodding?*

I'm sorry, she said. *I must have missed it.*

Her smell was on him in the morning when she left, her berry-scented lotion and the smell of her sweat. Even then, the moment she strode past him with Liza and her suitcase, he knew it was because of everything he hadn't done, everything he hadn't said. He wanted to grab her arm, pull her to the bedroom, shut the drapes on the morning sun and start the last night again. But by then she was at the car, and then she was gone.

"I want to ask you something," Stella said. "Has anyone ever touched your eye?"

Ramsy didn't answer. No one besides doctors ever had, and that was decades ago. Then he felt Stella's small, cool fingers on his scars.

"It's soft," she whispered. "Did you know that, Ramsy? The skin there is soft." Ramsy hadn't touched his scars in years except with a cloth in the shower, but now he raised his hand and followed Stella's fingers. The skin *was* soft, like the papery layers on lips.

"Alright," he said roughly, but when he pushed her hand away he did it gently.

After a while he spoke. "Have something belongs to you. Not sure it's the right time, but feels wrong to keep it anymore." He went out to his truck and got the shoebox of Lucy things. His hands shook as he unlaced his boots. He returned to the couch and handed the box to Stella. "Been saving these for years," he said. "Never had a reason. Just seemed like what I should do."

It was a mistake to have brought it, a mistake not to have burned or buried it when he could. But Stella was lifting the lid. "Oh," she said quietly. She took out the articles first and laid them beside her. She took out the flyer and unfolded it, staring at Lucy's face so long Ramsy wondered if somehow Lucy was staring back. Then she took out each of the objects she'd left at the bar, and only then did her eyes grow wet.

"People throw away such beautiful things," she said softly. "Why is that?"

She put everything back into the box and stood up. Ramsy stood too. "I'm sorry," he said. "I should never have—"

But Stella said, "Wait here," and went upstairs. She came down with Lucy's blanket in her arms. "I was going to give it to Serena," she said, "but it belongs with the rest." She folded it over and over until it became a fat roll that just fit under the lid. She slid the box under a corner table, where it would stay.

She was calm now, almost dreamy, as though relieved to have come to the end of something. "It doesn't seem fair," she said. "JT's dead, and the others are running for their lives. But here we are."

"Yes," said Ramsy. "Here we are." But for a moment he was in the mountains, his fingers feeling for JT's pulse. "It's not so bad," Ramsy said, "being here."

"But you're leaving," Stella said.

"Been thinking I'll stay on. Thinking this way for a while now."

"What about Liza?"

"She doesn't need me there. She feels guilty for what Marcie did. She feels guilty for what I did. But she's got another family now. We can visit."

"What will you do, Ramsy?"

"What I've been doing. I have the bar."

"Yes, you have the bar."

They sat without talking, a strange peace between them. Wind rattled the windows, and Ramsy looked up. Snowflakes as big as quarters were coming down thick, drifting in through the broken window, sparkling in the lamp's dim glow. "Snowing again," he said.

"I love snow at night."

"Yes," Ramsy said, imagining JT's body disappearing under a still, heavy cover of white, and young thieves stumbling through the mountains to their next stolen home.

"It's late," Stella said. "Let's go to bed." She rose from the couch and moved toward the stairs, and Ramsy followed. Halfway up, she turned around. "I don't want you to leave," she said.

"I won't," he said, and took her hand.

CHAPTER 15

Somewhere East of the Laurel Highlands

At night, they ate what they could, huddled close together for warmth, and talked about the homes they'd seen. There had been so many, in so many different towns, and after a while they all looked alike. These were the things they saw: carpets worn bald on the paths from door to couch to stairs. Dishes, locked up behind glass, that in other places, other towns, people wouldn't shed a tear over chipping. Calendars tacked to walls with every other Friday circled in ink, matching furniture so old and saggy that, were it not inside a home, it would be considered trash. They knew there were bigger homes, city homes, with art on the walls, shelves of leather books, homes full of things meant to be admired. But these were not homes that kept doors unlocked or let in the likes of them, and what they knew of them was equal to what they knew of dreams.

But now and then a house stood out, even in the towns they'd seen, and they remembered certain details. Like the nursery with a crib full of boxes and picture frames turned face down on the bureau. Like the bedroom with the dresser covered in saints—five deep, arranged tallest to shortest from back to front, all staring serenely at the bed. Like the house with the dolls peering mutely from every corner, dolls in wagons, dolls in chairs, and only men's clothes in the closet.

They'd been together years now. They no longer knew another life. Some part of them always wondered if the town up ahead would be the one they'd stay in, but when they got there it was the same as always: them looking in from the outside, their only glimpses of home the stolen kind. No one would admit a home was what he wanted. Each would say—and even believe—that the road was enough. But each had sat on a bed and looked around a dimly lit bedroom. Each had, for a moment, sipped a Coke on a couch and pretended he could stay. But then there were wheels in the driveway, or a key in the lock, and they remembered, as they slipped away, that the outside was the only home they knew.

The earth was finally soft. Ramsy pressed his hands into the dirt, patting it snugly over tiny buried seeds. It was early to be planting, but the winter had been long, and each morning he woke up yearning to immerse himself in the signs of spring: pink and brown worms curled and twitching in the dirt, the smell of the earth, the cold damp on his knees. He'd planted rows of carrots and lettuce in the garden, and neat beds of poppies and bachelor buttons out front. Leaning against the house were skinny new trees—Japanese maples. Stella had suggested them, and she'd stood with him on the porch, pointing out places where they could go. The delicate leaves would rustle prettily all year, but in the fall they'd turn fiery, red and orange and yellow, bursting into unexpected beauty as the weather turned crisp once again. Everyone always said there was such promise in springtime, but Ramsy had learned that it was the fall that brought the real magic. Things grew in spring, thrived in summer, and died in winter, but fall was an in-between time, when things grew exquisitely beautiful before the whisper of death took them away.

Ramsy stood and brushed off his hands. Around him was turned dirt like newly dug graves. For a long moment, he studied the house. Paint had been peeling off for decades, and stretches of bare wood showed from ground floor to attic. By the back door was a new stack of two-by-fours, bound with twine, and just inside was a remnant of thick green carpet Ramsy had bought last week. The house would never be a showpiece—they'd be lucky if the wiring held out another few years—but a sunroom full of African violets, maybe a small table and chairs, would be nice. He'd get to that—and the new kitchen fixtures, too—as soon as his planting was finished.

Ramsy headed inside to get cleaned up. The fish fry would be starting soon. Stella and Adrienne were waiting for him, sitting on the couch with their coats in their laps. Serena was already bundled into her carseat, and Adrienne leaned over to adjust one of the straps. Ramsy changed out of his work clothes, and together they headed for the church.

*   *   *

Along the sides of the churches and in damp black flower beds all around Shelk, crocus shoots had broken through. Tightly curled points of purple and yellow and white were already peeking out. Skinny daffodil leaves huddled in fresh green clusters, appearing almost overnight. The mornings were mild now, though there was still the threat of frost, and at night, if they remembered, the townspeople spread faded tarps over the tender buds. Tree branches were tipped in green now, weighted down by the first reappearing robins. Birdfeeders that had been overcrowded all winter went vacant as the ground opened up to the birds once more. It was spring, newly so, and baskets of plastic eggs and faded rabbit cutouts decorated even the dingiest storefronts. The air still felt damp and raw but it didn't cut through to the bone anymore. People turned their faces to the sky, to the sun, and let themselves believe that the sins of the winter had melted along with the last of the snow.

The polluted Youghiogheny River sparkled in the light. In another few months the snowmelt gushing down from the Laurel Highlands would turn the river rough and powerful, and professional rafters would descend on Ohiopyle State Park, twenty miles up the mountains, to experience the whitewater that was famous across the eastern United States. The river was already running strong through Shelk, saturating the banks almost as high as the railroad tracks.

There was promise in that strength, peace in the loud rushing water. A man standing in the middle of the Fair Street bridge, looking down, would understand that unclenching his fists, hiking one leg then the other over the rail, would bring him to the end of the line. That same man might choose to leave town rather than face that bridge, that rushing promise, every day for the rest of his life. And a man like that, always disliked but now, also, a widower to be pitied, wouldn't have to explain to anyone the reason why he left. Now that it was spring, now that the days were longer and the darkness somehow not quite so dark, people were finished with Jack Kurtz. They'd brought casseroles to his house after his wife was killed, their names written on masking tape on the bottom, and not one of them had gotten their dish returned. It cemented things, somehow. Gave them someone to blame.

*   *   *

It was the first of the annual fish fries the Catholic church put on every Friday of Lent. Inside the hall, people greeted Ramsy and Stella, nodded and smiled at Adrienne. Some of the women touched Serena's cheek when they passed, or squeezed her tiny socked toes, just as they would have done with any other woman's baby. There was reserve in their gestures, but warmth, too. Things were different now. They themselves were, too. The tangle of what belonged to whom and who belonged where had shaken itself out and fallen into a new kind of order.

What no one talked about were the kids in the mountains. They were gone, and everyone was sorry for how it ended, but it was spring now. Winter was over. Crocuses were blooming by the door of the church hall. Whatever had been taken didn't matter anymore.

Things were changing, yes, but except for Adrienne sitting among them, the fish fry was the same as it always had been: the same white paper tablecloths, the same doubled-up paper plates holding two planks of fried perch, a lemon wedge, and a pile of coleslaw.

It had been years since Ramsy had gone to a fish fry, and it was good to be out, all together, Ramsy and Stella and Adrienne and Serena. At first, when Adrienne decided to stay, Ramsy thought none of them would ever see the outside world again. At night, the gunshots from the mountains still rang in his ears, and he still dreamed about JT's body on the ground. It didn't seem safe to venture out, so for most of the winter they'd hunkered down at Stella's. Most of the time, Adrienne seemed happy enough to play with Serena and relax under Stella's care, but now and then Ramsy caught her gazing longingly out the window.

On Sundays, if the weather held, he'd drive them to Liza's. At first Liza asked questions, but not to judge or argue—only to understand. And so they fell into an ordinary kind of life, but Ramsy knew that it was fragile.

At the end of February, Stella said, "We can't hide forever. We've made our decisions. Shelk will have to face us sometime. I'm ready. Are you?"

Adrienne nodded, so Ramsy did too. Their long hibernation had been for her sake only. She was so young, her baby so innocent—they deserved protection from harsh words and angry glances. But they deserved a life, too. This was why she'd chosen to stay. And so one evening, before dark, they bundled Serena into her carseat and drove to the Rowdy Buck.

Stella led them in, Adrienne and Serena next, Ramsy following last. The room went quiet when they walked inside, as it had so many months ago when Kitty swept in with Emilian. But once they all emerged from the doorway, conversation started up again, quietly, and a few people offered tentative nods and waves. A few people stared, but it might have been as much about Ramsy and Stella as it was about Adrienne, Ramsy's hand on Stella's back, as odd a couple as Shelk could conjure.

In a booth by the window, they looked at the menus. They ordered a burger, a hot roast beef sandwich, a chicken pot pie. Their waitress was Meg Haggerty. She looked at Ramsy a few times from the kitchen, but she treated them like any other customers, refilling their coffee and taking away their empty plates just as she did up and down the row of booths. When they were finished eating, however, she brought over three pieces of apple pie along with the check.

"Must be a mistake," Ramsy said. "We didn't order pie."

"I know you didn't," Meg said. "Just wanted you to have it." She touched the very tip of her finger to the baby's blanket and flicked her eyes at Adrienne, giving her a tiny smile before she walked away.

And now here they were three weeks later, at the fish fry, winter behind them, good food on the table. The fish fry was filling up. Greetings were shouted across the hall. Bursts of laughter rippled from the corners. Stella and Adrienne stood up, their purses on their shoulders, heading to the ladies'. Adrienne held out the baby and Ramsy took her in his arms. She was sturdy now, with plump cheeks and rolls of fat at her wrists and tiny dimpled knuckles. Ramsy sat her on his knee, his arm tight around her.

"Ramsy?"

Ramsy looked up. Charlie Snyder and Ash Haggerty were making their way to an empty table in the middle of the room. Ramsy had seen them only once since that night on the mountain. He nodded at them while their wives pressed close to coo at the baby.

"How've you been, Ramsy?" Charlie asked. He stood at an angle, not quite facing Ramsy head on.

"Been alright," Ramsy said. "You?"

Charlie nodded. Ash did, too. "Got a grandson now," Charlie said, holding his open wallet toward Ramsy. In the picture, Charlie's young daughter held a fat smiling baby. "A son-in-law, too."

"Handsome little guy," Ramsy said.

"Been meaning to come up to the bar," Charlie said. "Been a busy winter. Keep meaning to, though. Will, one of these days."

"Bar's open," was all Ramsy said. "Not going anywhere."

The men looked at their wives. "We should sit down while there's still seats," Ash said. "Good seeing you, Ramsy."

Serena let out a little cry. She was tired. She'd need to sleep soon. Adrienne draped the baby on her shoulder and rubbed her back. She seemed different this spring, older, though she wouldn't turn sixteen for another two months. She held Serena with practiced arms now, took pride in keeping her warm and well-fed. Stella had less mothering experience than Adrienne, when you got down to it, but she still knew what to do, how to teach her. At times, Stella held Serena so close that Ramsy feared she wouldn't give her up. But when Adrienne appeared she always—if reluctantly—let the baby go.

Now, Adrienne took a breath. "I talked to a friend yesterday," she said.

Beside him, Stella tensed. Ramsy put a hand on her knee. "Who?"

"Her name's Kara. I knew her while I was with Emilian. She wasn't part of the group that came here—I knew her from before."

"Why didn't you tell me?" Stella asked.

"I wasn't sure I should," she said.

"Tell us, then," Ramsy said. "What does she want?" He didn't like the nervous look she had and wondered if this girl had asked for money.

"She wants out," Adrienne said simply. "Just like I did. I thought she could come stay with me for a while."

"Why now?" Ramsy asked.

"Shelk is the one place Emilian can't reach her—he's not crazy enough to come back here."

Stella jumped in. "Of course we'll help in any way we can," she said. "A friend of yours is always welcome here."

Adrienne nodded. "Thanks," she said. "I'm not sure when she'll come. Soon, she said."

"Is she fifteen, like you?" Stella asked. Her voice was casual, consciously so, and Ramsy knew that even in this town where Adrienne could now eat peacefully at a church supper, some things were never going to change.

*   *   *

Ramsy breathed in deeply when he unlocked the bar that night. The cool mountain air, the quiet, the familiar smell of stale beer and damp wood—it calmed him, steadied him, like breathing in the smell of Stella's shampoo or the warmth of her neck. In the past few months, he'd changed his home, given up his solitude. He'd welcomed all of it. But he still felt a wash of relief when he stepped into his bar. Here, he was as good as invisible. There was comfort in that, comfort in still having a place he could disappear.

Ramsy uncapped a beer and settled onto his stool. He wouldn't stay long tonight. One of these days, he knew, he'd close down the bar. He wouldn't need this refuge forever. For now, though, it was the one thing that had remained the same across all the years of his life in Shelk, and he held onto it.

He held onto JT, too, here at the bar. In the early days, he'd come here to grieve. It shocked him, the depth of his sadness. Each night he'd come to the bar certain it was over, that the sadness had finally dried up, or that at least the edges of it had pulled back enough so that he'd be able to breathe when he looked across the bar at JT's stool. He'd barely known him, wasn't even sure if JT was his name, had no sense of his history other than the few slivers he'd revealed. Still, he grieved, as much for JT as for what Ramsy had recognized of himself in him.

After a few weeks, he tried not to think of JT too often. What right did he have, when it was his own fault the boy had died? Oh, you could argue otherwise—Stella did—but the truth of it was that the boy was dead because of him. He should have tried harder to stop the men from going up to the mountains that night. He should have had JT sit among the men at the bar, been proud of their friendship instead of fearful and secretive. He should have offered JT a job—hell, given him his own job—so he could be free from Emilian for good. What had he really done for JT, in the end? Not a thing. Stella told him over and over that JT had to make his own choices, his own way, and that it was JT's choice that night on the mountain to step forward to reason with the men. He let her believe that her reassurances calmed him. But they didn't. Stella was the one who'd taken the risk, done the right thing.

JT was gone: that was the long and short of it. He could build a sparkling tower of reasons and explanations, but in the shadow of that tower would always be JT's body, bloody in the snow.

The bar stayed empty that night, as it had every night for over two months. Stella didn't come in anymore, what with the baby to help with at home, and the familiar faces had moved on. Things had changed after that night on the mountain, in the bar but in the town, too. Ramsy saw it in the way the townspeople nodded at Stella and smiled at Adrienne and Serena. Neighbors didn't bring over Christmas cookies or Easter bread, and no one shopped department-store sales with Serena in mind, but in their small gestures they indicated their acceptance. It was different for Ramsy. No one would run him out of town at gunpoint, but their distrust would linger no matter how many times they greeted him in line at the Shop N' Save.

Seeing Charlie and Ash at the fish fry reminded him of how his bar used to be. The men were still around, and Ramsy knew he'd encounter them again. But Jack Kurtz—he was gone for good. For a long time, Ramsy had thought he'd see him, and he'd imagined how it would be when Jack returned to the bar: a heavy silence, a debt of conversation Jack would feel obliged to pay. More often than he'd like to, Ramsy found himself remembering the Jack he'd seen through the window that November night, head in hands, pummeled by that empty house, that absent wife. But he couldn't separate him from the other Jack, the one in the mountains with the gun in his hands, aiming at Ramsy and then shooting JT when the fire went out. Ramsy finally heard that Jack had left town, and he was glad to know it. He didn't know how he could live with that much anger, that much pity, if Jack was just a few miles away.

As for Kitty—the state police concluded that one of the kids had shot her and taken the gun with him, and this was the easiest thing for everyone to believe. And even though Ramsy knew it wasn't true, he let them go on believing it. He understood that they had to believe it, to go on with the rest of their lives.

Charlie and Ash had come in a couple of weeks after that night on the mountain. They'd sat down with their coats on and barely met Ramsy's eye.

Finally Ash said, "Jesus, Ramsy, I don't know what to say to you. It wasn't right, what happened up there. Any of it. We were wrong, that's it."

And Charlie said, "It was the heat of the moment, that's all. No one meant to turn a gun on you. You're Ramsy, for Chrissake. One of us."

Ramsy nodded, accepting their apologies. They said he was part of this town, but Ramsy knew they didn't really believe it. That night on the mountain, it was JT he'd run to after the gunshots, JT he'd tried to help. Plus, Adrienne was living with him and Stella now. The town had come to a kind of peace with it, and with him, but it wasn't an easy peace.

"We'll be seeing you, Ramsy," Ash had said. But Ramsy knew they wouldn't be back. Spring was here now, and he couldn't say he missed them. They seemed like part of a life that was far away now, gone forever.

*   *   *

It was late when Ramsy got home, and Serena was asleep in Stella's arms. Ramsy made tea, and he sat in the living room with the paper. Adrienne curled up with a pillow and magazine on the floor like the child she was. This was life, then, Ramsy thought. This was what other people took for granted. It had come his way by such a gutted, twisted route that he still found himself straining to see ahead, fearful that the next bend in the road would be the one to topple the whole thing over. He thought this way for Stella, more protective of her happiness now than he'd ever been. But he felt protective of himself, too. Suddenly the world held promise, and so much of him felt raw and new.

It was close to midnight when someone knocked on the door. Stella had been dozing, but now her eyes flew open.

Adrienne looked hopeful when she sat up. "Kara," she said. "It has to be."

Another knock sounded, and Ramsy headed to the door.

Under the yellow porch light, a girl was crouched by a large woven bag, pawing through clothes and scarves and books. She had straight dark hair that hung loose to her mid-back, and she was clearly thin under her layered wrappings. When she heard the door open, she stood up quickly and brushed her hair behind her ear.

"Hello," she said seriously. "I'm Kara. Adrienne said to come here?"

A cold spring wind blew, and a few old fallen leaves scattered across the wooden slats of the porch. Tangled hair swept across the girl's cheeks, and she blinked her wide eyes as though startled in a car's bright headlights. There was a look on her face that said she could have come from everywhere and nowhere, as though she'd dropped out of the sky.

Ramsy opened the door wider. He would make her some food; he would pour some tea. He no longer had to hide the care he'd give. And if Stella studied the girl's face a moment too long, asked too many questions—well, she would. She always would, because she was Stella, because that was what she had to do, how she'd learned to go on living in the world. "Come in," Ramsy said, and stepped aside to clear a path. "We've been waiting for you."

ACKNOWLEDGMENTS

Endless thanks to Abram Himelstein and GK Darby at the University of New Orleans Press, and to everyone who participated in the University of New Orleans Publishing Lab for selecting *Each Vagabond By Name* and bringing it into the world with insight and enthusiasm. This book was lucky to find its home with you.

Over the years, my writing has benefited from many readers and teachers in Columbia University's MFA program and other workshops. I'm grateful to them for the many pages read, and the careful thought given. Thanks also to my long-ago poetry class at the Pennsylvania Governor's School for the Arts, where I first heard "A Vagabond Song." The haunting lines of that poem played a big role in how I imagined this novel.

I couldn't have written this book without my young daughters, Lucia and Greta, who, despite monopolizing most of my writing time, have given me the heart and perspective needed to write. Thanks to my parents, Larry and Marge Orlando, and sister, Molly Orlando, whose creativity, humor, and generosity have always inspired me. Finally, my husband, Andrew Littell, has read this book more times and in more iterations than should be expected of anyone, and his comments and ideas were crucial to shaping the story along the way. I'm grateful for his literary smarts, his endless encouragement, and so much else.

ABOUT THE AUTHOR

Margo Orlando Littell grew up in a coal-mining town in southwestern Pennsylvania. She earned an MFA from Columbia and has spent the past fifteen years in Manhattan, Brooklyn, Barcelona, Sacramento, and northern New Jersey, where she now lives with her husband and two daughters. *Each Vagabond By Name* is her first novel.

www.margoorlandolittell.com

Photo credit: Kathryn Huang